REBECCA JASMINE

THE COPPER KING'S DAUGHTER

A NOVEL

First published by Eversummer Media, LLC 2023

This novel is entirely a work of fiction. The names, characters and incidents portrayed in it are the work of the author's imagination. Any resemblance to actual persons, living or dead, events or localities is entirely coincidental.

First edition

ISBN: 9798988598411

This book was professionally typeset on Reedsy.
Find out more at reedsy.com

For my sister,
Angie Jasmine Wingett

Part One

Chapter 1

"What in blazes," roared the head captain, who came tearing down the stairs from the office. Three bells, then five, then three again, sharply rang. Electric lights throughout the mine flashed in time, signaling danger.

Perched atop a full load of iron ore in the mining skip cage, seventeen-year-old Jules Parker drew even with the platform, metal against metal screaming a high-pitched *screeeeech*. The cage jerked abruptly and shuddered to a halt. She threw her head back, looking for the source of the piercing noise, and spied the cause. The metal hoist wheel was stopped. Stalled. Deadlocked.

Jules' heart raced—she knew that when a hoist *wheel* stopped turning, it caused tension on the hoist *rope*, which then…

Her shoulders tensed just as a thunderous crack came from overhead. Flinging herself out of the cage and onto the platform, Jules landed on her hands and knees. Sharp gravel pierced her bare hands, scraping skin from her palms. Raking her long hair from her eyes, Jules peered up at the thick wood beam holding the three heavy metal hoists. A deep, angry fissure had formed in the main timber.

"Everyone, back away!" Vanorden jumped over the railing towards the shaft. "Now!"

Jules scampered to her feet just as the metal gate to the skip cage burst open, and a huge chunk of ore rock plummeted into the mine shaft, dropping, dropping, dropping…1800 feet to the bottom of the mineshaft.

Thud.

She turned to the hoistmen crowded around the collar, her eyes wide.

"Miss Parker!" cried the head captain from across the mine mouth. "Are you quite alright?"

"Yes, Mr. Vanorden," she shouted in reply. "The timber hasn't completely snapped. I'm fine!" Jules knew that the mine's headframes had catch-gear that prevented cages from falling back down the deep shafts, but the threat of a severed main beam was spine-chilling. "We're fine!"

Miners crowded near the stairway, far away from the wreckage. Vanorden walked quickly around the opening to Jules, mopping his brow with his sleeve. "What in tarnation happened?" he yelled, raising his voice over the din.

Jules took a deep breath in and out, then wiped her sweaty hands on her dungarees. She thought back to her morning down in the depths of the Metis mine, urging the men to work harder, to load more ore.

"I was working down below," she shouted. "I'd instructed Abbott's men to double load the skip cages in order to ensure that today's ore train was full before it left for the three o'clock freight to Bingham Junction." She bowed her head and pinched her nose. "I challenged the men. Whoever got their ore cart loaded first would get a free beer at the Mountain Saloon, courtesy of yours truly."

Vanorden closed his eyes and heaved a sigh. Jules glanced at the group of miners still standing by, catching the eye of a tall, dark-haired man. Their eyes held, but his gaze dropped to his feet, a look of guilt playing across his face. Jules winced and said, "Travis was the winner."

"Well, that ore train was full, sure enough," replied Vanorden, shaking his head. "We unloaded all those skip cages right as they came up." The incessant hoist bells clanged around them.

"I knew you would." Jules bowed her head at him. "Thank you." She placed a hand on his arm and mouthed silently, "I am so very sorry for the mess."

Vanorden squeezed Jules' hand. "We ain't had a full train leave for months, Miss Parker. In my opinion, you done good.

"But now let's have the men unload this last cage careful like, without tipping it even more than it already is," Vanorden instructed.

With a jerk of his chin at the skip cage, the miners finally moved slowly from near the stairs to the settled cage. Together, they gingerly began unloading the ore.

"That's right," nodded Jules. "Nice and easy." She held her palms outward and gently patted the air. "And turn off those bells, please." Vanorden nodded to the cager and the ringing promptly stopped, putting the headframe in a disconcerting silence.

"What is this?"

Jules turned around quickly when she heard someone approaching her from behind. A dark-suited man with a leather-bound ledger shading his eyes stopped. Gawking at Jules, he squawked, "Did I just see you, young lady, riding atop an ore load in a skip cage?" His mouth puckered into a deep frown.

"Well, maybe—"

"I have never, ever seen such a hazardous thing in all my years."

"It wasn't all tha—"

"Why, even the cages before this were overloaded to excess," he said, spitting his words. "Who's in charge here?"

"I am, sir," replied Vanorden, stepping forward.

"And who is she?" The man pointed at Jules, his eyes looking her over from top to bottom.

"I think the question is…who might you be?" asked Jules as she crossed her arms over her chest, exchanging a glance with Vanorden.

The man pulled his shoulders back, then withdrew a business card from his pocket and handed it to Jules, saying, "Wilfred Dory, Mine Inspector. Western States Division." Seeing Jules' grimy face and hands, he snatched his hand back, almost as if he didn't want to foul his own.

"This has got to be one for the record books…a woman—excuse me, a girl—causing massive damage to a mine headframe from absolute stupidity." Shaking his head, he opened up his leather book and pulled a pencil from his coat pocket. "And, this is exactly why women are not allowed in the mines." Dory made a wry face. "They are not capable of understanding the functions of machinery and are too dim to grasp the severity of their actions."

"It wasn't stupid," replied Jules, her eyes narrowing. "I was getting the freight containers filled so the train could take a full load down to Utah." She placed her hands on her hips and lifted her chin. "And this woman is entirely capable of understanding as much as any man. "

"You don't say," Dory replied, carving angry notes into his book. "So are you capable of understanding how irate Mr. Parker will be when he gets the violations report I will be submitting to the mining board and the labor unions? A report that could shut down this mine?"

Craaaack! The fissure in the main timber widened just as the last load of ore was scooped from the skip cage. A collective gasp filled the room as the miners once again scrambled away from the mine's open mouth.

"Now, now, Mr. Dory, no need for a violations report," came a firm reply from around the hoist house. AJ Parker walked toward the inspector, his hand outstretched for a handshake.

Dory's eyebrows shot up, and he grasped AJ's hand. "Mr. Parker! Thank goodness you are here. This vexing young woman has just caused potential risk to your workers," he spat. "Not only has she broken a myriad of regulations, but she also claims she works here!"

"She does, and she is correct about the ore headed to the station. That was the first full train I've seen in months," said AJ, eyeing the departed ore train in the distance. He turned back to Dory. "Plus, this vexing young woman happens to be my daughter."

"Your daughter? Why, I never imagined…" exclaimed Dory, looking from AJ to Jules. He tugged at his suit jacket's lapels. "But please, Mr. Parker, a woman working in mining? Preposterous! It just isn't done."

"Yes, I suppose," conceded AJ with a small shrug. "However, I treat everyone the same. Be it man or woman, each has to earn my respect. And until I decide differently, that is how it works here at Parker Copper Mining Company." As if waiting to be challenged, AJ stood glaring, a frown upon his face.

Tension was thick in the headframe, with the miners unusually hushed. Even when the clang of the hoist bells rang, signaling shift end for the workers, no one moved an inch.

AJ deliberately pulled two cigars from his chest pocket, offering one to Dory. "Care to join me?" AJ asked, his hooded eyes looking down at the mine inspector. Jules saw what Dory was greedily looking at: a green bill peeking out from within AJ's hand. Dory smiled, then accepted the cigar, placing the end in his mouth and the $50 bill in between pages of his leather book.

AJ struck a match against a wood post, then held it up, leaning into Dory and cupping his hand around the flame. "So, about that violations report," started AJ.

Dory took a draw on the cigar and tucked his book under his arm. "What violations report?" he asked with his eyebrow cocked. "Your company seems to be fine and in good order, Mr. Parker."

AJ nodded once firmly. "Wilfred, I know you are new to the West, and I hope it has been treating you well," he said, staring at Dory for much longer than was comfortable.

"But know this, I will treat you better," AJ said as he lit his own cigar. "Because I am AJ Parker and this is my company."

Three gray and black turkey vultures slowly soared overhead as AJ and Jules stood beside his auto, the late afternoon sun dropping behind the hill. Jules shivered but couldn't tell if it was because of the sudden drop in temperature or of the bad omen of the circling vultures.

AJ stared across the grounds with a deep frown rigid on his face. Finally, he said in a low, biting voice, "Jules, your little stunt has cost us both time and money." His arms crossed over his chest with his body stiff and unyielding.

In front of them, the last of the miners showed up for the night shift. AJ and Jules watched as each miner approached the entrance gate but were turned back, instructed to go instead to the Possum mine. With the Metis' main timber cracked, the mine would be out of commission until it was repaired, which could take weeks.

Jules turned toward her father. "But Father, the Metis can produce so much more than we are sending to the smelters each day. If we didn't have to pause mining operations because of train schedules and if the headframe were stronger, maybe steel, then we could get so much more out of her."

"At what cost?" AJ swiftly turned to his daughter, his face full of anger. "Do you have any idea how close we were to getting shut down?"

"I ... " stammered Jules, her cheeks burning.

"Parker Copper almost had to cease operation because of your recklessness."

"Bu—"

"Our hold on the mining business is precarious, what with Hailey

Mines breathing down our necks." AJ's eyes narrowed, and he leaned into Jules. She took a step back, her foot landing in a large, shallow puddle of slurry water.

"I've worked too hard to build this company into the greatest of its kind. Our success is based on my reputation, and I will not allow my name to be desecrated due to someone else's actions," he said sharply. "Even my offspring's."

Jules breathed in deeply, her heart beating hard in her chest. She heard the low, nasal whine of the circling vultures.

"You are reckless and irresponsible. You are immature in your thinking," continued AJ in a chilling voice. "And this is no longer amenable."

"What is no longer amenable?" asked Jules, her anxious face lifting to her father's.

"Having you work for the company."

"What are you saying?"

"I need assistance, not interference. I need someone who will work with me, not against me." AJ stepped to the side and said coldly, "I need someone else."

"But Father … "

A sharp clang rang out as the night-shift boss dropped a heavy metal lock against the entrance gates. He yanked against the chain twice, checking that it was secure. Then, with his hands in his pockets and chin lowered, he walked past Jules and her father, sliding a sideways glance at Jules.

The lights of the headframe flickered then blinked off, placing the mine in total darkness. AJ was right– she alone had done the damage, and now the Metis was no longer in production. Jules had nearly placed a death warrant on one of Parker Copper Company's mines.

She felt like she couldn't breathe, and her knees slowly buckled. Jules landed on her hands and knees in the grimy puddle, her head hanging with her long black hair draped over her guilty and ashamed face.

"Go home, Jules," said her father in a low voice, turning his back. "You are officially barred from the Parker Copper mines." He stepped past his daughter as darkness closed around them, then dropped his cigar in the slurry water, its ember dying out with a lingering hiss.

Chapter 2

A single shot rang out, the thunderous *ka-blam* flushing a parliament of magpies into the big blue sky, their angry cries echoing off the mansion's broad back wall.

Jules blinked her eyes against the sun's rays as she watched the luminous blue-black birds take to the heavens, chattering and cursing her. She raised the barrel of the Colt pistol and looked down the sight at the tin can that remained upright on the fence post 20 feet away. She turned her head and spit.

"Good lord, Jules, must you do that here?" Millicent Parker asked as she stepped out onto the back porch.

"Mother, this new handgun is absolutely fantastic. However did Father get Mr. Browning to give him one of his newest models?" Jules smiled and waved the gun in the direction of her mother.

Stepping quickly aside, Millicent answered, "I couldn't tell you." She motioned for Jules to lower the gun's barrel. "But really, I'd much rather live to find out, so would you please lay aside that cannon?" Her mother plucked a wilted blossom from a potted geranium.

Jules turned her head away, hiding her smile, and pointed the gun at the ground. Her mother had called the pistol a cannon, which Jules felt a bit melodramatic. She choked back a chuckle.

Jules ejected the metal cartridge and slid it into the pocket of her skirt, then looked through the barrel, making sure it was clear. She composed herself while she walked across the vast yard crowded with spiral-shaped juniper topiaries and rose bushes fat with blooms.

A breeze blew up the rise, where the Parker Mansion perched. The most glorious home in all of Butte—maybe even in all of the state of Montana—overlooked the lesser homes below. The expansive three-storey red brick manor had anchored the top of the hill for the past seventeen years, ever since construction had been completed in 1888, and her family had finally moved in with baby Jules. White wood trim outlined the many beautiful stained glass windows on the top floor like finely framed art, and enclosed the back porch, providing shade from an already hot day. Beyond the vast gardens lay acres and acres of untouched land overflowing with wildflowers, ponderosa pines, white-tailed deer, and meadowlarks.

A light spring wind lifted strands of Jules' long black hair, wrapping them across her eyes. She raked at the locks, tucking them behind her ear, her sooted hands leaving dark smudges across her forehead and cheeks. The sharp smell of burnt gunpowder lingered in her hair, and her hand felt slick and oily. Jules breathed in deeply, raising her face to the dazzling noon sun, the intense rays already turning her cheeks the color of copper.

The back door opened, and a petite brunette, her older sister Celeste, tagged behind a housemaid carrying a tray of iced tea in her arms. Two older women followed Celeste, one holding a parasol, the other a satchel.

"Mother, look who I've just discovered at the door," Celeste said, warmly. "Mrs. Harmon and Mrs. Abbott are here." She stepped aside, allowing the women to greet Millicent.

Millicent turned away from Jules and reached out to her guests. "Violetta, Beatrice, welcome," she said with a smile.

Jules smiled too. Hadn't she been wondering about the shift-boss Abbott's wife, back when she'd been… Jules despondently sighed, remembering a month prior when she'd last been in the copper mines. She headed for the patio, her skirt dragging behind her in the freshly cut grass while a hermit thrush gargled a flute-like song from the lilac bushes rimming the yard.

Jules climbed up the porch stairs, but stopped when Celeste met her with a look of disgust. "Oh no. Not with those filthy hands, you don't," she exclaimed, eyeing the dark smears across Jules' face.

"Celeste. It's just gunpowder," Jules replied, amused. She shoved a hand in front of her sister's face. "It's not as if I've been rooting around in the pig sty."

Celeste raised an eyebrow and said, "Yet. The day is young." With small, sure steps, she turned and headed for the shaded sitting area.

"Jules, Celeste is right. Go inside and wash up, then come join us," Millicent said as she took a seat on a wicker settee. She spread her voluminous skirt around her feet, the layers of fabric swishing the floor. Turning to the seated visitors, Millicent said, "Ladies, I apologize for my daughter. But she has always been a bit…"

"…Rambunctious?" asked Mrs. Abbott.

"…Uncouth?" replied Mrs. Harmon.

Millicent raised her eyebrows and folded her hands in her lap. "…Spirited," she replied. Celeste made a snorting noise, then reached out and lifted the lead crystal pitcher, filling four glasses. She tucked a mint sprig into each and then stirred with a long-handled silver spoon.

Mrs. Harmon took a sip of tea and patted her lips with a linen napkin. "Mrs. Parker, thank you for seeing us this afternoon. We did want to discuss a couple of issues with you," she said. "Are you sure that we came at an agreeable time? I thought I heard gunfire just as we arrived."

"Oh, that was me," Jules said as she looked over her shoulder at her target, mocking her from the fence post. She lowered her voice and spoke to herself, "Something really is bothersome with that shot—I should have hit it. Twenty feet isn't so far away." Beatrice Abbott covered her mouth with a gloved hand.

Millicent cleared her throat and reassured her guests. "Violetta, it's a pleasure to have you and Beatrice here at Parker Mansion." She looked over to Jules. "My youngest daughter was just trying out a new pistol."

"Miss Parker was shooting a gun?" Beatrice Abbott's eyebrows had climbed high up her forehead. "Dear me, I find that hardly respectable for a young lady. That kind of unfeminine behavior is exactly what the Anti…" From down the hill, a rooster cockle-doodle-doo'd a confusing call so late in the day.

"Yes, well," interrupted Violetta. She placed her hand on Beatrice's wrist. "We've just come to remind you of the upcoming policeman's ball. You've been so generous with donating in the past, and we hope that you will continue to do so." She smiled and inclined her head. "I know it's still quite far away, but we've set our sights on…"

"Set your sights," Jules repeated, rubbing at her chin. Maybe that was why she hadn't hit her target. Could it be that the fixed front sight was flawed?

Suddenly, she twisted around, pointing the pistol at the fence, gripping the handle with both hands, arms straight out in front of her. Her left foot slightly in front, she bent her knees ever slightly and with intense focus, looked down the barrel. Just as Jules pulled the trigger and muttered, "Bla….," a housemaid crossed in front of her.

"AUGUSTINA JULIETTE PARKER!" screamed her mother, jumping up from the settee.

"…aamm," finished Jules as the pistol hammer clicked.

Silence.

The six women on the porch stared at one another, eyes wide. Millicent drew in a sharp breath, and the air around them stilled.

"It didn't… The gun wasn't loaded," Jules stammered, her eyes darting from face to face. She rooted around in the many layers of her skirt until her hand closed around the cartridge. She slowly held it aloft.

Silence. Even the incessant chattering of the magpies had quieted.

"Yes, well… maybe I'll just put this back in Father's library," Jules whispered, her cheeks ablaze, as she tucked the gun into her pocket. She paused and faced the housemaid. "Trudy, I am really quite sorry for the fright," she said to the girl still standing in front of her.

"Yes'm," Trudy replied with an unsteady curtsy. She waved at the can, twenty feet away. "Miz Hazel told me to fetch that can o' beans from the fence post so's she can serve it for supper. You suppose I can do that now?" she asked after taking in a calming breath.

"Yes, please, do go about your work. I so apologize," Jules said, with a guilty smile. Seemingly used to the behavior, Trudy returned Jules' smile, then shrugged her shoulders and walked toward the fence.

Still tense, the women watched the housemaid walk away as a lone magpie shrieked from atop the porch roof, as if still irritated at the earlier shooting. From the edge of the yard, a group of whitetail deer stood alert with twitching ears, as two speckled fawns chased one another around a huge evergreen pine.

"Perhaps we should come another day," Violetta Harmon said in a shaky voice, her face devoid of color. She rose on wobbly legs and picked up her parasol, holding it in a death grip, her knuckles white. "Beatrice, dear, why don't you go ahead and just leave that reading material here for Mrs. Parker?" Violetta lurched from the seating area.

With a frown pulling her thin lips tight, Beatrice opened her satchel and removed a printed pamphlet from inside. She placed it on the glass tabletop and then looked to Jules with disapproval. A breeze ruffled the flimsy pages, so she slid her crystal goblet on top, the condensation from the glass marking a ring around the title: *Anti-Suffrage League Review.*

Jules glanced down, reading the front page:

"Join our new guild! Keep social order harmonious! Do not let women at the polls lest the boundaries of masculine and feminine, public and private, domestic and political be destroyed."

"What's this nonsense?" she asked under her breath. The Anti-Suffragists really thought that society might be destroyed by letting women have a vote. Jules barked a cough loud enough to send the deer near the edge of the yard fleeing, their tails pointed up to the sky.

Beatrice Abbott slowly stood, brushing hard at her skirt. She looked at Jules, then to Trudy, crossing the manicured lawn holding the can of beans. "Miss Jules, my husband sends his regards to you," said Beatrice as she made her way across the patio. She stopped and transferred her satchel to her other hand, then called over her shoulder, sounding a bit cutting. "He says it's just not the same in the mines without you."

"Really, Jules, your actions are just deplorable," said Millicent, returning from escorting Violetta and Beatrice to the front door. She let out a long breath. "You are fortunate that most everyone understands how... *spirited*... you are."

Jules laughed and replied, "Yes, most everyone. Especially Trudy."

"And the rest of the household staff," Millicent said. "Hazel was correct when she called you a walking calamity." Her mother shook her head. "From the day you could stand on your own two feet, they all knew you ran feral, dragging at least one of them along with you. Just like that bobcat they captured near The Possum last week."

"Mother, Butte isn't as wild as it used to be, and I think some people long for a little excitement. I never had to drag anyone—they all came along willingly." Jules hollered over her shoulder to the kitchen window. "Isn't that right, Trudy?"

"Yes'm. It's true, all right. Miss Jules does know how to have fun," came Trudy's reply.

"Really, Jules, I truly do not understand why anyone would fall in with your shenanigans," Celeste said. "I think you are incorrigible." She sat on the wicker ottoman and reached for a glass of iced tea. "I do love you, so take this question with a bit of sugar. But how do you expect to find a man to marry you when you go around shooting housemaids and generally acting like a savage? How do you expect to be happy?"

"Well, I don't want that," Jules replied, leaning forward in her wicker chair.

"Of course you do, dearest," Celeste said. "All girls want to be happy. Look how content I am with my own Bradley. And we've only been married a few years."

"I mean, I want to be happy, but I don't need to *marry* to be happy. I want to be my own woman—make my own money, live in my own house," Jules said. She snatched the Anti-Suffrage League pamphlet from the table and waved it in front of Celeste. "Maybe I even want the right to vote."

"Don't be ridiculous," Celeste said, pulling away from Jules with a frown.

"You don't be ridiculous," Jules replied, returning the scowl.

"*You* don't!"

"*You* don't!"

"Stop this nonsense immediately," Millicent replied shortly. "Both of you are acting completely beneath your station. I cannot bear to think that I've raised a couple of barbarians." Her steely light blue eyes halted the girl's argument.

Jules slid a glance at Celeste. "Mother, you know Celeste is the only one who gets my ire up in such a way."

"Yes, I know—thank god she is the only one. Nevertheless, do not ever forget that both of you young ladies belong to the Parker family," Millicent said, narrowing her eyes. Resuming its watch, the magpie on the porch roof cackled, as if mocking Jules and Celeste.

"Do you suppose any of the Rockefeller girls are harping at each other right now?" Millicent continued. "They may currently be the richest family in the United States, but in a few more years, *we* might be the richest." She sat down on the wicker settee. "You both had better start acting more gracious. Your father has worked too hard these years past, and I refuse to let either of you embarrass this family." Millicent looked pointedly at Jules.

Celeste moved next to Millicent and gathered her hands in her own. "Mother, I am dreadfully sorry. I do understand. My Bradley would be so disappointed to see how I was acting."

"Your Bradley?" replied Jules, leaning back into her chair and placing her feet upon the table. "You're worried about what a man thinks of you?" She smacked her forehead with her open palm. "Men and their big bazoos?"

Millicent closed her eyes and shook her head. "Jules, you have been in the hot sun far too long today and are speaking gibberish—I can only hope that you are ill."

"Of course I'm not ill, Mother," laughed Jules. "I just think that a woman is not less than a man. Shouldn't all people be equal, regardless of whether they are male or female?" The wicker chair squeaked as she leaned forward. "When I take over Parker Copper Mining Company..."

"When you what?" asked Millicent. "Really, Jules, do you think that is truly going to happen? Just a few weeks ago, you caused an incident that could have closed the company."

"But I was trying to increase the earnings," Jules quickly replied. She shifted in her seat. "I will allow women to work at whichever job they are proficient in when I inherit and run Parker Copper, as I am bound and determined."

"You know that might never happen." Millicent locked eyes with her daughter. "Not a single woman heads up a corporation—and probably won't. It's easier if we don't."

"Easier?" Jules stared back. "Over 50 years ago, at the Women's Rights Convention, the Misses Lucy Stone and Susan B. Anthony said that men and women should be equal in every way, and there is no such thing as a 'natural role' of a woman. They thought nothing about it being easy." She crossed her arms across her chest. "They said it because equal rights means women's rights—in work and in life."

"Must I remind you that you are no longer working at your father's mines?" Millicent asked. "You might reconsider what you are saying."

"I shouldn't reconsider equal rights at all," Jules said, agitated. She held up the Anti-Suffrage League pamphlet and crumpled it into a ball.

"Jules, equal rights for women are not going to happen anytime soon, so you should stop fretting about the issue. Just find a beau and get married like the rest of us," Celeste said, tugging at a curled lock of hair. "You've always had your head in the clouds and are a stubborn jackass."

Jules turned to her sister. "Well, it is you who has her head buried in the sand! Women are not second-class citizens—we deserve equal treatment. It will be by my own choosing should I decide to marry." Jules quickly stood, her eyes narrowed. She withdrew the Colt pistol from her pocket and aimed it at Celeste. "And did you just call me a jackass?"

"*Augustina*," barked her mother, her voice sharp and menacing. "How dare you threaten your sister with a weapon! You are utterly out of line!" Millicent jumped to her feet, knocking the wicker ottoman on its side. "Get out of my sight immediately."

"But, Mother," started Jules. "It's not loaded..."

"No. I want nothing more from you." Millicent held up her hand. "You will remove yourself to your room. Close the curtains against the heat, and lie for a rest until you come to your senses. Or until we do decide to marry you off and you become someone else's problem."

"But…"

Millicent cut her off. "What have I just instructed you to do?" she asked firmly. "Now."

Jules hung her head, her ever-present grin wiped from her face. "Yes, Mother."

"And return that evil firearm to your father's safe before you murder another can of beans—or worse." Millicent turned her back to Jules and picked up a glass of iced tea. "You are excused."

Chapter 3

Jules gathered her skirt around her and turned toward the porch door. Millicent called out to her, "Don't defy me again, Jules. Put the gun away now. If your father finds out what happened with Mrs. Harmon and Mrs. Abbott, he will be furious."

"I'm putting it away. You don't need to tell me twice." Jules pocketed the pistol once again, then glanced at Celeste, who wore a slight smirk on her perfect rosebud lips.

Jules entered the mansion's library, the two heavy double doors groaning when she pushed them open. Facing her was a floor-to-ceiling bookcase, crammed full of leather-backed books, the gold print on the spines glinting.

She was assaulted by the overwhelming fragrance of pure masculinity: cigar smoke, gun oil, newsprint, and sweat. Jules ran her fingertips across the arm of an overstuffed leather club chair. Although she still smarted from Millicent's reprimand, Jules was happy to be in the library. While the mansion's parlor may have been her mother and sister's domain, this was Jules' favorite room of all. After all, it was the owner of Parker Copper Mining Company, and her father, AJ Parker's favorite room too.

August Julian Parker claimed his first mine in 1870 in Butte, Montana. By that time, he'd already shown an immense aptitude for the mining business while working for already established mining companies. AJ was quite clever and a very resourceful worker. Whenever a mine captain gathered men together in cattle calls searching for mine hands, they would hear shouted above the crowd, "I'm AJ Parker, and I'm ready to work." And that's exactly what he did. AJ started on the bottom rung as a nipper—a trainee who brought supplies, hauled, mucked, whatever was needed. He quickly worked his way up to face-boss, in charge of men much older than him.

But, nine months later, when a supply wagon was leaving Bingham Junction for the new gold frontier further north, AJ saw an opportunity he couldn't refuse and hitched a ride to Alder Gulch in Montana.

Soon after arriving, AJ bought a silver mine in Butte and called it The Venturer. Even though he was aware it might be a risky enterprise, AJ knew he could work the mine and make some money off of her—but he had no idea how much. A few months in, as he drilled deeper searching for more silver, AJ discovered an enormous vein of copper iron ore.

The discovery of that ore was auspicious at the time. The country had exploded with the need for wiring for electricity, telegraphs, and telephones—all of it using copper wire. People began hearing him say, "I'm AJ Parker, and this is my mine." The lode AJ discovered in his mine, the Venturer, was found to be one of the largest deposits of copper ore ever known.

He began with only a couple of mines, but within a decade, he built an empire that outshone every rival in the nation. AJ Parker rose to become a multi-millionaire—and a true Copper King.

An immense oak coffee table flanked the leather seating, holding Butte's three newspapers. At almost 100,000 residents, Butte was the largest city between Chicago and San Francisco, and three daily newspapers were necessary to keep the growing population informed. Jules would regularly sit and read through each of them, learning all that was going on in their city and in the nation. She picked up the top paper, glanced at the date, April 15th, 1905, and read a headline that asked "Parker Copper Owner a Million Dollar Senator?"

Jules smiled and laid the paper on her father's desk as she thought of everything he'd accomplished. With 43 operational mines, Parker Copper Mining Company was one of the largest in the nation, perhaps even the world. AJ Parker also owned rail trains that hauled the iron ore and banks that held all the money that he made. Jules figured that her father's next achievement would most likely be in Montana politics. Maybe by this time next year, AJ could be elected as one of the state's two senators—and certainly he'd be better than the most recent halfwit to hold the seat.

Jules studied the newspaper photo under the headline. There stood AJ, Celeste, and Jules, arm in arm outside the Parker Bank & Trust building on Main Street downtown. Of course, her father looked commanding and influential in his impeccable business suit and black top hat—along with JP Morgan, John D. Rockefeller, and Andrew Carnegie, AJ Parker was amongst the richest men in the United States. He was, without a doubt, the most powerful man in the West.

But Celeste clung to her father, cowering from the automobile driving closely behind them. Jules remembered that the auto had backfired loudly—her sister had been dreadfully startled. Celeste's stark skin looked even paler beneath the halo of deep brown curls brushing across her cheeks, her bottom lip tucked behind her white teeth, her eyebrows drawn into an angry line. Was Celeste frightened or angry—or perhaps both? With her sister, really, sometimes they were one and the same.

Jules' photo, on the other hand, showed her facing the automobile, her mouth in a huge grin. She studied her image—while Jules was quick to smile, and even quicker laugh, in the newspaper picture, she did look a bit crazed.

But at least she didn't look like the sourpuss that Celeste often was, and Jules wondered when that had happened. They had both been happy-go-lucky when they were younger, but it seemed that Celeste had transformed when she'd turned eighteen and gotten engaged. Maybe after she'd married and had her own household to care for—with the supervision of the servants and the planning of social engagements—she'd been overwhelmed with the bore of it all. Yes, that certainly was enough to put a permanent frown upon anyone's face.

Jules sighed and faked a shudder—it was just months away from her own eighteenth birthday, that time when wealthy young women got married and presumably grew wretched.

Their demeanors weren't the only difference between the Parker girls. Even the way Jules looked was poles apart from her sister and, really, most other girls. Jules' long, black hair reached to the middle of her back, stick-straight, refusing to curl. As was the fashion, most women piled their hair atop their heads in a waterfall of curls, mimicking the popular Gibson Girl.

Jules really did try, occasionally letting a housemaid roll her hair with a heated curling tong. But once, when the maid accidentally overheated the tong and scorched Jules' scalp, Jules let out a yelp that rang throughout all of Parker Mansion. Jules had grabbed the curling tong and had threatened the maid, chasing her down the stairs, straight through the hallway. Upon reaching the kitchen, Jules ran smack dab into Hazel, who had her arms folded and was shaking her head.

"Miss Jules, you let Trudy alone now. She done nothin' but try to help you look more ladylike," Hazel had said.

Jules had thrown the tongs into the corner and laughed, "I don't know which is worse. Needing help to look more ladylike or getting branded on the head by a red-hot iron." She had turned and started back up the stairs, but stopped, leaning over the railing and called out, "Trudy, I am really quite sorry for the fright. I so apologize." Then, hitching up her skirt, she took the steps, two at a time, and disappeared into her bedroom, leaving Hazel chuckling but still shaking her head.

Jules tossed the heavy newspaper on the coffee table, where it landed with a thud, then walked to an enormous picture window overlooking the city. In just 15 years, Butte had grown into an exciting, bustling city from the small squalor of a mining town. It was a heady time in Butte with rich and poor mixing together, joined by what was brought up from deep in the earth.

Large cottonwood trees lined the street, the new green spring leaves almost glowing in the sunlight. From her vantage point, Jules watched the goings-on along Montana Street, which ran in a straight line directly to the mansion's front steps. An electric trolley rumbled almost the entire length of the cobblestone street, with another set of tracks crisscrossing along on Park Street. A couple of streets over lay Main, the street at the heart of Butte, where hundreds of shops, pubs, theatres, and civic buildings teemed with activity.

But it was the surrounding area that appealed to Jules the most. Punctuated with scores of headframes, she could almost feel the pulsing through the mansion walls. Considered the hearts of Parker Copper, the structures were used to bring up the lifeblood, the iron ore. Without the headframes, miners would still be hauling rock up in buckets, and Jules supposed that there was a chance that Parker Copper might not have grown to its vast size, had it not been for the headframes.

The tall structures ranged in height from 99 to 200 feet. Cables from a hoist house passed over wheels at the top of the frame and held an enclosed platform that was used not only to lower miners to their stations underground, but also to transport mules, equipment, and supplies. But most importantly, the headframes were necessary to bring *up* the loads and loads of mined Parker copper ore.

They were also called gallows frames by miners because they resembled gallows scaffolds used for execution by hanging, most often of murderers and thieves. But Jules preferred to call their's headframes as it seemed more respectful of the imposing structures that provided access to the riches below the earth.

Jules approached the window and looked over the mines. The Venturer mine was a second home to Jules—she'd been riding the cages and walking the tunnels since before she could read. Longingly, she reached out with one finger and outlined the great mine's headframe, tracing the long steel A-frame legs. Many outbuildings surrounded the Venturer, and an ore train lingered beside the headframe, the freight car's tops open, waiting to be filled, like mouths of nested baby birds.

After it had made AJ Parker's initial fortune in silver and then multiplied it tenfold, the Venturer had become Parker Copper's most significant mine and had been reckoned "the richest hill on earth."

Jules bowed her head forward and rested against the window. A weight in her pocket pulled at her skirt, and with a clunk, tapped against the glass. Jules pulled the loaded 8-round magazine out of her pocket and moved away from the window, laying it on the leather sofa. She withdrew the pistol and absentmindedly rubbed fabric from her skirt against smooth metal, polishing the muzzle.

Her head jerked round as the front door was abruptly thrown open, a commotion in the grand entryway alerting everyone that someone had come in. Jules could feel the energy in the mansion rise—AJ Parker was home.

"It's as hot as a whorehouse on a nickel night already! Hazel, bring a cool drink to me in my library, will you?" Heavy footsteps crossed the polished wooden floor, heading toward the library.

Jules smiled, still buffing the pistol, waiting for her father to enter his library. *Her father!* Her mother had told her that he would be furious at her fooling around with the gun.

Jules, eyes wide with panic, snatched up the gun cartridge from the sofa, slammed it into the gun, and swiftly clicked on the safety. Her head whipped around, calculating the distance between her and the gun safe—she wouldn't make it in time, before her father caught her.

Just as the library's double doors and the force that was AJ Parker blew in, Jules hastily sat down and hid the gun, tucking it deep between the smooth leather sofa arm and cushion. She spread her skirt and smoothed it over her lap, then dipped her head and positioned a smile upon her lips.

"There she is, one of my three favorite girls," AJ bellowed as he crossed the threshold into the library, shrugging off his waistcoat. He removed his felt bowler hat, revealing thick, black hair, the waves combed in by scented pomade.

"Father, " Jules replied demurely. "Welcome home."

"I'm glad to be home, dear," AJ said, placing a chaste kiss upon Jules, his bushy beard tickling her cheek. Hazel entered carrying a tray with a tall crystal glass filled with ice and a caramel-brown effervescent liquid. "Ah, Coca-Cola. Thank you, Hazel." He took a deep drink, then let out a belch as Hazel walked away. He set the crystal goblet on his desktop.

"You seem pleased this afternoon, Father," Jules said. "Have you had a good morning?"

AJ's lips drew up in a thin smile. "Well, if it takes paying out $30,000 for ownership of an ex-soldier's mining property to have a good morning," he replied. "Then yes."

Jules' eyebrows rose as she exclaimed, "Thirty thousand dollars! That's quite a large amount of money."

"Yes, quite." AJ nodded. "The property was sold to me from a Mr. Morgan Stickley, who had come into it last year. He's no miner and has only dug 45 feet into her."

"A Mr. Stickley, you say?" asked Jules. "That name is unfamiliar to me."

"To me as well," AJ replied. "I only by chance ran into him outside the Union Labor hall, and we started conversing. It was then that he told me of his property. He didn't even know who I was until I made him an offer to buy him out." AJ hid a smile. "He doesn't know at all what his mine might hold."

Jules grinned widely, her laugh pealing like a silver bell. "But you do."

"Of course I do, daughter. Stickley just mentioned the location, and I knew right away that it would have a copious amount of silver. And you know what is below the silver?" AJ said, his smile matching his daughter's. "A sizeable iron ore vein. I estimate that we just made upwards of $10 million on my $30,000 outlay."

Amazed at her father's keen business sense, Jules shook her head. It was no wonder people said that AJ could see farther into the ground than any other man.

"It does take hard work, though," AJ replied after he'd taken another sip of cola. "I will be toiling late into the night at Parker Copper, finalizing the contracts for the sale. That is why I am home now—I wanted to spend a moment with your mother before I have to go back into the office."

"Ah. You'll find Mother on the porch with Celeste. I was with them just a bit ago until I…" Jules hesitated.

"All right then, Jules, so tell me, what have you been up to today?" asked AJ, striding around the desk, his eyes studying her.

"Oh, nothing special," Jules replied, swallowing hard.

AJ sat heavily into his desk chair and eyed Jules from across the desk. He stroked his black beard. The grandfather clock in the corner ticked loudly. "Did you like it?" he finally asked.

Jules stiffened. "I beg your pardon?"

"The pistol. Did you like it?" repeated AJ.

"Why Father, I'm sure I don't know what you're—" started Jules, her eyes blinking quickly.

"Oh, come now, Jules. Don't take me for a fool," replied AJ. "I know my own library like the back of my hand. I certainly can smell the difference between a clean gun and one that has been fired."

Jules sat silent, her leg nervously twitching.

"Which one did you shoot—the .38 Special?" AJ asked. "Isn't that a little plain for you?"

"The new Colt pocket semi-automatic," Jules quickly retorted, then slapped her hand upon her mouth, covering it.

"Ah, I've not yet tried it." AJ tipped back in his chair, resting his feet upon his desk. "What did you think of it? And tell me honestly."

"It is fantastic!" Jules sat up. "The weight is manageable and well-balanced. The grip is solid. But Father, you must write to Mr. Browning and tell him that the front sight is flawed. That if he included a rear-sight, the aim would be accurate."

AJ smiled at his daughter. "Yes, I'll write him. What else do you like about the gun?"

"Semi-automatic is the way to go. Just think of having eight shots loaded at the ready!"

"Jules, don't forget that every gun is a dangerous weapon," AJ said, removing his feet from the desktop. He sat forward, leaning onto his forearms. "You only need one shot to do true damage."

"Yes, Father, I won't forget that." Jules nodded her head once. She looked to her father. "But tell me, with all the other guns you own, why do you even need one more?"

"Well, as you were saying, I was interested in the 8-shot semi-automatic. It might come in handy if trouble comes knocking."

"Trouble? What kind of trouble?"

"Not to alarm you, and certainly your mother already knows this, but we've been hearing rumors, Jules," AJ said, his face serious. He stilled as a housemaid walked past the library, carrying pressed linens.

"Rumors of what?" Jules asked quietly, as she sat higher in her seat.

"Sabotage, mostly. It's to be expected, I suppose, given our wealth and success. People want things of their own. And some would harm us to get it."

"I can't believe that, Father."

"Well, you had better, Jules. Be aware that some conspire to take all of this away from me." AJ gazed out the window at the Venturer headframe. "And the company is getting so immense that I soon won't be able to keep track of it all by myself. Especially if I'm to broaden my own horizons." He sat on the edge of his heavy oak desk. "Now truly is the time for me to get help in running Parker Copper."

Jules' eyebrows rose. Her father needed help running the company. Would he consider allowing Jules to take over? From a distance, she heard the ringing of hoist bells, signaling the movement of the cages in nearby mines. Jules took a steadying breath.

"Father, I am prepared to do that—to help you run Parker Copper," Jules said, resolutely.

"You?" AJ's face darkened. "Jules, I need someone responsible. Someone who would protect the Parker name and all it represents."

"I am…"

"I need someone responsible," AJ repeated. "And respectable."

"Responsible and respectable? Why does that matter?" Jules asked, jumping to her feet. "What matters is innovation, thinking of new ideas."

"See, Jules, that is immature thinking. I've been watching you, but you've not convinced me you are conscientious enough to run Parker Copper." AJ said, his voice low. "Maybe you never will be. Don't forget why you can no longer attend to the mines."

Jules felt her face flush. "But I am conscientious, Father! And I know more than anyone else about Parker Copper." She walked to the window. "Look! Did you notice that the Metis has been quiet for the last half hour?"

AJ rose from sitting on his desk, looking to where Jules pointed. "What the devil. Why is it—"

"The main timber has broken again. The engineers are trying to mend it right now."

"How did you even know the Metis had stopped?"

"I just knew. I felt it," Jules replied.

"Perhaps it is still damaged from the incident you caused last month," AJ said while crossing his arms over his chest.

"Well, Father, instead of merely mending the main timber, perhaps you should have replaced the Metis' old wooden headframe."

"Do not bring that up again, Jules," threatened AJ. "I'll not listen to talk of replacing the wood headframe with steel."

Jules frowned. "I don't understand why you cannot see the value in using new methods."

"Why?" asked her father, agitated. "Because I am AJ Parker. And this is my company." AJ snatched the newspaper from the top of his desk and pointed to the headline. "And, I make the best decisions for Parker Copper." He threw the paper onto the desk, where the pages scattered across the top.

Jules reached out and deliberately straightened the newspaper. "I would be using the newest technologies available if I ran a company."

"Well, you don't run a company. Perhaps the only level-headed one of my offspring might have." AJ slammed his hand onto the desk. "If

Gus had lived…"

"But he didn't. And I, your other offspring, learned instead. You let me sit in all your meetings and in all your council," cried Jules, turning to face her father.

"I wouldn't have if I'd known that you would damage my company with your carelessness."

"If I ran Parker Copper, I most certainly would not be careless."

"Take that crazy idea of running Parker Copper out of your head," AJ said.

"But I do have the idea," Jules said, wound up. "And the idea is not so crazy! Admit it, Father. Admit that it isn't crazy."

"Jules, stop this nonsense. I am warning you," AJ said, his face red. "Do not challenge me on this issue."

"I'll not challenge you if you'll not be so bull-headed! It is my right as a Parker to run Parker Copper Mining Company," Jules exclaimed. *"Am I not the rightful heir?"*

AJ grabbed the crystal glass half-full of Coca-Cola from atop his desk. He raised his arm and violently whipped the crystal into the library fireplace, shards of fine glass exploding against the stone hearth.

"DO NOT CHALLENGE ME," he roared, silencing Jules. The air in the library thickened, heavy with tension, the only sound coming from the copper mines.

"If Gus had lived, he would have inherited Parker Copper," AJ said lowly. "But he didn't. And none of my other children have shown me that they are able." Her father walked to the double doors and pulled them open. AJ held his shoulders stiff, his jaw clenched. "That is the end of this discussion. Now, take your leave."

Jules gripped her hands, halting her rage, and backed out of the library. Once her foot touched the polished wood floor of the entryway, she turned and raced outside, slamming the door behind her. Spinning away from her splendid home, she ran down the hill toward the bustling city, her feet tripping beneath her.

32

Chapter 4

Breathing heavily, Jules pulled up under a huge cottonwood tree, shaking with anger. "I am not immature!" she screamed into the vast blue Montana sky, punching the air and kicking the dirt surrounding the tree.

She fell to her knees and bent over panting, her forehead touching the cool, damp dirt underneath the cottonwood. "I am responsible," she said through clenched teeth, her body tense. Jules heard the constant ringing of the hoist bells at the Venturer mine, and with each ringing, her breathing calmed and her heart slowed. "And damn respectable."

Jules finally sat back up, and she brushed her hair from her eyes. She surveyed the outlying city—the green of the new spring mixing in with the bright colors of newly constructed buildings. She thought about her father and his aversion to new ideas. Wasn't that how their town had gotten on the map in the first place?

Once AJ discovered copper, his mining operation had expanded quickly. Butte had grown alongside to accommodate all the people pouring into town. With buildings crammed right up to the bases of all the headframes and roads leading to dozens of different neighborhoods, Jules wondered how it could get any bigger. From where she sat, Jules saw only rooftops of buildings butted against one another—not only mine structures like the hoist buildings and the dry houses, but white-painted two-room houses where miners lived with their families, and wood shacks where bachelor miners slept. A miner chose to live close to the mine where he worked—if his mine was prolific, he might live in the same house for years.

Jules slapped out at a fire ant crossing over her foot and scratched at the spot where the ant had sunk its sharp pinchers into her soft skin. She spied a solid four-foot line of the red-brown insects, looking like the train cars full of copper below her in the town.

Butte was where AJ Parker's empire lay, from the Venturer mine to the mines in East Camp, and over to the Angela and the Possum. From above ground, Parker Copper's forty-three mines looked out at one another. And from below ground, their warren of tunnels ran for over 5,000 miles.

The Outer Camp, far off to the west, contained just a single mine, but nonetheless, one of Parker Copper Mining Company's richest mines. Jules strained her eyes and found the headframe for The Only. Just as it had been for the last dozen years when AJ had instantly shut it down, the mine sat still and quiet. Silent. Jules propped her chin on her arms folded over her drawn knees and remembered that day twelve years ago.

Gus Melvin Parker was the only son, and upon his birth, as was the norm, became heir to Parker Copper. Even at a very young age, Gus had been called to join AJ in all Parker Copper meetings, as he would be required to take over the family business. He looked enough like his father that most everyone commented on the spitting image, yet he had brunet hair and was slight of build, like his mother. As he'd gotten older, little six-year-old Gus took to constantly wearing a miniature version of AJ's top hat partially because his father wore one, but really because it made him look taller.

On the day when politicians from the east arrived to take a tour of a mine rich with silver and iron ore, AJ Parker had selected The

Only. Compared to most of the other mines that sometimes ran inside temperatures above 100 degrees, the Only ran at a cool 65 degrees. And AJ knew that if his mines were good to the politicians, they would, in turn, be good to him.

They gathered in the Parker Copper headquarters, where AJ started the meeting with his trademark opening. "Welcome to Parker Copper Mining Company. I am AJ Parker," he'd say. "And this is my company!" He talked about numbers and geography and history—things that weren't easily grasped by Gus. Nevertheless, he'd sat through his father's oration, as was his duty, being the son and heir of Parker Copper.

But when the guests had all departed for the tour, leaving Gus behind in the relative safety of the boardroom, he had doffed his top hat and simply walked to the mine himself, sure that his father had forgotten to invite him.

A crowd had stood outside The Only mine, eager to catch a glimpse of powerful politicians from the great East Coast. From the headframe deck, the group with AJ piled into the cage of the chippy—the hoist used for both men and materials, rather than raw ore—and AJ made a production of ringing the bells himself, rather than allowing the cager to do his job. Nine bells rang to the hoistman, who answered back, then started lowering the cage down the narrow shaft.

AJ explained to his guests that he'd just gotten word from the mine foreman that they might have stumbled upon a new discovery, and that they should be blasting within a day. Preparations were underway, as they could tell by the supplies riding past them in the other cages: a large, heavy crate loaded with dynamite; a mule crammed vertically into a cage, trussed up like a Thanksgiving turkey, braying in loud hiccups.

Reporters from across the state tried shoving into the cage with the politician's group, but were instead resigned to riding the miner's skip cage, occasionally hollering across the shaft, "Mr. Parker, what's the haps down here? Can you tell us some news?"

Up above, an excited crowd, eager to be the first to hear news of a rich new vein, gathered around the tight deck area near the chippy hoist. No one noticed the young boy with the miniature top hat, peering into the darkness of the shaft where the miner's skip cage had gone down minutes before.

It was a fluke, really. No one would have realized that the soil surrounding the open shaft was loose. And no one would have guessed that the photographer accompanying the reporters would have missed the ride down the skip hoist.

But when he had come upon the young Parker boy, leaning over and intently peering into the black hole, it must have been one of those moments he couldn't pass up. Just as Gus leaned in further and called out "Poppa?" the word ringing throughout the deep shaft, the photographer snapped the photo. The brilliant flash of the ignited magnesium and potassium chlorate powder caused a small explosion above his head, which startled young Gus, who looked up in surprise and proceeded to slip, dropping with the loose soil far into the mine shaft 3,500 feet straight down.

The photographer, distraught after realizing what he'd done, flung himself into that same opening, to his death. When AJ and the politicians and the reporters returned from the tour to the 3500 Station hoist, they discovered the photographer and Gus' crushed corpses, the photographer's arm eerily embracing Gus' body as if he'd try to save him well after the fall.

After arriving back at the surface, distraught and with his son's body cradled in his arms, AJ Parker had closed The Only mine forever.

Jules leaned against the cottonwood and rested her head back. When

Gus died, there was no other son to join AJ in his meetings, to take over the family business. Celeste was unquestionably uninterested, so Jules had taken to showing up at her father's office, situating herself in a corner chair, quietly listening. At first, AJ had ordered her out, but when she wouldn't ever leave, instead raising her chin in stubbornness, he acquiesced and let her sit, ignoring her.

It was during those hours that Jules soaked in everything she heard. She quietly learned how to identify a fault and a vein. She quietly learned what and how to mine for the greatest profits and how to deal with the labor unions. She quietly learned it all.

But then, after a while, she couldn't be quiet any longer.

There was the time during a board meeting when discussing Parker Copper's second-largest mine, the Metis, that twelve-year-old Jules stood up, without being called upon, and declared that the foreman from the Metis ought to be monitored as he'd surely been short-shifting his men. She said that the miners were unhappy and were no doubt going to start complaining.

Sure enough, a few days later, when the labor union officials came to the Parker Copper headquarters and demanded to talk with AJ about providing full eight or ten hour work days, her father had slid a glance at Jules, one eyebrow cocked. Jules had spoken up and assured the union official that they'd already addressed the situation and could monitor the full number of hours a miner worked based on the number of candles he used per day, down inside the dark mines. One candle was for eight hours, two candles for ten hours. The labor official shut up his trap right then and there and walked out the door. It was after that that her father finally began asking her opinion.

Yet now, years later and bursting with even more knowledge, Jules would not be running Parker Copper Mining Company because she was labeled *reckless* and *irresponsible*. Frustrated, she kicked out at the line of fire ants, scattering them in all different directions except their own hill.

Chapter 5

A petite girl with sharply trimmed bangs brushing at her almond-slanted eyes quietly approached Jules. She tossed a small package in the air, which Jules easily caught.

"You brought cigarettes?" Jules asked, a grin finally upon her face.

"I saw you sitting up here like a troll, silently fuming, so I came right up," replied the Chinese girl. Balinda Chang, also seventeen years old, had been Jules's best friend since they were girls, and Balinda's mother had worked for the Parkers. Since then, Mr. Chang's business, the Chang Noodle Parlor, had grown so busy that Mrs. Chang left the Parkers to work at the restaurant.

The Chang Noodle Parlor was the largest restaurant in all of Butte and had made Mr. Chang a prominent business owner of substantial wealth. Balinda's father developed qualities that garnered respect from those in Butte's upper class: education and a keen business sense. And while his daughter also possessed those qualities, she had another that was even more valuable. Balinda could read people's personalities and emotions just by looking deep into their eyes.

Her mother had said that eyes are windows to the soul, and that some of her family had a knack for figuring out a person's intentions— almost like a farmer able to read the weather. It was a trait that was handed down by her side of the family, and Mrs. Chang said that was why they had all married well and were successful in both family and business.

Since she was a young girl, Balinda had heard the stories of how back in China, Aunty Ping had saved the family fortune when she'd warned one of the Mai daughters against marrying a man who had been chosen for her. Ping claimed that he was a fake and was only after her dowry so he could use it for gambling. It had caused a rift in the families until they'd found out Ping was right. After that, all the mothers in their town consulted with Ping before any relationship decisions.

"I didn't need Aunty Ping to figure out that you needed a bit of cheering," continued Balinda as she sat next to Jules. "You're kind of obvious."

"Lucky me," Jules said, shaking two cigarettes out into her hand. "Wherever did you get a pack?"

"I took them from Sammy's jacket pocket," Balinda replied, shrugging. Then, noticing Jules' cocked eyebrow, she huffed a laugh, "What? I left a couple of coins in return."

Jules struck a match against the tree trunk, lighting the two slim cigarettes at the same time. She held one out to Balinda but swiftly tucked it into the palm of her cupped hand as a governess and her three wards strolled by. She whispered shortly, "Balinda, try to look inconspicuous."

"Hallo, Miss Parker," the governess called out with a hearty wave and toothy smile. "Good to see you!"

"And you as well!" Jules replied, waving her empty hand. As they watched them head for town, the children said over and over, "We just saw Miss Parker!"

Balinda sighed. "When you are with the town's beloved Parker girl, it is impossible to be inconspicuous."

"Just keep a lookout," Jules said, elbowing Balinda in the ribs. "Wouldn't do for someone to see a couple of girls smoking—especially the town's beloved Parker girl." Balinda returned an elbow to Jules, then sat with her back against the cottonwood.

Jules settled against the tree, thinking of Balinda's family. They were part of a large population of immigrants that made up Butte. Decades before, thousands of Chinese citizens had come to the United States seeking their fortunes. When the gold rush had made many men giddy, the Chinese men were no different and went to the areas known for the riches buried deep in the ground or sitting in streams, waiting to be plucked from the cold, flowing water. The areas in Montana were some of the richest they'd ever encountered, so the Chinese called Butte's hills *Gam San*—Gold Mountain.

The industrious Chinese found other work besides working in the mines. They provided the bulk of the labor to build Montana's first railroad systems and soon enough opened dozens of businesses that included restaurants, laundries, fresh vegetable farms, doctors' offices, and stores that carried Chinese goods. Most of the original Chinese had families, their children taking over and expanding the family businesses, growing Butte's own Chinatown to over 2,500 residents.

"And how is our fine number one son, Sammy?" Jules asked.

"Oh, you know, Jules, he is the same as ever—discontent. He's trying so hard to get in with Walter Liu and his group. It's very hard to just stand by and watch."

Jules did know. She'd often watched Sammy scurrying behind Walter, almost as if he were kowtowing. Sammy was a good guy, so it was hard for Jules to see him trying so hard to get in with Walter's tong, a Chinese sworn brotherhood. Sammy was at the age to belong to one of those organizations, and he'd chosen Walter's group over the dozens that were showing up in Butte.

"Is it at all dangerous?" Jules asked. "I thought tongs were a lot of gangsters."

"Not all tongs are crime gangs," Balinda replied. "They started out in China as benevolent secret societies. But a few years ago, there was tension between the traditional Chinese who came over directly from China and the first-generation Chinese who were born here. That's when fighting between tongs started." Balinda shrugged. "And over time, some tongs got into crime—like gambling and prostitution, and drugs."

"I hope Walter's tong isn't that type," exclaimed Jules.

Balinda smiled. "It is not. Walter's father owns the Chinese bank here in Chinatown. They have been very generous to our community."

"How does your father feel about Sammy joining a tong?"

"Well, he doesn't like it one bit," Balinda replied. "Just because a tong doesn't partake in criminal activity, doesn't mean it won't get involved." Jules nodded while Balinda continued. "And I suppose Sammy is trying to challenge our father."

"Ah. I know something about that, alright," Jules replied. She inhaled the cigarette smoke and blew a perfectly formed smoke ring.

"Another fight with your father, I presume," Balinda said.

"Yes, and this one was a doozy," replied Jules. She recounted the argument in between slow puffs on the cigarette. Finally, when the cigarette was burnt down, she stubbed the end into the dirt. "I know my father thinks I am immature and will, at any given point, sully his good name, but everything in me knows that I can run his company. That given the chance, I would do the job better than anyone." She stared out over the city and rubbed at her forehead. "What's worse is that my mother and Celeste are hell bent on marrying me off."

"Oh, the horror," Balinda said with a grin.

Jules laughed. "Balinda, who would even marry me?"

Balinda smiled at the dirt smeared across the top of her friend's face. "Jules, your father is wrong. You are not at all immature. You are delightful..."

"Ha!"

"…and presentable…"

"Ha!"

"…and would make someone a wonderful wife."

At that, they both started laughing. "I am most certainly none of those things," Jules said.

"And neither am I. Maybe that's why you are my truest friend," Balinda replied, reaching out and clasping Jules' hand in her own.

The honking of a flock of geese in the air mimicked their laughter. They looked up into the cloudless sky at the wide "V" headed north. "Just like clockwork. They know it's spring," Balinda said. "They always know."

"Yes, they do seem to know when the time is right," agreed Jules. She tilted her head, then said after a beat. "How do you think we will know when the time is right?"

"Right for what?"

"For anything, for the future."

"For the future?" Balinda's eyes lit up. "I know of something that will help us know our fate, our fortune. You must come down to the noodle parlor with me. We've just received a special shipment from my uncle in California. It came on today's train."

"What is it—"

"It's something new he's invented and is already taking San Francisco's Chinatown by storm. Maybe we will be able to find out about the future after all." Balinda pushed herself up and brushed the dirt from her skirt. She held out her hand.

"I hope that whatever it is can help me figure out what to do about the fight with my father," Jules said.

Balinda sighed. "You know what needs to be done, Jules. Apologize to your parents tonight while at dinner. They'll forgive you. As they always do."

Jules smiled and grasped Balinda's hand. She pulled herself up and hugged Balinda. "Do you want to sneak these back to Sammy?" she asked as she held out the pack of cigarettes.

"No, you keep them," Balinda replied, walking briskly downhill. "He'll only just give them to Walter, and you need them more than he does. Now, come on!"

They hurried downhill for 10 minutes, crossing Broadway and Park streets. When the streets flattened out, they came to the bustling area of Butte that made up their Chinatown. With sure steps, Balinda crossed in front of slow-moving automobiles and fast-moving horse-drawn wagons. She pulled Jules along, darting amongst the crowds of shoppers, then entered Chinatown on West Galena. An older man wearing a white tunic and soft black fabric shoes swept the walk outside his storefront. He looked up when Balinda walked past. "Good afternoon, Mr. Lin," she said, smiling. Hot, damp air escaped from the open transom window above the front door, the smell of starch heavy in the air.

"*Ni hoa*, Miss Chang," he replied, dipping his head. He kept it lowered and said, "And to you also, Miss Pahk-ah."

Jules stopped and smiled. She loved how the Chinese pronounced her name—it seemed so exotic. She lifted her hand, shading her eyes against the sun's glare as it reflected on the polished front window.

"How is your laundry business, Mr. Lin?" she asked.

"Very good. Very good," he said, nodding. "Many wagons going out every day—coming back very full." Jules smiled, stepping aside just as a laundry wagon pulled past, loaded with soiled clothing from the many families just outside Chinatown. The Lin family had been in business for years, as were a dozen other Chinese laundries, providing a service at lower rates than the traditional steam laundries they quickly replaced. Jules heard shouting from behind the building as Mr. Lin's sons ran out and began unloading the truck. Upon seeing Jules talking with their father, the boys stopped and called out, inviting her to ride with them on their next run. Jules clapped her hands and promised to join them another time.

Balinda tugged at her arm. "Come, Jules, let's get to the noodle parlor." The friends turned, waving goodbye to the Lins, then continued down the street. They crossed in the middle of the block to get into the shade provided by the tall brick buildings lining the street. Mixed voices carried out of all open doors of the ground-floor shops, the top floors quiet with the tenets working in the shops or at the many mines surrounding Butte.

Jules slowed and peered into the open door of the joss house—the temple where many of the Chinese still worshipped. An immense gong stood next to an altar, the smoke of incense joss sticks hanging still and thick. The large, open main hall was dark, but many candles flickered, casting dancing light across the surrounding red walls. Jules knew the Chinese believed that evil spirits were always present, so a light was constantly kept burning to keep the evil at a safe distance away.

"Balinda, would you like to stop?" Jules asked, pointing into the joss house.

"No, let's just get to the noodle parlor," Balinda said, exasperated. "Good lord, Jules. I thought you wanted to know about your future!"

"But, maybe we should light a candle while we're here. You know, keep the devils away." Jules shrugged her shoulders.

"Keep the devils away? What could possibly happen? Let's do it later—come on!"

Jules threw her hands up, surrendering. "Ok, ok! I'm coming." She followed Balinda down the street and saw an old woman carrying a red lantern slip into the alley. Jules glanced down the gloomy passageway and saw a lean-to shack propped against the brick siding of the joss house. Made of thin sheets of wood and other leftover construction pieces, and attached like some kind of parasite, the shack was dependent upon the brick building to keep it upright. But the old woman was nowhere to be seen. Certain she'd seen the old crone, Jules squinted far down the alleyway. Where did she go? Jules shrugged, then hurried to catch up with Balinda.

Balinda and Jules arrived in front of a three-storey brick building, with the smells of fried garlic and onion coming from the open windows. Balinda grasped Jules' hand and pulled her into the alley and the restaurant's back door. Wooden crates stacked haphazardly along the walls seemed ready to tumble under the heavy loads of fresh carrots, onions, bok choy, and some strange-looking mushrooms. Burlap bags crammed full of rice rested against the crates, the Chinese lettering on the outside printed with bright red ink.

They entered the kitchen and were immediately assaulted by the heat coming from the blazing stoves. The cooks shouted to each other as they whisked noodles, meat, and vegetables in the large, sizzling metal woks. The first time Jules had been in the noodle parlor kitchen, she thought the cooks were arguing, what with the yelling and clanging of heavy pans and chopping of cleavers. But in the midst of it all, one cook might say something, and then they would all throw back their heads and laugh gustily, their mouths open wide, eyes closed tight. Even though she never understood what they said, Jules would join in as she couldn't help but laugh as well.

The swinging door from the dining room burst open, and a busboy staggered past carrying a washtub loaded with dirty dishes. And then from around the corner came a lovely Chinese woman dressed in a sleek, fitted dress embroidered with flowers and vines, her hair twisted in a bun at the nape of her neck. The many jade bracelets encircling both her wrists clinked as she carried a large platter of more dirty dishes.

"Daughter! Where have you been?" she asked, displeased.

Jules stepped in front of Balinda, taking the platter into her own hands. "Mrs. Chang, please don't be angry at Balinda, it was my fault." Jules turned and brought the platter to the dishwashers, who rapidly scrubbed and rinsed at huge porcelain sinks. She wiped her hands on her skirt, then reached out to Balinda's mother, grasping her hands in greeting. "She was helping me."

Mrs. Chang shook her head. "You girls. Always thick as thieves. When we were at Parker Mansion—"

"Yes, always," Jules interrupted. "And by the by, my mother sends you her love. She would love for you to come to tea sometime soon. She says you wait too long between visits. "

Mrs. Chang's expression softened, and she pressed Jules' hands. "Ok, you tell Mrs. Parker I come visit her this week." Balinda grinned behind her mother's back.

"Mama, can I show Jules what Uncle sent this week?" Balinda asked. Without waiting for an answer, she pulled Jules away and down the hallway to a dimly lit storeroom. "Wait right here for me."

Balinda stepped out of the storeroom carrying a small blue and white ceramic dish piled with a few small, light-colored crisps, folded and bent in the middle. "Here, take one. A sweet for the sweet," she said, holding out the dish.

"What are they?" Jules asked.

"They're called cookies of destiny. They're quite new," she answered. "My uncle from San Francisco just started making them in a small bakery in their Chinatown. Go ahead, take one."

Jules peered at the dish and selected a cookie. It was lighter than it looked, almost delicate. She raised her eyebrows at Balinda, opened her mouth, and inserted the cookie.

"No! Not the whole thing," Balinda cried, laughing. "You're to crack it in the middle and take out the paper. It has your fortune on it." Balinda laughed so hard that she bent at the waist, her arms wrapped around her middle.

Jules retrieved the cookie from her mouth and held it up still intact, then they stood in the hallway, shaking with laughter.

When they'd finally stopped laughing, Jules held out the cookie and asked, "Well, shall I try it?"

"Please," Balinda replied, choking back another laugh. "I think you'll find the flavor pleasing." She selected a cookie for herself. "Go ahead, check your fortune—see what the future has in store."

With a quick twist, Jules cracked the cookie of destiny in half. She held up the half without the slip of paper and again raised her eyebrows at Balinda, who nodded once. Jules slipped the pieces into her mouth, tasting sugar and almond.

Balinda clapped her slender hands, her palms together, fingers pressed lightly together. "Now your fortune," she said, her eyes bright. "What does it say?"

Jules unfolded the thin slip of paper and held it between her fingers. She cleared her throat and read aloud, "*If you speak honestly, everyone will listen. If you speak dishonestly, no one will listen.*"

"Oh, that is a good one," Balinda replied.

"But what does it mean? I always speak honestly, and yet *no one* ever listens. Either that, or I just get in trouble for whatever I've said."

"Maybe you need to be more honest with yourself," Balinda said.

"That's what I'm saying. Maybe I'm too honest about what I think and say," Jules said, shaking her head. "Do you really think these fortunes could come true?"

"I don't really know—but I got one this morning that said, "You judge a book by its cover." Balinda's eyebrows wiggled up and down.

"Well, that is indeed true," Jules said, smiling. "So maybe there is something to these cookies of destiny after all." She slid the fortune into the pocket of her skirt. Jules sighed. "I suppose I should get back home and face my parents. I will certainly speak honestly and only hope someone will listen, although I am not holding my breath." Jules turned to Balinda, hugging her. "Thank you for the sweet. Oh, but just a thought. Because of the fortunes, maybe you should tell your uncle to instead call them *fortune cookies*. I'm quite sure they are going to be a big hit with your customers."

Chapter 6

J ules walked down the dark hallway crowded by white aprons hanging from hooks and freshly laundered tablecloths bundled with red ribbon. After pausing in the doorway, allowing her eyes to adjust to the afternoon light, she stepped into the alley, still thinking about her fortune.

Just as she took another step, a group of four young men rounded the corner, running at full speed. Before Jules could move, one of them hurtled into her, entangling their arms and legs, her skirt wrapping around them like a net. They fell onto the street in a heap.

What in the world? It felt like the time they were branding cattle on the Rankin ranch, when a calf slipped out of the ropes and plowed right into Jules as she stood watching.

"Oh my," Jules exclaimed, trying to push herself to her knees. "I am dreadfully sorry to have—"

"Stop them! We've been robbed!" A door slammed, and she heard excited shouting from the Chinese bank across the street. Footsteps ran toward them.

"She devil! Get out of the way!" a Chinese boy of about eighteen years of age yelled. He kicked out, catching her on her hip. As he tried pulling apart from Jules, a .38 fell from his pocket, spinning near her. Jules gasped and scampered away. She reached out and flung the gun out of his reach, toward the edge of the alley near the crates of vegetables.

"What's going on here?" demanded Jules, hurrying to stand. "Who are you?"

Ignoring her, the three remaining young men began yelling in Chinese, gesturing wildly with their hands to the one on the ground behind her.

"Kai, the Liu's are coming!" yelled a young man with black hair that flopped in his eyes. He held up a bulging cloth bag. "Come quickly!"

The one called Kai jumped up from where he and Jules had fallen to the ground. Jules felt his eyes travel over her, and she raised her hand to her chest. His handsome face was cruel, his boyish, round cheeks contradicting the viciousness in his eyes. She stared back at him, their dark eyes locked as she heard more people running.

Kai broke the gaze and then jerked his head down the alley. "Zhang Yong, you have the money—let's go!" he said to the boy with floppy hair.

Riled, Jules said, "Absolutely not! You cannot steal from the Liu's!" She confronted Kai, her hands clenched at her sides.

"The Liu's belong to us now." Kai turned his head and spat at Jules. He grabbed the arms of the two boys standing near her and yanked them to run. As they turned on unsteady legs, Jules lunged out, diving to hold onto their legs like an alley cat pouncing upon a scurrying rat. They dragged her along as they tried to flee, her skirt mopping the grimy street.

"This is none of your business," hissed Kai. He stepped back and struck out with his foot, kicking Jules hard in the stomach. She cried out, her arms dropping from the boys' legs. She saw one of the boys quickly hand something to Kai. He eyed Jules with malevolence, and she thought he might strike out at her again. But instead, he turned away, tucking something into the waistband of his trousers.

Suddenly, an ear-splitting BANG rang through the air. Jules flattened onto her stomach as the gunshot resonated throughout the tight alleyway. She frantically crawled to the stacks of crates along the wall and ducked behind.

"You cannot do this to us!" shouted a young Chinese man dressed in a black suit and tie. Jules peeked around the crate. Walter Liu stood at the entrance to the alley, waving a pistol over his head.

"Oh, yes, we can! Our brothers were right," Kai yelled. "The Liu's are too easily robbed. You are weak." He laughed with the other three boys.

Walter's face flushed, and he raised the gun, pointing it at Kai. "Devil!" he screamed. "That money belongs to us."

At that very moment, Kai reached into his waistband, withdrawing a .38. With a smooth movement, he pulled the trigger, the shot exploding. Jules looked up in time to see Sammy Chang throw himself at Walter, knocking him to the ground. The bullet ripped through Sammy's shoulder, spraying blood across Walter's face.

"NOOOO!" cried Mr. Chang as he emerged from the front of the noodle parlor, his face contorted in horror.

Kai quickly turned to run. But the floppy-haired boy, Zhang Yong, paused behind him with a frightening calm. He pointed his gun at Sammy, who lay groaning atop Walter on the ground.

"Stop!" shouted Jules, her ears still ringing from the previous gunshots. Something glinting under the crate near her caught her eye, and she snatched it up, raising it in a fluid move. She cocked the hammer, aimed, and pulled the trigger.

The bullet slammed into Zhang Yong, spinning him away from Sammy and Walter. He screamed in pain and then dropped to the ground, blood staining his white linen tunic. Kai looked back, swearing. He ran to his friend.

Police sirens wailed in the background as people from nearby businesses flooded into the street.

"You! *Guilao!*" snarled Kai. "Don't get involved in the things you know nothing about, white girl. Go home to your ghost dolls."

"Grab him," Walter yelled, struggling to stand. He seized hold of Kai's pant leg.

Kai pulled away from Walter's hands as the police sirens got louder. Swearing again, he looked to where Zhang Yong lay still and bleeding. He shrank back at the growing crowd. Then, with a howl of anger, he turned and ran away down the murky alleyway, alone.

With her eyes wide, Jules breathed heavily and stood paralyzed. Her grimy skirt, smelling of rot, was plastered against her, speckled with blood. Jules watched the pool of blood under Zhang Yong spread. She felt bile rise in her throat.

"Miss Parker!" Mr. Chang ran up. "You mustn't be found here. Follow me! Quickly!" Jules' legs turned watery, and she staggered back, but Mr. Chang steadied her as she weakened.

"But, Sammy… the money… this…" Jules gripped the gun.

"Quickly! Before the police arrive!" Mr. Chang held up the cloth bag full of money. "The stupid boys dropped it—I will return it to the Liu's." He pulled Jules by the arm for a door open in the side of the brick wall to the noodle parlor.

"What? Where did this doorway come from?" she blinked in confusion.

Balinda appeared in the secret doorway, waving Jules closer and demanded, "Jules, come on!" With her friend in sight, Jules finally shook her head, then ran for the doorway. She looked behind her at Mr. Liu and Walter carrying Sammy, blood dripping from his shoulder. But beyond them lay Zhang Yong, trembling with his eyes closed.

"I said, come on!" Balinda repeated with urgency. But Jules turned back and ran to Zhang Yong. She grabbed him by his tunic collar and dragged him through the doorway. Jules gently leaned his head against the damp brick wall just as the first police car drove into the alley. Balinda quickly pulled the door behind them, shrouding them in darkness.

Jules followed Balinda down two flights of wooden steps into a dimly lit hallway. Mrs. Chang approached her carrying a small lantern. She raised one finger to her lips and shook her head. They could hear a ruckus from above their heads. "Where is everyone?" yelled one of the police officers. Car doors slammed as more police cars arrived.

With her eyes adjusted to the dark, Jules could just make out where they were. Violet light filtered from overhead, purple glass blocks in the cement above their heads. The air was cool and damp, the floor pressed dirt.

Mr. Liu and Walter laid Sammy onto a pallet of blankets. His eyes flickered, and he groaned. Dr. Ts'ui came up beside them and knelt beside Sammy. Jules spied a bowl of hot water and some towels nearby.

Jules shivered. She wondered how the doctor had gotten to them so quickly. But when she looked past him, she saw many hallways leading in and out of the room where Sammy lay. Just like Parker Copper's maze of mine tunnels that twisted for miles, it seemed as if an entire city might exist down here, beneath the streets of Butte's Chinatown.

"The wound is clean," Dr. Ts'ui said quietly. "The bullet passed through without hitting a vein." He bent lower over Sammy's shoulder.

A moan came from up the dark staircase. Jules placed her hand on Dr. Ts'ui's arm. "There is another boy at the top of the stairs who has been shot. He needs care," she said. "Please mend him as best you can, then, when he is stable, return him to his family. I will stop by your office tomorrow to pay for his treatment."

"What? He doesn't belong with us," Walter cried. "He is a thief."

"But I am no murderer," Jules replied, holding up the gun she still clutched in her hand.

"We need to get up to the restaurant," whispered Mr. Chang, resting his hand on Sammy's leg. "The police will be there asking questions."

Mrs. Chang nodded and looked at Balinda."Stay here with your brother. And keep Miss Parker hidden until the police have gone." She handed Balinda the lantern.

"But I should go talk to the police," Jules exclaimed. "I saw that boy shoot Sammy."

"And you also shot one of the members of the Five Brothers," Mr. Liu said, walking up to Jules and retrieving the gun she held. "They won't forget you."

"The Five Brothers?" Jules asked. "What is this all about?"

"It's beyond you, years in the making," Mr. Liu replied, his face serious. "Have you heard of triads?" Jules shook her head.

Balinda came close to Jules. "Triads are in the old country. They are the groups involved in crime—the tongs here evolved from them. Like I said before, some tongs are legitimate, but some tongs are trying to take over and gain power. They have ties to their brothers back in China."

"Kai said something about their brothers—right before he shot Walter." Jules shivered again. "All the more reason I should go to the police."

"Miss Parker, I am in your debt for saving Sammy's life. But you must keep all this secret—we don't want to damage your reputation," Mr. Chang said. "You are a society woman. The daughter of AJ Parker."

"That is exactly why I should tell the police!" she replied.

"But you are not at Parker Mansion. You are in Chinatown."

Jules stared at Mr. Chang.

"You may be accepting of us, but others in this city are not so. You must remember who you are, your standing, and what you have been born into. Being involved in a war between Chinese factions is not something that befits someone of your status."

"But…" continued Jules.

"Do not do anything to jeopardize yourself. Or us," Mr. Chang said.

"Respectfully, Miss Parker, it is not for you to decide, so you will not say anything to anyone."

Chapter 7

Jules perched on an overturned wooden crate, the dappled light casting a violet hue over her. A blanket covered her shoulders, keeping the damp from permeating her bones. Sammy lay next to her, his breathing shallow but steady. Dr. Ts'ui had stitched and bandaged the oldest Chang son, and Balinda applied a cool cloth to her brother's forehead.

From down a dark hallway, Zhang Yong quietly murmured in Chinese. Dr. Ts'ui had administered some kind of tea, which slowed Zhang Yong's bleeding and put him into a fitful sleep. The doctor promised to come back after darkness fell, when it would be easier to move Zhang Yong undetected.

Balinda had told Jules to stay beneath the streets until the area was clear and the police had moved on. But besides that, they hadn't spoken much at all. The only sounds were water dripping somewhere down the cramped hallways and the scurrying of rodents.

After about half an hour, no more voices were heard above, so Jules stood and quietly crept toward the wooden stairs.

Balinda's soft voice called out, "Jules, please. Remember, not a word to anyone."

Jules nodded and replied, her eyes dark and serious. "Of course not. I promise." She pushed against the solid door, and it gave way without a sound. Once out in the alleyway, Jules leaned against the secret door, making sure it closed, the seams fading into the brickwork without a hint. She ran her hand over the bricks, shaking her head in wonder.

Jules' thoughts whirled. So much had happened, and the day wasn't even over yet. Jules thought about Sammy throwing himself in front of Walter. What a wild and impetuous thing to do. Jules thought briefly that maybe she was the pot calling the kettle black since her father had called her wild and impetuous just a few weeks ago.

But Jules knew that she was like Sammy—loyal. If she had to fight for Balinda's family again, she would. If she had to fight for her own family, for Parker Copper, she would. Even though she'd shot someone, and it weighed heavily on her conscience, Jules knew she would do it again. She'd do anything for her family.

She turned away from the hidden door and brushed at her filthy skirt. A rustle came from her pocket. Jules reached in and pulled out the slip of paper with her fortune. *If you speak honestly, everyone will listen. If you speak dishonestly, no one will listen.*

Jules shook her head again. Just earlier today, she'd told her mother and sister of her desire—her *need*—to run Parker Copper. And then she had tried speaking honestly with her father, but had been basically kicked out of her own house. And now, when she told Mr. Chang that she wanted to go tell the police what she'd seen, he had ordered her to keep her mouth shut.

If you speak honestly, everyone will listen. If you speak dishonestly, no one will listen.

That's what her fortune had said. But just what part of that was actually going to come true?

Chapter 8

"Really, Jules, your behavior yesterday was impossible. Father was so upset—I heard him telling Mother," Celeste said, adjusting the sash on her skirt. "And then you just disappeared until dinner was served! What were you thinking?"

"Of course you heard, Celeste. That's what you do—eavesdrop," Jules said, pushing the brim of her elaborate hat off her forehead.

Celeste frowned. "However else am I supposed to know about what goes on in that house?" she asked.

Jules leaned far over the platform, peering down the train tracks, the ribbons and flowers drooping forward as she bent. "Let's just drop it and wait for Bradley to arrive," she replied. Jules clasped the bonnet to her head, saying under her breath, "Damn this blasted hat."

From deep in the crowded station platform, they heard someone call out, "Hey, Miss Parker! Love your hat!"

As the hat tipped again into her eyes, Jules replied, "Thank you so much for noticing!" But then, she snatched it off her head, waved it in the air, and called out, "You can have it for a two-cent piece!"

"Don't love it that much," came the reply, which was followed by laughter from the crowd.

"Your loss," Jules joined in laughing, and she pulled the brim over her ears.

Celeste shook her head and said, "All I'm saying is that you are going to end up alone, a spinster, if you keep up your ways." She reached out and grabbed hold of Jules' sleeve, pulled her upright, then brushed at her skirt. "I mean, really, you do like boys, don't you?" A herd of mules near the platform raucously stamped their hooves, leading Celeste to brush harder than she'd planned.

"Of course I do," Jules said. "I just haven't met any that interest me. The boys here in Butte are just that—boys. All of them with their overbites and acne and conversations consisting of two words." She turned, eyeing the pack animals. "And if any are mature enough to be considered a young man, most of *them* just want to tell me what to do." A mule brayed behind them.

"Well, someone's got to do it," mumbled Celeste.

A piercing train whistle blew in the distance. The crowd roused and began moving toward the tracks, filling every inch of the station's wooden platform. Celeste stiffened with dread as bodies rushed past them, stirring dust into the air. Shouts and laughter rang through the station, the din barely covering the sound of the approaching train. As the crowd surged, Celeste swayed back and forth, like a stalk of wheat in the wind. Losing her balance, Celeste tumbled backwards. Jules saw her reach out to steady herself, her hand landing squarely on the grimy belly of a drunken miner, his hands and face filthy with sweat, dirt, and god-only-knows what else.

"Hey, hey there, Beautiful," the miner slurred, pressing Celeste's hand more firmly onto his thick belly. "Ain't you ace-high? How about us go share a pint or two?" He leaned close into Celeste, his sour breath enveloping her. Celeste looked as if she might faint.

Jules stepped forward, soundly pushing the miner away from Celeste. "Move away now, Matty Kelly," she demanded. "Nothing for you here." She placed her hands on her hips. The miner started to resist, but his eyes cleared for a moment, a glimmer of recognition flashing across his face.

With a smile full of crooked, yellow teeth, "Is that you, Miz Parker?" he asked Jules, his words slurring. Without waiting for her reply, he moved away from Celeste, his dirt-encrusted hand held up in a small, pathetic wave. "Nice to see you. Sorry for the trouble," he murmured as he backed away into the crowd.

"Oh! This is always such a clutter," exclaimed Celeste, her breathing uneven. "You are a dear to accompany me, Jules." She fanned her face. "Now, please see if you can spy my Bradley. As soon as we find him, we can get out of this god-forsaken chaos."

With a whoosh, the train from Idaho pulled into the Butte station. Bodies rushed forward, the crowd of people pressing forward, trying to get closer to the train. The conductors shouted "Butte! Butte, Montana!" as they lowered steps from the passenger cars to the station platform. With ear-splitting screeches, heavy metal doors to the freight cars pulled open, and dozens of wagons, the mules whinnying and hee-hawing, backed up for loading. Newspaper boys stirred from sitting on the side of the road, jumped up, and began shouting the headlines on the newspapers they held aloft.

Jules looked at the train, rising up on her toes, and straining for a glimpse of Celeste's husband. From one of the passenger cars, Jules spied a family of Chinese debarking, their speech sounding sharp and staccato amongst the other voices. Behind them, a line of people followed—a young mother holding her crying baby, a couple of businessmen dressed in typical dark suits, one carrying a top hat and cane, an older couple, their weaving steps making it seem like the train was still moving. But just as Jules was about to turn away, her gaze was drawn back to the train. Backlit from the sun shining through the doorway and almost glowing, Jules looked to the most handsome man she'd ever seen.

Tall and lean, he stood above the others, stepping off the train. At first glance, because of the way he carried himself with such self-assurance, Jules thought that he was much older than she. But when he grabbed the side handrail on the train car and merrily swung out onto the platform, Jules realized that really, he must only be older by a couple of years.

He walked further onto the platform, the spring light glinting on his sun-bleached sandy brown hair, making it seem as if dusted with gold. Even from so far away, Jules could see his eyes framed with thick eyelashes, his thin, straight nose, and prominent cheekbones. Good lord, he really was attractive. He raised his arms overhead and stretched, like a mountain lion just awakening from a nap. Jules inhaled sharply. Yes, he was very attractive.

She watched him walk away from the emptying train car, his plain, yet well-cut clothes hanging nicely on his slender frame. The handsome stranger abruptly stopped and tilted his head, as if listening to something. He then turned quickly and, in two steps, was kneeling at the base of a stand of holly bushes, their dark green leaves sharp and prickly. Jules watched as he reached into the thicket and withdrew a ball of black fur—a tiny black Labrador puppy yelping pitifully. He spoke a few soft words to the pup, then took something that looked like jerky from his pocket, and held it to the puppy that eagerly nipped at it with pointed little teeth.

The stranger cradled the puppy in one hand and ran his handsome cheek across the pup's furry neck. He looked over the heads of the crowd to where the newsboys stood, waving their papers in the air. The stranger approached the group, still stroking the puppy's head. When one young boy noticed what the stranger carried, he dropped his papers to the ground, near an overturned crate, yelling, "Buster! How 'dya get outa the crate?" He reached his skinny arms up to the stranger and accepted his puppy with a huge hug and smile.

The stranger clapped the newsboy on the back and said, "I've got a weakness for these dark-haired little mischief-makers." He handed the newsboy some silver coins, pointing to the pup. Jules heard the boy yell, "Yessir! I'll make sure to get him a proper bed and some good food. Thanks!"

Jules found herself entranced, blatantly staring, when a cart, piled high with luggage and boxes, wheeled in front of her, cutting off her line of sight to the good-looking new arrival. Not ready to look away yet, Jules craned around the cart, looking quickly over the passengers unloading the train, but he, the handsome stranger, was already gone.

"Do you see him yet?" asked Celeste, breaking the spell that Jules was in.

Jules blinked quickly, her eyes wide. "Did you see him too?"

"Bradley?" replied Celeste. "That's what I'm asking you, Jules."

"No, no, that's not who I'm talking about," Jules said as she rose on her toes, her neck stretched high, searching the crowd for that crown of golden, sandy hair. Jules shook her head. He was gone.

Ignoring Jules, Celeste said, "I do hate when my husband has to travel for business, but I suppose that is what it takes to be successful in the banking industry."

Jules sighed. "Celeste, Bradley works for Father's bank," she replied, then stepped up onto a small stack of bricks lying near their feet. Jules craned her head, looking over the fray. "He could spend his time wearing nothing but an apron and riding a llama around singing The Star Spangled Banner, and he would still be successful."

Celeste shot Jules a dirty look, then shoved against her sister. Once again, Jules' enormous hat tilted forward over her eyes, obscuring her vision.

"Why you…" Jules said angrily. But suddenly the hair on the back of her neck stood. With her hat pushed back, Jules looked out over the crowd once more and saw a dozen dark, wicked eyes watching her.

Kai and his group of Five Brothers stood silently in the shade of a box elder tree, their hands clasped behind their backs. They watched

Jules for what seemed like hours. Jules' heart raced when she saw Kai mouth, "Now I know you, *guilao*."

From behind Kai, a floppy-haired boy stepped out, his arm clutched around his heavily bandaged body. Zhang Yong! Jules stumbled back, off the brick pile. They knew who she was. And they were following her.

"Celeste, we have to go," stammered Jules, in a panic. "We have to go now!" Without looking, Jules turned away from her sister and smacked right into someone standing behind her.

"Gah!" shrieked Jules.

"Whoa there, I gotcha."

Strong arms grasped Jules, holding tightly before she would have toppled over. Jules looked up and stared straight into the most stunning hazel eyes she'd ever seen. Surrounded by a halo of gold-dusted hair, the handsome new arrival stared back at Jules.

"Oh!" she exclaimed, as all sound muted from her ears, except for the sound her heart made, like the explosions underground in the mines.

A chunk of hair dropped across his forehead and over one eye, another hooked behind his ear. Jules thought that maybe he'd been a couple of weeks too long without a haircut. Not that it was a bad thing, but only because it hid too much of his strong square jaw and high cheekbones.

He tilted his head to the right, the corner of his mouth pulling up in a small smile. They remained balanced against each other in a kind of unmoving dance until he reached up and brushed a strand of Jules' long, dark hair off her cheek.

"Hey, Miss Parker? Everything ok with you?" The question, called out by a train attendant, brought Jules out of her dream. Upon feeling a strange man's touch, Jules jerked and quickly pulled away, standing upright.

"Why… how dare you!" she gasped. The stranger knelt to one knee, his hand reaching out beneath him, lifting something from the ground.

Celeste quickly ran to her sister's side. "Unhand her, sir! Or I shall have to summon the police!" Celeste moved close to Jules, stepping soundly on her elegant hat, crushing the brim and smearing mud across the crown.

"Really? I suppose if you must, go ahead and call the police," he said, laughing and standing up. His eyes danced. "They'd soon figure out that you two young ladies might be full as a tick, stumbling around like that."

"What are you saying?" Celeste drew herself up. "Are you implying that we're drunk?"

Jules noticed that he only smiled—the one that lifted the left side of his mouth. "I'm not implying anything. But most ladies I know who smoke cigarettes usually do it while sitting in a saloon." He held up a pack of cigarettes. Jules quickly patted her pocket—sure enough, they were hers. Or rather, Sammy's. Jules' eyes widened.

"Celeste, my dear! Is everything all right?" Bradley strode toward them, pushing against the crowd.

Gazing at Jules, the handsome stranger stepped back. With two fingers, he raised the cigarettes in a kind of salute, then with his long fingers, tucked the pack into his front shirt pocket. And with that dazzling and glorious smile again, the handsome stranger turned and walked away.

Jules finally took in a breath—she realized she hadn't been breathing. She reached down to retrieve her filthy hat, then stood back up and watched the stranger navigate the crowd and out of her sight.

"Bradley," replied Celeste, rushing to her husband. "I am ever so happy to see you." She grasped his hands as he leaned over and placed a kiss on her cheek.

"My dear wife, I am happy to see you as well," said Bradley. He turned to Jules. "Are you quite all right?"

"Yes, quite, thank you, Bradley," replied Jules, adjusting her skirt. "I just, well, slipped after climbing on those bricks to get a better view for you." She glanced over to the stand of trees where the Five Brothers had been—it was empty.

"Heh, heh. Yes, well, perhaps that will finally learn you to act like a lady," chuckled Bradley. "Do keep away from climbing on rocks, will you, Jules?" He tilted his felt bowler's brim lower, shading his eyes from the bright sun as he looked out over the crowd.

Celeste placed her hand lightly on Bradley's arm. "What are you looking for? Did you leave something in the passenger car?"

"No, no, dear, not some*thing*," he replied. "I'm looking for some*one*." Celeste raised her eyebrows questioningly.

Bradley leaned in close to Celeste and Jules. "Talk on the train was that we had a big shot passenger with us. Some kind of major player from a wealthy East Coast family with business and political connections."

Celeste pursed her lips in a smile. "I wonder who it might be! Surely Mother will know of this man soon enough—and before long, he will be amongst our guests at Parker Mansion."

Jules grimaced. "Oh great—yet another flannel-mouthed, fancy-talking, old geezer to entertain."

Bradley chuckled. "Would you rather he be a flannel-mouthed, fancy-talking young man? Then might you be more inclined to entertain him, Jules?"

"Probably not," Jules answered, while she watched a group of men in severe black suits and top hats climb into an automobile waiting for them at the side of the street.

Bradley placed Celeste's arm in his and stepped away from the train station. "Now, speaking of Parker Mansion, let us be off. I have much to tell your father of my trip."

Jules turned to follow, but suddenly found herself surrounded. The Five Brothers crowded tightly against her, moving in a slow crawl. Staring straight ahead, Kai said through the side of his mouth, "It is not often that a debt is created and paid the same day, Miss Parker." Jules walked slowly, her eyes on the back of her sister's head.

"As you see, Zhang Yong will be fine," continued Kai. "But I warn you once more, do not get involved in something you know nothing about. You do not want to have another obligation to the Five Brothers." He stopped and looked at Jules with his evil eyes. "Because the next time, it may not be so easily wiped."

Jules swallowed hard and nodded quickly. "I understand."

"*Ting hǎo*," replied Kai. "Good." After a long look, he drifted away from Jules as the rest of the Five Brothers disappeared into the crowd.

Sorry that she'd shot Zhang Yong, but relieved that she'd ask Dr. Ts'ui to care for him, Jules wiped her damp palms on her skirt. She felt as if she'd dodged a bullet and certainly would not ever want to again be beholden to the Five Brothers. Jules ran quickly to catch up with her sister and brother-in-law.

When they stepped into the cool, dark entryway of Parker Mansion, Jules heard her father's voice, coming from his library. Hazel approached Bradley, welcoming him and taking his topcoat and hat. Jules removed her hat, her fingers trailing the soiled ribbon that had previously choked her.

Grimacing, Hazel held out her hand, "Miss Jules, may I take that… hat… from you?"

Jules crushed the hat to her chest and replied, "No, no, thank you. I'll take this to my dressing room. It has suddenly become my favorite hat." And a hat that would certainly serve as a reminder of the handsome stranger she'd just met.

Bradley moved in the direction of the library while Celeste and Jules turned for the grand stairway, their heels clicking on the polished wooden floor.

"Greetings, Mr. Parker," called Bradley as he pulled open the library's double doors. "And…and…"

"Greetings to you as well, Bradley," AJ's voice boomed. "Come right in. There is someone I should want you to meet."

Jules and Celeste paused on the stairway. Someone else was with AJ in his library? As if reading their thoughts, AJ leaned out the doorway and bellowed, "Jules, come join us." Used to being beckoned by her father at any time, Jules looked at her sister and shrugged. "Coming, Father!"

Still holding her grimy hat, Jules entered the library, her hair windswept and tangled. Bradley stood just inside the doors, strangely quiet and tentative.

"Ted, I'd like you to meet my precious daughter, Augustina Juliette Parker," said AJ, looking from Jules to the tall, dark-haired man standing at his side. "And Jules, please say hello to Mr. Theodore Jackson." The fine-looking guest smiled widely, a deep dimple showing on each cheek. His face was boyish, with round eyes rimmed with thick, black eyelashes and a full fringe of hair combed low across his forehead.

Jules dipped her head and said with a small smile, "It's a pleasure to meet you, Mr. Jackson." She approached him with her hand outstretched.

"Please, call me Ted," he replied, catching Jules' hand and holding on a bit before giving it a squeeze. His dark eyes appraised her. "Your father has been telling me all about you."

"Has he?" asked Jules, glancing quickly at AJ.

"Why yes, he said that you know everything about Butte and

suggested that perhaps you might be able to tour me around," replied Ted. "Seeing as I am new to town."

Jules nodded, saying, "I do think you'll find Butte an interesting city. We have such diverse neighborhoods."

"Did you find that in one of your diverse neighborhoods?" asked Ted. He eyed the filthy hat Jules held in her other hand. "Perhaps the alleyways in the, what do you call that seedy area… the Cabbage Patch?"

"Oh, this? No, no, it dropped off when I stumbled after climbing up on the brick pile…" began Jules.

"Ahem!" growled AJ, interrupting Jules as Ted's eyebrows climbed high. "Bradley, please come over and shake hands with Mr. Jackson." AJ looked over to his son-in-law. "You two will surely be working closely." Bradley threw his shoulders back and strode over to Ted, his hand outstretched.

"Mr. Jackson, very glad to meet you," he said. "You say you're to be working for Parker Copper?"

Ted gave Bradley's hand a firm shake, clasping his elbow with his other hand. "Why, yes, Mr. Parker has hired me on as the new Vice Director." Ted inclined his head at AJ. "Of course, I'm thrilled to be here."

AJ settled on the edge of his massive oak desk. "Ted and I have been corresponding over these past few weeks—he wrote me from Colorado, where he was working for Bull Ridge Mining. Lucky for us, I was able to steal him away to come work for Parker Copper Mining Company. I've been explaining to him that I'm looking at further exploring my future in politics, and I need a first-rate man to help run my company." All three men nodded in agreement. Upon hearing the news that AJ had hired someone to help him run the company, Jules bristled.

"Well! Since you first-rate men have it all figured out, I suppose I should go rest or tidy up or some other irresponsible nonsense," said Jules. She looked at her father, who leveled his eyes at her. He glared and, with a short shake of his head, silenced her. Jules turned toward the doorway, her chin tilted up and her hands on her hips. "Good day, gentlemen."

"It was a tremendous pleasure meeting you, Augustina," called Ted as she stepped away. Jules turned back, meeting Ted's gaze. "I do look forward to you guiding me throughout the town." His warm smile lit up his face, melting Jules' frosty anger at her father.

"As do I, Mr. Jackson," she replied, returning his smile. "But please, I'm called Jules by my friends."

"Well, Augustina," Ted said, still staring at her. He moved one arm behind his back and bowed low. "I would hope that we become much more than just friends."

Chapter 9

"Imagine that," said Millicent as she and Celeste sat, supervising the housemaid curling Jules' stick-straight hair. "I knew your father was hiring a young man from Colorado, but I had no idea he was so very attractive!"

Jules tried nodding her head, but instead just pulled at the curling tong. The sharp smell of singed hair filled the air. "Imagine that," she replied.

And imagine the fact that she'd met another—entirely different— very attractive young man. Who was the sandy-haired stranger whom she'd run into at the train platform? And if he were truly trying to come to her aid, why then had he waved her cigarettes around, teasing her so? Jules remembered the feeling of his strong arms, circling her waist, holding her close. Her blouse still wore hints of his fragrance—a bit of sandalwood and the slightly nutty and musky ambrette. Jules could still feel his long fingers brushing at her cheek, lifting her hair away. She smiled.

"Mother, I think we may have broken through the calloused shell!" exclaimed Celeste. "Why, I think that Jules may be smitten with Mr. Jackson!"

"It is absurd for me to be smitten," replied Jules. "Mr. Jackson merely requested me to show him around. And I must take the task seriously."

Jules thought back to the conversation she'd had with her father a couple of hours prior. When Bradley and Ted Jackson left Parker Mansion, Jules had approached her father in his library. She pleaded with him to let her take over as Vice Director, that it wasn't too late to send Ted back to Colorado. AJ had stiffened and refused to allow it; his mind was made up. But he did make one concession. He said that he had been thinking long and hard about Jules' experience and love for Parker Copper, and it had made an impression on him. So he'd come up with a solution—he'd created work for her within the company.

She would conduct tours, attend parties, and be available for anything else that might be required of visitors. She was to act as the foremost contact for all things having to do with Parker Copper—outside the mines.

Jules had been devastated. Tour visitors around? Attend parties? None of it was remotely sufficient to her in terms of being involved with Parker Copper. But AJ had been clear that it was this, or nothing at all, having to do with his company. And he left it off by saying that if Jules could prove herself to be respectable and responsible at the work, then he might reconsider allowing her back in the mines.

Upon hearing that, Jules had thrown her arms around her father and had said in a sure voice, "I will do my best for Parker Copper."

So that was why she was sitting still, allowing Trudy to fry her hair. Millicent and Celeste could go on thinking that she was getting dressed to impress the handsome Ted Jackson, but Jules knew it was all part of her job.

"But he said that he'd hope you'd be more than friends," cried Celeste, jumping up from the settee, still thinking of Ted Jackson. "I heard him myself."

"Of course, you heard it yourself," said Jules. "You were practically falling into the library with your ear pressed so hard against the door."

Millicent laughed. "I think Celeste is correct. And since Mr. Jackson is joining us for dinner this evening, we want you to look your best. So sit still and let Trudy finish curling that hopeless hair of yours." Beneath Jules' bedroom, the kitchen staff was busy putting an elaborate dinner together. They could hear the clatter of trays being placed on the countertops. A clank rang out as a silver serving-piece dropped into the cast-iron sink.

Jules sighed and looked into the mirror. "I don't know why it's so important to train my hair into doing something it's not willing to do."

"Because a woman's hair is her glory!" answered Millicent and Celeste together, both of them unconscientiously reaching up and patting their own styled tresses. Her mother continued, "Always remember that, Jules. Men expect us to look a certain way, and it begins with our hair."

"It still doesn't make sense to me," said Jules. "What does it matter what we look like? I'd rather be comfortable—I'd even shear off my hair if I could." Celeste inhaled sharply and placed her palm against her forehead. "And these corsets and chemises and skirts allow for no freedom. How will I be able to ride a bicycle, let alone drive an automobile?"

"You won't," came an icy reply from Millicent. "Jules, it is time for you to get it into your thick head that there are certain ways that women, especially of our station, are expected to act and dress. Your father and I have given you all kinds of leeway throughout the years, but now that a possible suitor has come into your life, I am bound and determined to make you presentable."

"But, Mother, he's not a suitor," said Jules. "He is a Vice Director."

"If a man is interested in a young woman, he is a suitor. Jules, I am not budging on this. Your father was correct—you've gone from being *spirited* to being wild and impetuous. From this moment on, you will act and dress like a lady." Millicent approached Jules and placed a firm hand on her shoulder.

The din from the kitchen below continued when the sound of shattering crystal pierced the air. Jules remembered her father's anger when he hurled his goblet at the fireplace hearth. "Egad," said Millicent, removing her hand. "I hope that wasn't your great-grandmother's decanter."

Jules thought of the fight, just days ago, with her father. Of how angry he was that she'd presume to take over the company. He must have had Ted in mind all along—a young man who was responsible and respectable.

Jules didn't feel that men were any better than women. She felt that everyone was equal, regardless of gender or race. But the fact was, most of society still thought that men were superior and that all women were faint-hearted, foolish, and rash.

Jules knew her battle was hard because she was one of the ones considered foolish and rash. But maybe that was the point—she wasn't doing anything to disprove the notion.

Well, that would change tonight. Perhaps she was a woman, but she would no longer be foolish and rash. She would act like a lady, and she would be responsible and respectable. She would do her gender proud.

"Mother, I'm not saying that you and Celeste might be right," said Jules in a quiet voice. "But if I'm to provide service to Parker Copper, then my aim is to act and dress like a proper lady."

AJ had just made a concession to Jules by giving her a foot back into the company. He'd extended an olive branch. So could she.

Jules looked up and gazed into the mirror, this time with a look of resignation. "Trudy, you've missed a lock here on the side. Could you please curl it and tuck it up? And then let's try to put a little color onto my cheeks and lips." Reflected in the mirror, Jules saw her mother and Celeste grin wildly and clasp hands.

With her hair piled on top of her head, tendrils strategically dangling here and there, Jules stepped down the staircase. Her new evening gown flowed softly over her hips, flaring at the hem, a short train trailing the stairs behind her. The open neckline, embroidered with ivory pearls, and lightly fitted bodice showed off Jules' smooth skin, the beautiful pale blue satin contrasting deeply with her black hair. Music played softly from the drawing room, the sound of gentle laughter drifting out. Jules entered the room and selected a glass of rose-colored champagne from a servant's tray. She lifted it to her mouth, sipping the cool, bubbly wine.

"Good evening, Augustina."

Jules turned and looked up into the face of Ted Jackson. He was dressed in a black dinner jacket with a white shirt, its three-inch collar standing stiff. Jules smiled and answered, "Good evening, Mr. Jackson. Do you mind?" and without waiting for an answer, she lifted up on her toes, reached up, and adjusted his black silk bow, which had been tilting to one side.

He returned her smile and answered, "Ted, please." He patted his tie. "And thank you for that. I'm still not fully unpacked, and I had to rush this afternoon to even find my dinner-wear."

"Well, you look fine," said Jules, taking in his pomaded hair and his dimples deep in his freshly shaved cheeks.

"And you look stunning," replied Ted. Jules felt a blush creep onto her cheeks. Ted lifted his own glass of champagne and took a drink. "Tell me, who are your guests tonight?" His dark brown eyes scanned the crowd.

Jules surveyed the drawing room, checking out the familiar faces. "Most of them are business associates of my father's—no one truly of note. They are here for cocktail hour only." She took another sip.

Then, from in front of the fireplace, a dark-haired, burly man in his early 20s spoke sharply, "I am telling you to mind your own business. Go chat with the other women." He tugged at his brown suit vest, stretched tight across his soft belly.

The handsome young woman he spoke to removed her hand from his arm, her large diamond wedding ring glinting in the firelight. Hanging her head from the reprimand, her thick blonde hair drooping, she said sensitively, "Dell, we are in the finest company, you should…"

"Don't start with me again, Martha," he derided. "You do not tell me what I should do. Now go off." Mopping his sweaty brow with an already damp handkerchief, he turned his back to her and joined in with a group of men standing nearby.

Ted looked at Jules, his eyebrows raised in question. Leaning close into Ted, Jules said softly, "That is Mr. and Mrs. Dell Fleming—they were married six months ago." Jules sighed. "Martha and I used to be great friends—we attended school together. I thought we had quite a bit in common back then."

She smiled, remembering her first day in elementary school. Jules had gotten caught tripping a boy who was cheating during their outdoor activity of Mother-May-I. Since it was her third time getting in trouble that morning, the teacher, Miss Sutter, had sent Jules to the coat closet, where troublesome students spent the rest of the day in detention. Jules wasn't the only one in the closet—that's where she met Martha.

It turned out that Martha came from a prominent Butte family. Her father had run a large construction company that serviced Butte and the surrounding area. When he died in a tragic train accident when Martha was a young girl, her brothers took over and grew it to be the largest business of its kind in all of Montana. Their family dinners included discussions of camber, dead loads, and national building codes, amongst other mechanical talk.

Jules and Martha had become fast friends and remained so throughout their schooling. When they weren't horseback riding or hunting squirrels in the wooded area around Parker Mansion, they often studied together. During their early years, Jules and Martha would compete against one another, seeing who could figure numbers quicker, or who could get the correct spelling for Latin words faster.

And as they got older, Jules found that Martha was as interested in business as she was.

Their discussions frequently ran to the philosophy of new business. Martha had followed the careers of many industry titans, like Andrew Carnegie and J.P. Morgan, and felt that Jules' own father was a rival. She felt that with the new technologies springing up, many of the industries in Butte would have a chance to prosper. And since Parker Copper was already an industry leader in mining, there was a huge opportunity to grow even larger.

Technologies such as the blast furnace and the open-hearth process in steelmaking were already making mass-produced steel inexpensive, with Mr. Andrew Carnegie owning one of the most extensive iron and steel operations in the country. Then, just a few years earlier, Jules watched Carnegie merge his company into U.S. Steel, which became the first billion-dollar company in the entire world.

Jules could barely comprehend it—a billion-dollar company! Who knew what else the future might bring? Jules felt that they had only reached the tip of the iceberg with what Parker Copper could achieve. But while eager to point this out to the company's board of directors, Jules had yet to actually speak on the topic.

Martha had sat in with Jules on one of AJ's Parker Copper board meetings. She'd been fascinated and had asked Jules if they could listen in on more meetings, which Jules was more than happy to encourage.

Yes, Jules had enjoyed their friendship—until Martha met Dell. He was the son of a wealthy Great Falls businessman and had been off to college at the University of Texas. Upon his return to Montana, he'd come to work for Parker Bank and Trust. Dell was determined to find a wife who could quickly connect him with Butte's prosperous families, and he'd proposed to Martha after knowing her for only one week. And then quite soon after, he'd been invited to sit on the Board of Directors of Parker Copper Mining Company.

Jules had tried spending time with Martha and Dell, but there were too many things about him that she didn't like. Besides his unrelenting perspiration problem, Jules thought that he was a lout, especially in how he treated others. More often than not, Jules had seen him cuff his driver if they weren't moving as fast as Dell wanted. And, he was the type to grope any pretty young girl who happened to pass by him. But probably the worst was that Jules had often overheard him telling Martha she was unattractive and dim-witted, which Jules knew was so very opposite of the truth.

It really started after they'd married. Martha had quit coming to Jules with business ideas and discussions of emerging practices. And then she'd stopped asking Jules to bring her to any more Parker Copper meetings. When Jules had asked her why, Martha had answered, her eyes dull, "With my husband sitting on the board, he won't allow it. I'll be at home. Maybe you might join me for tea?"

Ted's hand upon her elbow jolted Jules from her reverie. "While I do not know him in the least, he does seem a bit of a buffoon," Ted said, smiling, his dimples again appearing on his cheeks. "Perhaps it would be best to sit far, far away from him during dinner."

"Luckily, Dell will not be joining us later. We are having a smallish family dinner afterwards," Jules replied, returning his smile. "Mother informed you, did she not?"

"Smallish? I saw what looked like an entire army in the kitchen," said Ted, rocking back on his heels. A chef, in a white coat and toque, rolled a tray laden with two full hams and a beef brisket past the open door, headed toward the dining room. "Are all your family dinners this… smallish?" A servant sidled up to Ted and refilled his glass.

Jules laughed and lifted her glass to Ted. "Welcome to Parker Mansion."

With the string quartet playing lightly and the soft sound of laughter floating throughout the drawing room, Jules and Ted approached a group of men surrounding AJ, the talk of their competitor, Hailey Mines, turning heated.

"They're cutting corners, I tell you," said George Ferguson, the Head Engineer of Parker Copper. "I've heard tell that rather than using steel, they are bringing in timber from Utah—wood that has been felled from the pine beetle epidemic.

"There is no proof of that," replied AJ.

"Yet," said Ferguson.

"Ah, well, if someone were to find evidence, I would reward him handsomely," AJ said, taking a sip of champagne. "But I know that scoundrel Hailey, and he will never be caught red-handed. I am sure he has many devious plans that none of us might ever know to what extent." AJ turned to Ted and Jules. "What say you to that, my fine young man?"

Ted shrugged. "I'm sure I don't know, sir. But as your newest employee, I will certainly be vigilant." As AJ began introducing Ted to the men standing around them, Jules watched Dell Fleming sidle up next to them, an eager look upon his sweaty mug.

Jules backed away from the group and drifted to the drawing room window, overlooking the headframes to the north. Most of them were still made of timber, but they were sure and strong. Jules hadn't really considered fully what the upshot might be if they had all steel headframes, but it was something that she thought her father might have to contemplate at some point soon.

But as of now, with Parker Copper Mining's executives standing around drinking fine wine and conversing amongst themselves, the company's thousands of miners continued to enter the mines, riding cages in those strong timber headframes, loading and unloading the many tons of Parker iron ore.

Bradley approached the window and said, "Is that truly you, Jules? I barely recognized you." He raised his hand as if to stroke her newly coiffed hair. She stepped quickly back, "Oh no, you don't. Do not touch this hair—it took hours upon hours to fashion." Bradley raised his hand to his mouth and coughed lightly, a smile playing at his lips. Jules glanced at Ted and noticed him watching her, and she felt herself blush.

"Jules, look who has joined us," called Millicent from the door of the parlor. She waved Jules away from the window. Jules weaved her way through the many guests and arrived at Millicent's side just as a young woman shrugged off her evening coat.

"Jeannette!" cried Jules, reaching out with both her hands. "I am ever so pleased to see you." She placed a kiss on both cheeks of the young woman. "It's been so long, let me take a good look at you!" Jules stepped back and gazed at the young woman who stood a full head taller than she. Their newly arrived guest, Jeannette Rankin, carried herself with a sense of confidence that was also warm and genial. Her mousy brown hair was upswept in a chignon that revealed dark, heavy eyebrows and a large, straight nose. She wore a plain evening gown, adorned with a few velvet roses and ribbons. "Are you here in Butte for a spell?" asked Jules.

Jeannette smiled warmly at Jules and replied, "No, I'm afraid not. I'm actually headed to Helena tomorrow. But I did want to come by and give your mother and father regards from my own."

"And how are your parents?" asked Jules. "And of course, your brother and sisters?" Jules thought fondly of the summers she spent on Rankin ranch. Jeannette and her siblings always treated her as a younger sister, even though she really was just a ward of the family while Millicent and AJ were traveling.

"Oh, thank you for asking, Jules," replied Jeannette, smiling. "Everyone is fine. Mother and Father are still out on the ranch. You know this is the beginning of their busy season." A look of guilt flashed across Jeannette's face, and Jules felt bad for her friend. She knew Jeannette missed helping out since she'd been away at university for the past few years, working toward a degree in biology.

"They'll do fine; they have lots of help." Jules placed her hand on Jeannette's arm. "But tell me about you, what are you up to now?" AJ and Ted strolled near them.

"Well, as I said, I'm headed to the state capital." Jeannette's eyes gleamed. "I've sent word to the Montana legislature that I would like to speak to the lawmakers about voting rights for women," said Jeannette. "I am representing a group called the 'Equal Franchise Society.'" Jules' eyes widened, and she caught a glimpse of Martha, whose eyes looked as big as hers.

AJ stepped closer, smoke from his cigar obscuring Jules' view of Martha. "Miss Rankin, I am not so certain that Montanans are at all eager for equal rights. You'll most likely be wasting your time in Helena."

"Ah, respectfully, I must disagree," replied Jeannette. "I think that many—not just women but men as well—are ready to dispel the idea that a woman's place is in the home. Rather than merely marry, bear children, and obey our husbands, we are ready to get better educated and hold worthy jobs."

"Not to mention having a vote," scoffed Ted, as he drew close to Jules.

"That is correct, Mr…" Jeannette raised her eyebrows. She held out her hand.

"Jackson. Theodore Jackson," replied Ted, shaking Jeannette's hand. "Please, call me Ted."

"Mr. Jackson, Ted," smiled Jeannette. "You are new to Montana, are you not?"

"Why yes, quite," he replied. "I've just arrived from Colorado."

"Then let me counsel you that we Montanans are a sturdy lot. What with all the family-owned farms and ranches in our fine state, everyone must pitch in…with equal work. I know countless women who can lift as many hay bales as their husbands. And then they go in and put supper on the table." Jeannette tilted her head. "The least we can have is a say in our laws—with a vote."

The parlor had gone quiet.

Ted cleared his throat. "Some feel that women are too frail and vulnerable, and if women get the vote, they may become more masculine."

"It is said they grow beards," laughed Dell Fleming from the crowd standing near.

Jeannette joined in laughing and said, "Well then, there must be some very hairy ladies in Mr. Jackson's home state. The women in our neighboring states of Wyoming, Idaho, Utah, and, yes, Colorado, have the right to vote."

Jules felt Ted tense up beside her. "Quite," he said softly, with a frown.

AJ barked a laugh. "Jackson, seems you got out of Colorado just in the nick of time." Everyone smiled as the tension melted. The string quartet struck up a lively tune, and guests once again mingled.

"Jeannette," said Jules, sipping her champagne. "If you require any assistance while in Helena, you should send word to my Father. He has been spending a lot of his time in the Capitol recently." AJ slid a long look at his daughter and puffed on his cigar.

Jeannette accepted a glass of champagne from a passing servant. She took a sip and turned to AJ. "Mr. Parker, I'd heard a rumor you were interested in pursuing a Senate seat."

AJ nodded, his eyes veiled.

"Perhaps if I run for Congress, you and I will be serving Montana politics at the same time," said Jeannette, raising her glass as if in a toast.

"A female member of Congress?" Dell laughed, still lurking beside them. "That is absurd."

"Is it? Perhaps what is absurd is the fact that men make up all laws, even laws that concern women. Perhaps if women could vote, they might pass laws that are more gentle and sensitive to the needs of the people. All people."

Jules remained rooted, her hand over her lips, hiding a small smile. The parlor had once again gone silent.

A shrill bell rang out, effectively breaking the silence, announcing the end of cocktail hour and the beginning of dinner. Without a word, Dell turned and walked away from Jules and Jeannette.

AJ leaned close to Jeannette and placed a kiss on her cheek. Jules saw him give her a wink before he turned and walked among his departing guests.

Jeannette raised her eyebrows. "Well, I sure can clear a room," she declared, shrugging her shoulders. "And now I suppose I must clear out myself." She leaned over to Millicent, kissing her cheek. "Thank you for having me, Mrs. Parker. I am sorry if I've upset anyone here at Parker Mansion."

"Don't worry, Jeannette," replied Millicent. "In our household, this subject is discussed even more than the weather forecast." She cast her eyes at Jules. "Good luck, dear," said Millicent as she and Jules walked Jeannette to the front door. She hugged her. "I do mean that sincerely."

Millicent turned to her other groups of guests, making small talk and thanking them for stopping by.

Jules' eyes burned as bright as the stars that dotted the big Montana evening sky. She leaned in and hugged her friend hard, holding on for longer than necessary. "Jeannette, if women get the vote, I will vote for you," whispered Jules. "I will be the very first in line to vote for you."

Chapter 10

The wooden walkway was as sturdy as any other along the busy city street. Jules stomped a booted foot atop a plank, a dull *thunk* resonating across the boards as pedestrians jostled past. Jules walked the length, amazed that Jeannette had built the walkway all by herself.

Even though her father, John Rankin, owned the building, he hadn't been able to collect rent as it sat empty for months. When Jeannette realized it was because no one wanted to cross the filthy mud in the building's front, she took it upon herself to build the walkway. Immediately after she'd completed it, the building was fully occupied with boarding rooms on the top floor, and Butte Cigars and Fishing Tackle and Café M&M on the ground floor.

"This is such fine workmanship," said Jules, leaning against the hand railing. "Jeannette is an amazing woman. I just know she's going to be successful in politics. Mark my words." A tinny bell rang, and the mouth-watering smell of grilling meat wafted as patrons of the cafe pulled open the door beside them.

Balinda nodded in agreement. "I knew it the minute I met her."

"Now, where did she leave…" asked Jules as she rounded the corner of the building. "Aha, she did leave them as she said she would. Balinda, look, they're here."

Balinda joined Jules in the alleyway where they stood before a stack of large, printed placards mounted on wooden sticks. "Equal Franchise Society," she read aloud. She took a step back. "Oh no, Jules. You are not going to…"

"Of course I am," replied Jules, grabbing a sign and lifting it to her shoulder. "We've got to get the word out, to convince people that all people are equal, regardless of race or gender."

"But Jules, I'm not so sure this kind of public support is such a good idea. A Parker picketing on Main Street? If your father finds out, he'll be furious."

"When isn't my father furious?" asked Jules, rolling her eyes. "Come on, grab a sign, and let's get out there."

"No, not me," replied Balinda. "Obviously, I do agree with equal rights for all. I mean, look at me—a Chinese woman. But I'm uneasy picketing, publicly damning people for not treating me the same as a white man." She placed her hand gently on Jules' arm. "Please reconsider what you're planning on right now. Remember your promise to your mother that you'd start behaving yourself."

"But Balinda, my hair is curled and I'm wearing a nice frock," replied Jules. "I am doing what I told my mother I would do."

"You know what I mean," said Balinda. "Celeste told me that the new Vice Director, Ted Jackson, has expressed interest in you. He's probably looking for a woman who conducts herself a certain way. Don't spoil this, Jules."

"We don't really know what Ted Jackson is looking for," called Jules. "And since when did you start listening to Celeste?" She held the placard in the air and stepped out onto Main Street.

The street teemed with businessmen out on their lunch breaks, women running errands, and store owners sweeping the front stoops of the various shops crammed next to each other.

Jules held her chin high, her hair still elaborately curled and piled on her head from the previous evening. Even though she *had* pledged yesterday to behave herself, to act like a lady, she was exhilarated from her brief conversation with Jeannette. Jules felt certain that acting like a lady and demanding equal rights should not be mutually exclusive, but that both could coexist.

Balinda waved goodbye and drifted toward Chinatown, her hands held up in resignation. Then continuing with sure steps, Jules walked down Main Street past Butte Security Bank Loans, Red Bird shoe shop, and the Owsley Theatre. She held the placard high. A slight wind came up, ruffling her coiffed hair, and she tucked a tendril into the bun, patting it into place.

"Equal rights for all!" she cried out. "Women want a choice!" A group of society ladies stopped their window shopping and stared at Jules, covering their mouths in astonishment. An automobile slowed on the street, the men hollering and booing from inside.

Jules' eyes shifted side to side as a small mob gathered, following her slowly down the busy street. As a trolley car trundled by, a young man leaning out the back blew a raspberry, the sound of contempt obvious.

She stopped in front of one of Butte's largest department stores, Hennessy's Mercantile, and pumped the placard up and down. Jules cleared her throat and spoke out, "I agree with the many esteemed women before us who said that the choice for equal rights is vital if society is to move forward for a better future! Women want the right to control their earnings, to own property, and, in the case of divorce, take custody of their children. We want a choice for broad-based economic and political equality and for social reforms!" Jules looked at the men and women surrounding her, their faces filled with disbelief.

"Choice! Women want a choice," she yelled again.

A gigantic man stepped out of the Lucky Saloon and approached

Jules. She recognized him as a mine foreman from Hailey Mines, Timmer Foley. His shirtsleeves were rolled to his elbows, exposing his huge, muscular forearms. His thick neck disappeared into his massive head, where a vein in his forehead bulged.

"You want a choice?" he barked, spit flying from his mouth and catching in his thick, whiskey-dampened beard. Beer stained the front of his shirt. "The only choice a woman needs is whether to be in the kitchen barefoot, pregnant, or both." Foley crossed his arms across his immense chest. The crowd grew.

Jules closed in. "Mr. Foley, you may not know this, but it has been said that women voters would have a civilizing effect on politics. Not only would we work for improved wages and working conditions for women, but we would also tend to weaker members of society. And we would support, ahem, controls on alcohol." She blinked and waved the placard in front of Foley's face. "So, yes, we want a choice."

Foley pressed close to Jules, his rank odor causing her to wrinkle her nose. "I'll give you a choice. You can agree to either this…" He held up one finger and placed it in front of his lips. "…Or this." He moved the finger away from his lips and clenched the hand into a fist, waving it in front of Jules' face.

At the absurdity of what he'd just suggested, that she either shut her mouth into silence or be punched in the face, Jules burst out laughing.

"You laughing at me?" Foley's face turned beet red, steam coming out of his ears.

"Why, yes," laughed Jules.

Enraged, Foley abruptly reached out, his meaty hands grabbing Jules' by the hair. With a yelp, Jules was pulled over at the waist. "Shut up, you damn bitch," he bellowed. The crowd stepped back.

Livid, Jules inhaled quickly. Her scalp ached, tender still from the hours under the red, hot curling tongs—and now her lovely curls were scrunched in the filthy hands of Timmer Foley. *A woman's hair is her glory* rang throughout her head. Jules' eyes blazed. She clenched her teeth.

"Do. Not. Touch. My. Hair."

Foley's hand instead tightened, and he leaned over Jules, his rank beer breath enveloping her. "You think you can make me, little lady?"

Jules drew a deep breath, then dropped the placard to the ground and rapidly lifted her head in one fell swoop. The top of her head slammed against Foley's chin, knocking him back. Unbalanced, he dropped the handfuls of hair, releasing Jules. She twisted around, facing him, and kicked out hard at his shin.

"Ahhhh!" he screeched and bent down, grabbing his leg. With Foley's head now level with her waist, Jules swung together her arms, her palms open, and clouted him decisively on his ears. Foley dropped to the ground, clutching the sides of his head.

Breathing heavily, Jules moved away from the swearing man. Jules looked out over the crowd and watched the society ladies back away, shaking their heads and whispering behind their gloved hands. The men, most of them with small smirks, began drifting away, leaving Jules standing alone.

When she looked into the Hennessy Mercantile's polished glass window and caught a glimpse of her hair in disarray, hanging about her face, and blood from Foley's chin staining her blouse, Jules sighed and shook her head. What part of this was ladylike? She certainly wasn't off to a very good start with her new behavior.

At the sound of the electric street trolley's brakes screeching to slow for the dispersing crowd, Jules' shoulders dropped, and she felt suddenly worn out. She slowly picked up the placard she'd dropped and stepped over Foley, still clutching at his ears. With her hair now hanging over her eyes, Jules couldn't see anything—especially not Ted Jackson just inside Hennessy's, watching her from amongst the fine menswear, a frown forcing his dimples deep into his smooth cheeks.

Chapter 11

Jules dragged the placard beside her as she walked away from Hennessy's. She brushed at the dirt covering her skirt when she felt air cooling against the back of her legs. Jules rubbed at her forehead as she realized she had a large rip in the back of her skirt. Damn that Timmer Foley! Jules stamped her foot in frustration. She couldn't walk all the way home with her backside available for all to see, could she? While Parker Mansion was many blocks away, Jules knew there was someplace much closer she could go. Looking up the street at a tall, imposing building with a copper-clad cornice winking in the sun, Jules sighed heavily.

She held the placard behind her, covering the rip in her skirt, and started walking toward Parker Copper Mining Company headquarters.

An arched entry led to the elegant lobby of Parker headquarters. Bustling with activity, people passed by the large windows set within thick oak-trimmed ivory-colored plaster walls. White marble floors lead to a wrought iron staircase with the same marble treads, but many people chose to stand in line and wait to be shuttled to the upper floors by the only passenger elevator in the entire state.

Jules glanced at the queue and quickly decided to take the stairs up to her father's office on the top floor. He would surely be furious at her disheveled appearance, but what other choice did she have? Jules thought she would wait in a quiet corner and catch a ride with her father when he departed for home. At least she could sit down and effectively hide the gaping hole in her skirt. Holding the placard behind her, Jules quickly climbed the stairs, taking them two at a time.

She entered the top-floor central office just as someone walked into her father's own office, leaving the dark oak door slightly ajar. "Good afternoon, Georgia," Jules said to one of AJ's three secretaries. "I'm just here waiting for Father. I can make myself comfortable." Used to seeing Jules around, Georgia just smiled and nodded, then continued tapping away at the heavy steel typewriter upon her desk.

"Dillie," shouted AJ from his office. "Make certain that the telegraph gets to Hearst in San Francisco right away. If he doesn't come up with the funds within the next few hours, our deal is dead!"

The secretary sitting at the desk next to Georgia looked up. "Yessir," she said.

"DID YOU HEAR ME?"

Dillie jumped to her feet in a panic. "Yes, Mr. Parker! Right away, sir!" She brushed past Jules and then ran out of the central office, her heels clicking rapidly down the marble stairs.

Jules moved to a tufted leather armchair just outside AJ's office. She tucked the placard next to her feet, then sat back into the deep cushions, wrapping the fabric of her skirt beneath her. Twisting round in the chair, Jules tried to get a glimpse of the person her father was meeting with.

She heard AJ say, "Hello, young sir," followed by his usual trademark saying, "I am AJ Parker, and welcome to this, my company." Jules smiled as she pictured AJ standing in front of his enormous desk, his arms outstretched wide.

"I am honored to meet you, Mr. Parker," came the reply. "Random Ferris Buckley." Jules imagined them shaking hands, and then heard AJ and his guest sit, the leather in their chairs squeaking.

"Now, what can I do for you?" asked AJ. "...Mr. Buckley."

"I am here to tell you of the benefits of using steel," the visitor said, his voice sure and confident. "And once you hear me out, you will surely decide to utilize steel in all of Parker Copper's headframes."

"I will, will I?" asked AJ, his voice already skeptical.

"Yes, you will. You see, I come from a line of engineers from the East who are already creating remarkable structures using steel," he said, the pride evident in his voice. Jules' ears perked up as she recalled Bradley talking about the East Coast major player who was on the train with him when he came back to Butte.

"And just who are your people?" asked AJ.

"My father and uncle are both successful civil engineers. My father was educated at Columbia College, my uncle at Rensselaer Polytechnic Institute."

"Um-hm," said AJ. "Go on..."

"Well, while analyzing the steel industry with them, I've found that the use and output of steel is expanding so quickly in the United States that the growth rate here has surpassed even Great Britain and Germany. What with the latest technology now, companies using steel are contributing to the rapid expansion of urban infrastructures across the nation. Factories, railroads, bridges..."

"Carnival rides?"

"Why...yes," replied Buckley, uncertainty finally hinting in his voice.

"I know of your uncle, George Washington Gale Ferris."

Seemingly thrown off guard, Buckley asked slowly, "You know Uncle Gale?"

"Believe me, young man, if I were in the market for a Ferris wheel, I would have my attorneys draw up a contract with you this very instant," replied AJ. "But since I am a real businessman, I'll kindly ask you to take your leave. I'm a busy man and I've no time for folly."

"But Mr. Parker, using steel for your headframes is certainly not folly! Steel is already being used for railroads and bridges, and many office buildings in the large cities," said Buckley quickly. "I can help you bring new technology to an old industry—copper mining."

Jules sat up in her chair. It was as if the guest in AJ's office had been in her head. Hadn't she just been telling her father to swap out the old wood headframes for steel? Her father ought to go into business with this man!

"Why should I convert to steel, or introduce new technology, when my company has been exceedingly successful thus far with heavy, timber headframes?" disparaged AJ.

"Well, because you will be lucky to see an increase in production!" said Buckley.

Of course, Buckley was right. While steel used to be very expensive to produce, the past few years had seen new technology like the electric arc furnace that had made it less expensive and produced steel with great strength and durability. The only logical result of using steel would be an improvement in what they were currently taking out of the Parker Copper mines.

"I'll be lucky to see an increase in production?" repeated AJ, his voice hard. "Mr. Buckley, I haven't become one of the richest men in the United States by being lucky."

"I didn't intend that…"

AJ held up his hand, stopping his visitor midsentence. "I am not interested."

"How can you not be interested in new ideas? Don't be bull-headed," challenged Buckley. Jules swallowed hard. Buckley had said exactly what she'd told AJ in his library. Uh-oh.

"Get out of my office," yelled AJ, standing to his feet. "If I ever see the face of anyone else who thinks as you, I'll throw them out as well!"

"But… but…"

Jules lifted the placard in front of her face, cowering behind the Equal Rights sign just as AJ roared, "GET OUT!"

And with that, the door flew open, and a handsome young man with sun-bleached hair charged through. He slammed the door behind him, then stormed away across the tapestry-covered floor.

Still covering her face, Jules heard AJ bellow from behind the glass window, "Whoever is waiting for me next better not be wanting to discuss preposterous ideas on new technology, that is for goddamn sure."

Jules jumped to her feet and grabbed the placard. She held it behind her as she raced to the stairs. Walking home with a torn skirt was a great deal more preferable than walking into her father's office and getting torn to pieces.

Chapter 12

After Jules made it back to Parker Mansion with no further ripping of her skirt or any other sort of embarrassing incident, she found a note from Ted Jackson asking her for a tour of Butte that very afternoon, as he had a few hours of free time. Furthermore, the note said he'd be by to pick her up before the dinner hour, then perhaps after the tour, they might stop off at the Le Havre, where he could treat her to a fine meal in return for her time.

Pleased that she would finally be able to begin her work for Parker Copper, as her father directed, Jules was admittedly more pleased that Ted had asked her to dinner. Jules couldn't deny that Ted was very attractive, as her sister and mother repeatedly reminded her. But he also seemed quite intelligent and already very engrossed in the operations of Parker Copper. He'd been in Butte for two weeks and had barely set foot out of the mine's offices.

Jules adjusted the pins in her hat while she stood on the mansion porch, waiting. The late May afternoon was beautiful with the sun warming the porch swing and purple bearded iris in the pots lining the steps.

A Rambler automobile pulled in front, and Ted Jackson jammed on the brake, then jumped out. He strode up the walkway toward

Jules. "Augustina," he said. "I am quite sorry I am late, but there was a pressing issue that needed resolving at headquarters." He smiled and his cheeks dimpled.

"Mr. Jackson, no need to apologize," replied Jules. "I completely understand."

"Well, now that it's been resolved, let's get moving before anything else comes up." He held out his arm, the elbow crooked. "And, really, please call me Ted."

Jules accepted his arm and they walked to the car together. He opened the door, and Jules stepped through and sat. "Thank you," she said with a smile. "Ted."

They drove slowly down Montana Street. Jules pointed out a large, stately house set back from the road. A gardener trimming the bushes around the fence looked up as they slowed. He snipped a brilliant red rose from a stem and hurried to the car with it extended in his gloved hand. "Miss Jules," he said. "Nice to see you takin' advantage of the fine weather."

"Why, thank you, Nat," Jules said, her face lit up. "You do such a good job here. Keep up the nice work, as I'll surely now expect a rose each time I come by." The gardener grinned and bowed before he walked back to the yard.

Jules turned to Ted and said, "That is where Martha Fleming grew up. You remember meeting her?"

"Ah, yes," replied Ted. "She of the churlish husband."

Jules laughed. "You do remember her." She pointed at the street crossing in front of them and said, "And this is Park Street. Turn here and we'll go down to Main."

As Ted turned the corner, a group of miners stood waiting to cross the street. They spied Jules riding in the car. "Hey, Miss Jules," one called out. "When you goin' to have 'nother contest for loading? I already drank that one beer."

Jules leaned out of the auto and waved energetically. "Hi-ho, Travis! Soon, I promise."

Another miner called out, "Can't be soon enough, Miss!" Then they all crossed and disappeared into the dark entry of the Mountain Saloon.

Ted pressed the gas, and they motored along Park Street. "They love you, don't they?" asked Ted. "The people here."

Jules tilted her head. "I suppose so," she replied. "I love them too. There is no other place I would rather be than here with the people of Butte." She looked at Ted. "Well, except the mines."

Ted raised his eyebrows with a grin. "Really, the mines? Well then, how about we skip Main Street and go someplace you'd rather." He reached over and squeezed Jules's knee, then honked the horn as they gathered speed, headed for the Venturer headframe.

"And here is where Matty Kelly forgot to put his pants back on after he'd showered at the end of his shift," Jules said, pointing to the dry house. "He walked all the way to his boarding room with his drawers flapping in the wind before someone pointed out to him that he was half naked." She laughed. "That was the day he discovered a new vein that was just under his drill. Nobody even knew it was there—it was a huge surprise and I suppose Matty was in a bit of a shock."

They had been sitting in Ted's car for an hour, parked at the base of the Venturer mine while Jules told story after story. Ted encouraged her to talk, bombarding her with questions about the goings on. More than once, he'd expressed his amazement at how much she knew— Jules thought Ted was maybe more than a bit impressed.

And she was more than grateful. It had been so long since Jules had been involved in Parker Copper, and she didn't have anyone at all to talk with. Once she'd been banned from going to the mines, she felt like part of her had died. But with Ted appreciating her knowledge and expertise, Jules felt fully alive again.

"Augustina, I must apologize once more," said Ted, pulling a pocket watch from his jacket. "Time has gotten past me, and I fear we've missed the dinner hour at Le Havre. It's just that I was so engrossed with listening to you."

"You mustn't apologize for letting me ramble," replied Jules. "It has been my absolute pleasure."

"Well, I do aim to feed you, so might you suggest another establishment where we could dine?"

"Of course, I know of someplace," smiled Jules. "It's not quite so fancy as Le Havre, but the food is even better."

They parked the car in front of Chang's Noodle Parlor, and Ted pulled open the door, allowing Jules to enter before him. A white ceramic cat figurine sat in the window, its paw up in a kind of wave.

"Miss Parker, very nice of you to join us tonight," said a Chinese man, dressed in a suit and tie, standing behind a pedestal.

"Mr. Chang," replied Jules, grasping his hands. "How wonderful to see you. And where is…"

"Jules!" cried Balinda, hurrying out from behind the kitchen doors. She ran up and hugged Jules hard. "What are you doing here?"

Jules pulled back from her friend. "We've come to dine," she replied as she stepped aside. "Balinda, let me introduce you to Ted Jackson."

Ted stepped forward with a smile and held his hand out to Balinda. She grasped it in her petite hand and held on, looking deep into Ted's eyes.

"It's a pleasure to, uh…" said Ted as he tried extracting his hand. Balinda's face was a mask while she held on.

"And you are here to…" she asked as her eyes examined Ted's face like a hawk soaring over a grass field, searching for something.

"Dine, of course, " replied Jules, pulling them apart. "Come on,

Balinda, seat us at the front window." She wrapped her arm in Balinda's and then turned toward an empty table.

Once seated and their orders placed, Jules noticed that Balinda had disappeared back into the kitchen. But she promptly put her friend out of mind as soon as Ted started again questioning her about Parker Copper.

"What's the story about the Metis headframe?" Ted asked after taking a sip of hot tea.

"Ah, the unlucky Metis," replied Jules. She leaned back against her chair and told Ted all that had happened in the past months. She wrapped up by saying, "So, the main timber has been repaired again, and I can only imagine that it is fit to carry many more loads."

Ted nodded his agreement and held up his teacup. "Let's toast to that," he said.

Jules smiled and held up her cup as well, just as a gentle *taptaptap* came from the window next to her. She looked out the window to two lovely young women, dressed in similar chic blouses and skirts, their matching faces full of cheer.

"Genevieve! Josephine!" laughed Jules. She waved and mouthed hello through the glass. The twin sisters mouthed hello in return. They met eyes with Jules, then shifted their gaze to Ted. Genevieve's lips pulled up in a wicked smile, and she nodded before giggling and pulling her sister away from the window and bustled away from the Noodle Parlor.

"I can assume those were more friends of yours?" asked Ted as he stroked his chin.

"Ted, I am sorry for their girlish behavior," started Jules. "They are my friends from school. I never quite know how to react to them— sometimes I think I'm from a whole different planet."

"Perhaps that is what makes you so charming," came Ted's reply.

Jules felt her face flush. "Oh, you can say that now because you've spent only a couple of hours with me." Jules tucked a lock of hair behind her ear.

"While it is still early in our relationship, I should look forward to the rest of our time together…" began Ted, reaching out and grasping Jules' hand in his. He leaned over the table. "…If it is even halfway as enjoyable as these past couple of hours."

Chapter 13

"Don't do it, Jules," her sister said, grimacing. Celeste, sitting in the window seat of Jules' bedroom, studied her tapered fingernails, her French manicure still perfectly intact, even after a week.

"Oh, Celeste, be quiet," replied Jules, fastening the top button at her waist. She was feeling grand after her time with Ted and wanted some solitude to reflect on what he'd said at the end.

"You're going too far now. A lady does not wear trousers," said Celeste.

"Well, a lady should—especially if she is going horseback riding. It just makes sense, seeing how sitting astride a saddle is impossible in a skirt," said Jules, pulling on a pair of mud-caked, worn work boots. "Why should men have it easier?"

"*Because*, Jules. Just *because*." Celeste placed her hand on her forehead, shaking her curls. "Please don't get caught. I mean it—don't let anyone see you. It's a beautiful spring day, and many ladies will be out strolling and window shopping."

"I used to wear these clothes in the mines, and everything was just fine," Jules replied.

"If everything was just fine, what are you doing here at home instead of at the mines?" retorted Celeste under her breath.

Ignoring her sister, Jules said, "Why would anyone in their right mind choose window shopping over pounding across the prairie on a powerful beast, riding at full tilt, the dust and dirt soaring around them?"

Celeste picked at her cuticles. "Why would anyone in their right mind, indeed," she replied sarcastically.

Jules looked at her older sister, shaking her head. How had they turned out so different? Celeste was lovely, with her petite features and hair of perfect ringlets. But despite their physical differences, Jules knew they were even more different in their beliefs and opinions. While her sister desired to marry a nice man, keep him content and socialized, then to do the same for her children once they came along, Jules desired with all her heart to run a highly successful business—Parker Copper.

But society women did not work. While certainly no law existed saying that women must not work, women of the upper classes would never have taken an actual job. They *provided* jobs to other women as housekeepers, cooks, and nannies.

From an early age, Celeste and her friends had played with dolls with their miniature houses, decorating rooms exactly how they would end up setting up their own homes when they grew up. The girls, in exquisitely trimmed dresses with smoothly plaited hair, all chatted about current fashions and gossiped about other girls for what seemed like hours. And Jules would sit alongside them, never uttering a word lest she say something unfortunate that would embarrass Celeste, and result in a shrill reprimand after her friends had gone home.

Jules closed the door to her wardrobe and peeked at her reflection in the mirror hanging on the door. She couldn't understand what the big deal was—she didn't look so bad in miner's clothing. She realized that no other woman would be caught dead wearing what she currently wore, but Jules honestly felt the most comfortable dressed this way, and probably always would.

After Gus had died, when Jules finally started accompanying AJ to the Parker mines, she wore her normal skirt with its wide sash and mutton-sleeved blouse. Upon seeing her, the miners would immediately stop working, their usual banter and chatter dying down to nothing. And even though it wasn't typical to remove their candle-topped hats while inside the mine, one or two of them would doff them in greeting, as if he were a gentleman with a top hat out on the street. Jules was certain she made them uneasy because she was in a man's place—females had never been allowed in the mines before. When she was there, it would often be so quiet that she could hear the swish of her skirts as she walked behind her father.

But unexpectedly, one day, as she walked along the tracks, a trolley heavily loaded with ore passed by so closely that a bolt had snagged at the fabric of Jules' ample skirt, pulling her along, dragging her for over 15 feet. She hadn't been hurt, a bit bruised is all, but she quickly realized the mines were not the place to wear floor-skimming skirts and dresses.

She remembered the first day she'd taken to dressing like a miner, when she and her father had entered the Original mine. Jules had tucked her long straight hair up into a cloth miners' cap, and she was dressed in canvas trousers, a thick cotton shirt, and heavy leather work boots.

All the miners had been their usual boisterous selves, with Matty Kelly telling one of his usual off-color jokes.

"Mr. Parker," Matty had yelled over the din in the mine. "Have yer heard the one about the portly woman carryin' a duck, who walks into a pub? The bartender says, 'What'r yer doin' with that pig?'"

AJ stopped, smiled, and shook his head. "No, Matty, haven't heard that one." The miners surrounding them turned to Matty, grins already creeping upon their lips.

"How about you, boy-o," Matty had called out to Jules, "Do yer know it?"

When Jules had stepped out from behind her father and removed the cloth cap, her hair tumbling down across her shoulders, you could have heard a pin drop. The air in the mine stilled, and she heard a shovel drop to the hard floor with an earsplitting clang. Jules had looked from miner's face to miner's face and seen a dozen slacked jaws and blinks of absolute shock. They'd really thought she was a man.

She'd tucked her cap under her arm, hitched up the back of her pants, and said, "…the woman says, 'that isn't a pig, that's a duck. And then the bartender says, 'I was talking to the duck.'"

Matty Kelly's own jaw was dropped so low, Jules thought she'd seen his tonsils. "And Matty…" she'd laughed. "…that's *Miss* Boy-o to you." Then she'd positioned the cap back on her head and jumped a ride on a passing ore trolley, enjoying the sound of her father's laughter mixing in with the miners, ringing off the hard rock walls.

So as she stepped out of the kitchen and into the side yard, wearing trousers and work boots, Celeste's admonishment still ringing in her ears, Jules yanked on her leather gloves. She couldn't wait to get away from her irritating sister. Jules pulled an apple from her pocket and extended it to a chestnut colored horse hitched to the fence post. Upon seeing her, Spirit nickered, bobbing his head up and down, and Jules finally smiled.

"Hi, boy," Jules said softly. She approached the Thoroughbred stallion. "You ready for a bit of fun today?" She stroked his nose as he crunched the apple. Ever since she was a little girl, Jules loved being around horses, especially at Lewisia Stock Farms, her father's breeding farm. At any given time, there might be upwards of 50 Thoroughbred horses housed in the stables. Beautiful, powerful animals. Jules had raised Spirit since he was a colt at Lewisia, and they knew each other well.

Jules swung up into the saddle, relaxing into the leather's embrace. She tilted her face up to the sun and inhaled deeply. In the way that some girls loved the smell of clean linens and baking cookies, Jules loved the smell of dirt and horse. She nudged Spirit into a cantor, her hair already spilling from the long braid trailing down her back.

Across back acres of flat, golden prairie, Jules rode the outskirts of town. With Parker Mansion set on the outer border of Butte, the wild yonder acted as an extension of her own backyard. While AJ could certainly have afforded to build on the 2500 acres, he'd purchased it expressly for conservation of natural land. Jules knew it would remain wild and grassy and wind-swept long after she was gone.

As if feeling Jules' exuberance, Spirit plunged through rivulets fed from underground springs, splashing mud high across Jules' cheeks. He coasted by silver buffaloberry thickets, heavy with spring berries, the thorns grabbing and ripping at Jules' pant legs. With her eyes tearing from the rush of the wind, Jules laughed wildly, the argument with her sister all but forgotten. Nothing could be more glorious.

Jules and Spirit ran together until they neared Continental Drive, a brand new street that ran along the border of the conservation land and would lead into town and across Main. Not yet even half finished, the workers had only just pulled out loads of large boulders and rocks and had laid them to the side in a huge, jumbled pile.

"Whoa there, Spirit," said Jules, as much to the horse as to herself. "Could this be the ringing rocks that I overheard Hazel talking about?" She aimed the horse toward the rock pile, recalling the conversation she'd had with Hazel just a few weeks ago. Apparently, whatever it was about the way the pile rested, or maybe it was the makeup of the rocks, but when hit with a hammer, the rocks chimed melodically. Jules thought perhaps it might sound like when the gong at the joss house was rung. She pulled back gently on Spirit's bridle and coaxed him to a walk, wishing she'd thought to bring along a hammer.

With the day starting out so lovely, without a cloud in sight, the sun from the south had already heated the boulders and baked the dirt dry. Spirit's hooves kicked up dust as they ambled along, creating little poofs at each step. Still feeling content from their wonderful ride, Jules sang out, her voice thin but pleasant,

"In the sweet by and by,
We shall meet on that beautiful shore;
In the sweet by and by,
We shall meet on...."

But, suddenly, on the last refrain, Spirit stopped dead in his tracks, his nostrils flaring.

Just as she heard the harsh, dry sound, she looked down at the dirt road and saw the triangular head of a tan and black prairie rattlesnake. Coiled upon itself, with its unblinking slitted eyes staring at them, the snake's tail swished rapidly, rattling a warning. Spirit screamed and reared up on his hind legs, his front legs pawing at the empty air, dumping Jules cleanly from her saddle. Backwards she tumbled, landing flat onto the parched earth. She scrambled onto her feet, her eyes darting around for the rattlesnake. She wheezed in a breath when she realized that the rattler had been frightened as well, and had swiftly slithered off before Jules had even landed.

"No, Spirit! Come back!" yelled Jules as she watched the beautiful horse running away at a full gallop, his saddle empty. "Damn it!"

Jules rubbed her backside, where she'd landed, then brushed away the dirt on her seat. Luckily, she hadn't been hurt. But now she supposed she was walking, rather than riding a horse. With a sigh, Jules shaded her eyes and looked across the flat land—it was only a couple of miles back to Parker Mansion. She could follow Continental Drive until it crossed Main downtown, then climb up the hill to her home. Jules wiped the sweat from her brow, smearing dust across her eyes, creating dark rings like a raccoon's. She started walking west.

After 20 minutes, Jules could already sense the bustle of the city. An electric trolley rumbled across steel tracks, the overhead cables snapping and clattering. Music and laughter poured into the streets from pubs, already filled with first shift miners coming off the job. At three shifts per day, eight hours each, a mine crew was always getting off as another came on. Celebrations ran throughout the day and night at the many saloons that dotted Butte.

At hearing a far-off horse whinny, Jules said to herself, "Dammit, Spirit," and thought that perhaps next time, she'd ride a bicycle instead.

A few more yards took her to the top of a rise on the street, and she stopped looking out over the intersection of Continental and Main, where several people rushed past. Celeste had been correct in predicting that many would be out on such a fine day. A group of young women whom Jules had attended private school with walked arm-in-arm. The twins she'd seen while with Ted, Genevieve, and Josephine Alder were with Anna MacDonald and Charlotte McGuire. They stood in front of the Hennessy's fine department store, peering in the window. All of them were marvelously dressed, especially Genevieve and Josephine, who always wore fashions from Paris, where they often vacationed. And hurrying from behind them walked her good friend Martha Fleming. Jules hadn't chatted with Martha since the cocktail party at Parker Mansion a few weeks ago, and she longed to catch up with her.

Jules picked up her pace and was just a block away from her friends. She was about to call out to them when a hand abruptly reached out, seizing her arm and pulling her into a dark alley.

"Augustina! What are you doing?"

Jules placed her grimy hand over her heart. "Oh! Ted, you surprised me!" She smiled, and her heart brightened at the sight of the tall, dark, handsome fellow in front of her.

"You are lucky I came upon you this minute," he replied.

"Don't you mean that you're the lucky one?" she smiled. But then Jules tilted her head to the side and looked at Ted's eyes. Instead of looking pleased to see her, they seemed disturbed.

"You don't want anyone seeing you in that get-up, do you?" he asked, gesturing at her miner's clothes.

"Get-up?" Jules repeated, her brows drawn together, questioning. Before he could answer, the group of Jules' friends called out from across the street.

"Oh, Mr. Jackson," Genevieve cried, waving her petite hand in greeting. Ted brusquely forced Jules deeper into the dark alleyway, with one hand pressing her head down low against the filthy brick wall. He turned toward the group of ladies and, with his free hand, doffed his hat.

"Good afternoon, ladies," he answered genially.

"Where is your girl Jules this fine day?" Josephine asked, her voice a high trill.

"Oh, I am sure she must be home studying her French," replied Ted. "Or perhaps she is creating a lovely arrangement with the new spring flowers."

"Ah, yes, that would be it. Do tell her hello for us?" Genevieve said with a wave. "Until we see you again—*au revoir!*" Ted bowed low until they turned the corner and were out of sight. He released Jules from her spot against the alley wall, and she was finally able to stand upright. Perplexed, she leaned back against the wall, her eyes blinking quickly.

"Did you really just hide me away and pretend I wasn't with you?" she asked hesitantly.

"Of course!"

"Of course?" Jules repeated.

"Augustina, you are a beautiful young woman," started Ted. "But you often make it very difficult for me to see that beauty." He moved closer to her. "A man needs to put his beloved on a pedestal, in a kind of unattainable love. She must be something to strive for, someone to adore." He looked out of the alleyway at Jules' school friends, his eyes traveling over them with admiration. "You must try harder to show me your beauty. I do so want you on that pedestal."

Embarrassed, Jules hung her head. Her knotted hair tumbled over her shoulders, and she tucked a strand behind her ear, smoothing it back.

"Do you want to be with me, Jules?" Ted tipped her head up so he could look into her eyes. His dark eyes burrowed into hers. Jules breathed out and searched Ted's face. Look at him—he was absolutely everything Jules' mother wanted for her husband and everything her father wanted for Parker Copper. He was perfect.

"Of course you do," Ted said when Jules didn't answer. He took out his monogrammed handkerchief and brushed at her lips. Leaning in slowly, Ted pressed his dry lips against hers. His tongue snaked out and pried open her own lips, licking lightly at her teeth.

"Oh!" Jules stopped breathing and leaned closer to Ted. But before she could get nearer, he stepped back.

"Please, Augustina, not so close. My suit is quite new," he said.

"I am sorry," Jules said in a quiet voice. After a pause, she added hesitantly, "Ted, when you waved out your greeting to the other girls, did you truly mean to thrust my face against this filthy alley wall?"

In the dim light of the alleyway, they stared at each other until finally Ted sighed and pulled her to him in a hug. He wrapped his arms around her and rested his cheek on her hair. Jules could sense an apprehension from Ted's embrace, and she stood still in his arms, trying not to let the dirt from her dungarees rub onto his suit too much.

"Wait right here for me. I'll go fetch my auto and drive you home," he said, pulling away, leaving her question unanswered. He kissed her lightly again, then took a step toward the street. "Promise me you'll wait right here," he said, pointing at the spot where she stood in the alleyway. Jules glanced around them, at the garbage and puddles of foul water. Ted brushed hard at his suit and placed his hat at a jaunty angle upon his head, then walked into the sunlight, leaving Jules standing near a pile of trash, alone.

Chapter 14

Ted delivered Jules back to Parker Mansion, where she spied Spirit contentedly munching on some green delicacy in the side yard. She'd never have gotten into that mess with Ted had Spirit just calmly walked around that rattlesnake, and they'd gone happily on their way. Jules sighed heavily and reached for the door handle.

But Ted was outside the auto, already opening the door for her. "Augustina, isn't that one of your horses there?" he asked, looking at Spirit.

"Yes, it certainly is," replied Jules. "His name is Traitor."

"Is that so?" replied Ted, sounding indifferent. "I thought you would be delivering him back to Lewisia soon, given that the horse races are this month."

"I thought that as well," she answered. "That is why I was on my ride this morning, because he was going back this week. Well, that and other things." She stepped out of the auto and looked up to Ted.

"Thankfully, you got in that one final ride," Ted said. "I imagine your riding days are over, now that the races can occupy your time." He laughed. "And maybe instead of looking like a muckraker," his eyes swept over Jules, "you'll consider dressing like the proper young lady that you are." He reached out for Jules' hand, then raised it to his lips.

Jules softened at Ted's kiss. While she'd been hurt over his comments in the alleyway, she hurt even more to think that he was embarrassed to be seen with her. Jules knew she wasn't as pretty as Celeste, and that she made it hard for men to see her beauty, especially dressed as she was. But she must be doing something correctly, for he had kissed her and wrapped her in a hug.

And hadn't Ted asked her if she wanted to be with him? Of course she did—he had said it himself.

"Have a nice time at the races this week, Augustina," Ted called out as he climbed behind the wheel and firmly closed the auto door. He pulled away from Parker Mansion. "I'll be with you in spirit!"

Upon hearing his name, Jules' magnificent chestnut horse held his head high, laid back his ears, and snorted.

While horse racing was among the oldest of organized sports, often called "The Sport of Kings," the out-of-control cheating and deception during betting was fairly recent. Just a decade ago, it seemed as if everyone was in on it, from the jockeys who were paid off to slow their horse, to the bookmakers who would buy true information from trainers, but then spread false information to gullible bettors in order to improve their own chances of not having to pay out.

AJ Parker loved horses as much as Jules did, and back then, when he'd seen what was happening to the sport, he refused to tolerate the corruption that was happening. Naturally, he decided to take matters into his own hands and turn horse racing back into a respectable sport.

And so, AJ Parker built Montana Silver Downs racetrack.

Silver Downs was located just east of town and was accessible by Butte's electric railway. The 50 acres of groomed gardens offered not only a dance pavilion, but also a small zoo and a man-made lake stocked with fish. The impressive Copper Clubhouse offered fine food and drink while the Olympia beer garden in back provided flowing draft beer and ale to the many miners who gathered to celebrate winners—or mourn losers.

But of course, the real draw was the horse race track.

The track itself was a fenced oval, running for an even eight furlongs. The grass aprons bordering the mile-long track provided a manicured, bright green border next to the brown of the dirt track. On the spectator side of the fence arose a three-storey building with vast, multi-level grandstands. The top and ground levels were open to the sun and rain, so one and all wore hats. Straw boaters bobbed for as far as the eye could see, in an ocean of matching hats.

But the middle of the grandstand, protected from the weather, housed the exclusive boxes of prominent Butte families. Resplendent with bentwood chairs and cloth-draped tables topped with silver vases of fresh flowers, the boxes were filled with women eager to show off the latest fashions. Many wore slim skirts with sophisticated white blouses and intricately decorated hats, and their men were seen in handsome three-piece suits, stiff white collars tight around their necks.

When Jules arrived at the Montana Silver Downs early that day, the grounds were already teeming with exquisite creatures—both equine and human. She spent the first hours visiting with the families in their box seats, but as soon as she could, she made her way past the paddock where a handful of horses grazed and back to the stables.

The stable bustled with energy, all the trainers and their horses preparing for the afternoon competition. Heads shorter than Jules, jockeys in their fine uniforms walked past, eyeing each other, looking for some sign of an advantage. Each was a master strategist, constantly crafting their plans early on and reconstructing them during the actual race. Their profession took bravery and cunning as much (or even more so) as miners who were lowered into the deep, dark mines each day.

A jockey, striking in the blue and gold silks of Lewisia Stock Farms, approached Jules as she entered through the large barn door, his helmet in his hands. "Afternoon to you, Miz Parker," he said.

"Why, Mr. Boland, good afternoon to you as well," Jules replied, tilting her head in greeting. "How was your weigh-in?"

"Fine, thank you for inquiring," replied the jockey. Not to be mistaken for merely a diminutive man, Boland's compact body moved like a racehorse itself, all sinewy muscle. They walked through the stable toward the back stall, to a beautiful pure white Thoroughbred, Smooth Ivory, her father's number one racehorse. Amongst the great racehorses in the history of Silver Downs, the best horse yet, Ivory, was the biggest winner at 13-for-13. She nickered as Jules approached.

Jules smiled and reached out and stroked Smooth Ivory's nose. The horse's well-chiseled head bobbed on her long neck, her slender legs pawing at the ground. At 16-1/2 hands, Jules had to stretch up to see over her withers. "Early, Ivory is gorgeous—she looks the best I've seen her. Is she ready to run today?"

"I'm sure she is, Miz Parker," replied Early. "But I ain't never trained with a filly more feisty than this one—she got a mind of her own, alright. I don't rightly always know what she's liking at one time or the other. The good thing is she's faster and more agile than most of the geldings. Now that's for certain." Jules nodded. A female who has a mind of her own and is more spirited than her male peers? Surely that is why she and Smooth Ivory were so comfortable together. As if reading Jules' thoughts, Smooth Ivory blew gently through her nose.

Early leaned against the stall. "I'm sure you already know this, but today aims to be Ivory's last race, seein' how Mr. Parker is focusing more on his standardbreds now."

"Yes, I did know that. And it seems that all of Montana is aware as well," said Jules. "The fairgrounds are already teeming with people come to attend the races. I've heard betting on Smooth Ivory is the highest it's ever been."

"Sure looks that way," agreed Boland. "People likely forgot how it was ten years ago when betting wasn't so legit. A lot of 'em have most of their wages riding on Ivory. I sincerely hope horse racing's shady past really is history."

Jules nodded in agreement. "Well, at 2:1, Ivory should be a sure bet."

Early grinned. "I'd be betting on her, too, if we jockeys were allowed. But since it's against the rules, I guess I'll just do my best to win some money for the great people of Butte." He placed his helmet atop his head, tipping it back. "You best get up to the Parker Box, Miz Jules. Race going to be starting soon."

"Oh no, Early, I'm a real railbird—I'll be down front in the stands. I like to be close to the track when Father's horses run. More action." She winked.

Boland raised his eyebrows. "Be careful, Miz Jules. It can get pretty rowdy down there on the ground with all those miners and such."

"Please, Mr. Boland, don't worry," replied Jules. "What could possibly happen?" She smiled. "Best of luck to you!"

"I'll need that luck, what with all the pressure for me to win for the town people—I'm gonna have to ride better'n I ever done." Early squared his shoulders as he turned away from Jules and Smooth Ivory.

Jules sat alone on a wooden stool next to Smooth Ivory's stall, a shaft of sunlight filtering across her. She thought about how her father would have enjoyed being in the stables with her, but AJ was back in the state capitol for a few weeks. Her mother had accompanied him this time around, as she did more and more now that AJ was considering entering Montana politics.

And of course, Celeste was nowhere near. She'd stayed back at Parker Mansion since even the thought of the race crowds would bring on her fainting spells. Jules had left her sister sitting on the front porch with a cool lemonade and a half-finished needlepoint that was to read "Cleanliness is next to godliness."

Then there was Ted. Although they'd spent the past few weeks together—almost every day since the incident in the alley—this afternoon, he was at Parker Copper Mining Company's main office taking care of business while AJ was out of town.

Jules had thought long and hard about what Ted said about her trying to show her beauty more. Jules remembered how he had admired her school friends as they strolled along the busy street. The Alder twins had been dressed immaculately, as they always were, that day in matching crisp puffed-shoulder blouses, tight cuffs buttoned at their wrists. Black leather belts had cinched in their tiny waists, and ankle-length skirts had skimmed their slender hips. Their long hair had hung down their backs in single braids, topped by elaborate hats framing their delicate, identical faces. Jules, on the other hand, had been hiding in a dark alley, wearing muddy boots and miner's dungarees. But still, Ted had chosen her.

So Jules decided that she would put more effort into her appearance. Each morning, she spent considerable time choosing her outfit, making sure that it was fashionable and flattering. She went shopping and bought the very same clothing that the Alder twins wore that day. And, she had Trudy style her hair with the hot tongs of torture.

Jules did want Ted to find her attractive and appealing, and if it was as easy as dressing well, then she'd do it. Because there was something more that Jules wanted from Ted. And that was for him to continue to be interested in what she had to say.

Ted and Jules had spent their days driving around Butte. She showed him St. Mary's girls' school, the large public library, and at least a dozen theaters. And they'd spent a long hour walking around the courthouse, with its red copper doors and roof. Jules especially loved the stained glass rotunda, while Ted was engrossed with the gallows frames behind the building that were used to hang criminals.

During their drives out of town, to the old mining camp Alder Gulch, and then up over the Rocky Mountains Continental Divide, Jules recounted history and stories of all the surrounding area. They had enjoyed each other's company, and Jules could feel Ted's affection for her. He would compliment her on her knowledge of her hometown, and when he'd pull his automobile up to Parker Mansion at the end of each day, he would kiss her cheek and tell her how much he'd enjoyed spending the day with her and that he was already looking forward to the next day.

Ted was an excellent driver, very cautious and safe, slowing for curves in the road and putting up the convertible top when the wind blew up too briskly. But one day, when the morning bloomed beautifully, Jules had suggested they take out bicycles or horses for their tour. Ted had frowned and had just replied that he would pick her up promptly at 9:00 a.m. in his auto, and this time, would she have completed her breakfast by then, please? At first, Jules had felt chastised, but that day Ted had commented that she had a "pleasant demeanor" and she really was "beautiful, if not a bit too slender." He had smiled when he'd said it, his dimples deep as craters on his cheeks.

Jules had understood what her father had found appealing about Ted. He was very bright and quite sure about himself—just the kind of man AJ was looking for to take over his company.

So, now Ted was at the mines, running Parker Copper, and here was Jules, with nothing to do but attend the races in a new outfit and shoes, her hair curled to perfection. It was turning out exactly as AJ had wished.

Chapter 15

"Ah...choo!" A sneeze sounded from the other side of the stable's tall brick wall. A smile played at Jules' lips as the sound brought her out of her reverie. While she, herself, was not allergic, Jules could only imagine how difficult it would be to be around the race track if one were sensitive to horses. The unfortunate person sneezing from outside had been having a bit of an attack, with this last one coming after a string of five in a row.

She rose from the wooden stool, gave Smooth Ivory one last pat, then walked past all the other horses and out into the bright outdoors. Immediately, she felt the liveliness of the crowd gathered for the races. Jules surveyed the grounds, which were as packed as downtown Butte on St. Patrick's day. People called to one another, a few words exchanged, with everyone holding tight onto a racing bill.

Sure enough, everyone knew it was Smooth Ivory's last race, one to remember. Jules glanced at the bookmaker's tote board and took in all the familiar horse names. They'd all raced against each other in the past, but none had beaten Ivory. Yes, betting for Ivory was still an easy win at 2:1. Jules' eyes followed each horse's race standings until she came to a new name. A last-minute substitution, Galileo, was running in place of Northern Lights. Jules consulted her racing bill. Lights was a late scratch? He was a magnificent horse, and she hoped nothing bad had befallen him.

The name Galileo seemed familiar to Jules. What was it? Jules remembered that he'd been around a couple of years back and had been a very promising racehorse. He was a striking animal with a deep black coat and a fine symmetrical body. He'd had some minor physical setbacks early on in his career, but most thought that Galileo was just not as mentally tough as other racers. Once in the paddock before a race, Galileo wouldn't want to leave—it was a battle just to get him onto the track. No matter what the trainers and jockeys had tried, Galileo seemed destined to be an Also Ran, typically finishing in sixth place or worse. He couldn't be counted on to bring home many winnings.

Jules studied the tote board. Galileo had betting at 35:1—surely again, he wouldn't be much of a competitor. With a flick of her tail, Ivory would swat him away like the black flies that were so bothersome to her.

"Hey, Miss Jules," called out one of the miners who worked at the Venturer. "You bettin' on your pa's horse?" He flicked a silver coin into the air, then caught it again.

"You know I'm not allowed, Cole," Jules replied. "You do it for me. Here are some coins I was going to use to buy a sausage."

"If'n Ivory wins, you could buy a lot more dogs."

"If Ivory wins, I'll buy you a victory sausage." She laughed with a wave. "I'll even throw in some sauerkraut."

The Call to the Post trumpet fanfare rang throughout the stadium, indicating that the race would be starting soon. Jules moved with the throngs to the lower stands. She pushed her way to the very front of the stands, against the railing, just feet away from the dirt track where the horses would soon be pounding past. Many of the spectators had had the same idea and were shoulder to shoulder, their bodies crushed close. Jules thought that her parents and Ted would have a fit if they knew she was mixed in with the teeming masses.

Jules rested her hand against the wooden railing, steadying herself as the crowd pressed in near. She heard grunts as people tried to get tighter and felt someone come in close behind her. Oh! Jules' eyes went wide. Really? Was there really someone's hand grabbing her bottom? Jules tried moving to the side—and yet the hand definitely still rested there. Through the many layers of her skirt, the hand almost burned against her, the rank smell of old whiskey and cheap cigars wrapping around her. Maybe she shouldn't have been there along with the masses!

Unwilling to let some cad spoil her day at the races, Jules pulled her shoulders back. "Oh no, you don't," she said under her breath. Jules took a quick step backwards, stepping squarely onto the foot of the dastardly culprit and with a quick jab of her bent arm, elbowed him sharply in the stomach, causing him to make a sound something like "oooph." Immediately, his hand disappeared from her rump, and for a moment, Jules had a bit more room around her. Thank goodness the scoundrel was smart enough to move off. Jules raised her chin in triumph.

But damn, wasn't he persistent? Already, he'd crammed in close again. Jules could feel him pressed close, maybe not as close as before, but she could smell his scent of sandalwood and ambrette. Jules' eyes widened again. Sandalwood and ambrette?

"Ah-choo!"

Jules turned around and came face to face with the stranger who had come off the train that day and had caught her from falling when she smacked into him. A day's worth of facial hair grew on his cheeks, only emphasizing his high cheekbones and strong chin. Those eyelashes rimming his hazel eyes seemed too full and lush for a boy.

"Ah-choo," he repeated, sneezing into his bent elbow. "Good thing this spot opened up. Great view." He smiled playfully at Jules.

"You! Don't tell me it was your hand on my bottom?" Jules accused.

The stranger held up both hands. "No, ma'am. That was Arvid Malone. And I don't think he'll be groping anyone again soon. Seems he can't barely breathe correctly since you got him in the solar plexus." The stranger grinned and burst out laughing. Jules couldn't help herself and, giddy from standing so close to the handsome stranger, started laughing as well.

When their laughter finally subsided, Jules, a smile still upon her face, said to him, "I'm Jules." He tucked a racing bill into his back pocket, rocked back on his heels, and said in a clear voice,

"An emerald is as green as grass;
  A ruby red as blood;
  A sapphire shines as blue as heaven;
  A flint lies in the mud.

A diamond is a brilliant stone,
  To catch the world's desire;
  An opal holds a fiery spark;
  But a flint holds fire."

His hazel-colored eyes danced. "Those kinds of jewels?" he asked, his lips pulled in a mischievous grin. Jules, one eyebrow cocked high, shook her head. She studied him through her eyelashes.

"I'm Rand Buckley," he said. "It's nice to finally know you."

"Finally?"

"Now then, you don't think I could forget once having you in my arms, do you?" he asked, as Jules blushed red and ducked her head. "Almost seemed too good a fit," he said, almost to himself.

Jules' blush deepened. "I... it...we..." she stammered.

He looked her up and down, his eyes shining. "You are very lovely with that pink upon your cheeks—it complements the lavender coloring of your dress." Jules felt a smile creeping up on her mouth.

"Ah-choo!"

"Mr. Buckley, do you think it's wise for you to be here, given your apparent allergy to horses?" Jules teased.

"Rand, please. And in case you didn't know it, a filly named Smooth Ivory is running today for the last time. She seems to be an easy bet, and I thought I'd come try to make some winnings." He jingled some coins in his pockets.

Jules smiled. "Yes, I'd heard, Rand. So you and the rest of Butte have all bet on Ivory."

"Oh, no," he replied. "I'm going with Galileo."

"What? That's crazy! He's running at 35:1. Why would anyone in their right mind bet with those odds?"

Rand stared at her, their eyes locking and taking Jules' breath away. Her heart pounded as if it would escape her chest and roll away onto the racetrack. He said, "Sometimes you gotta take a chance." Around them, people, anxious for the race to start, started chanting, "Let 'em run! Let 'em run!"

Jules turned from Rand's slow grin, unsure of whether he was teasing her in return, and moved away from him, alongside the track railing. Rand followed her, and the smile dropped from his handsome face.

"Listen, I know this may seem crazy, but I've been thinking about you ever since the first time I laid eyes on you," he said in a quick breath. "There's something special about you."

"Oh, please, Mr. Buckley, does that line work on all your women?" Jules frowned, sure now that he was mocking her.

"No! I've never said that to another woman before," he objected. "I'm serious. It's like I said—it's almost like we're a perfect fit. Please, how about I take you out to the theater? Or for a stroll? Or to church?

Something… anything?"

"But I don't even know you!" objected Jules.

"Sometimes you gotta take a chance." His eyes bore into hers. "Please."

Jules took a deep breath, then smiled sweetly. "How's this for a chance. If your horse, Galileo, wins, I'll accept a date with you." Jules blinked innocently.

"I'll take those odds." Rand nodded once, then held out his hand. "Let's shake on it."

Jules clasped his powerful hand, covering it with both of her smaller hands, and was shocked at the electricity that flowed between them. Almost like being caught outside just before a thunderstorm, Jules' heart raced, and goose bumps covered every part of her body. She had never experienced anything like it before. It took her breath away.

But then, as she looked up into his face and sensed that same familiarity, her heartbeat slowed and thumped against her chest. All sound muted from the crowded stands, and all she could do was gaze into this stranger's eyes and hold his hand in both of hers. It seemed as if everything was in slow motion: the horses walking past, the woman to her right with her head thrown back, laughing gaily, and a lone red balloon floating up out of the stands, into the big blue sky of Montana.

"Yes," she said as if spellbound. "I suppose sometimes you've got to take a chance." And then at that moment, a piercing signal bell clanged, and the flag was dropped. The horses were off the starting line.

The race started as planned, with Smooth Ivory jumping to the forefront. She led the pack around the first turn, then easily pulled ahead of them all. It seemed she had the race all but won already.

But who was this? Jules stood on her toes, her eyes growing wide. Galileo had come up from 8th place and was actually gaining on the leading pack. The crowd was going wild, watching the muscular black horse covering ground. He passed Deep Storm on the inside and moved up into third place, just shy of Valiray, coming into the last stretch.

The crowd was chanting "Smooth Ivory! Smooth Ivory!" but Jules heard Rand cheering behind her, "Let's go, Galileo!

The horses and their riders passed by the stands on the straight run home, so close that the horses' guttural breathing and their thunderous galloping deafened the spectators at the rail. Jules could see her jockey Early's neck straining as he leaned up and over Ivory. She saw him frown and glance behind, aware of how close Valiray and Galileo were. "Smooth Ivory! Smooth Ivory!" yelled the crowd. Early leaned further, his bottom out of the saddle, shouting and egging Ivory on.

But now, Early was leaning forward too much, and he clutched at his whip. Jules gasped. She knew Smooth Ivory better than anyone. It was too much weight near her withers. And Ivory balked at the whip.

Valiray came neck and neck, and Jules thought back to Early fiercely saying he had to win for the people of Butte. Jules screamed, "No, Early!" just as he flicked Smooth Ivory's hindquarters. Jules saw Ivory's head pull up, and she faltered. The great racehorse caught the tip of her hoof on the dirt track. And stumbled.

Just inches behind Ivory, Valiray spooked madly and pulled up on his hind legs, dumping his jockey from the saddle.

A collective gasp came from the stands as Galileo darted past both Smooth Ivory and Valiray and crossed the finish line in first place.

"Atta boy!" hollered Rand as he pounded the air with his fist. He lifted Jules into his arms. "We won!"

He swung her around laughing, his strong arms holding her tightly against his muscular body. Jules, heady from being in his arms, pressed against him, feeling him tight against her chest. Jules leaned into his embrace, resting her small waist in his cupped hands. With the sun gleaming off his gold-flecked hair, completely unable to resist, Jules wrapped her arms around his neck and buried her face in his hair.

When he finally set her down, both with breath heavy and ragged, he spoke to her, his confession solemn on his face, "I've never met anyone who has so stolen my thoughts and captured my heart."

Intoxicated, Jules' thoughts swam around in her head. *He'd meant it for her!*

Rand brought his face close to hers, closing his eyes, his thick eyelashes brushing at the tops of his cheeks. His lips parted, and he leaned in closer as Jules, her heart pounding, tilted her face up to his.

"THIS GODDAM RACE WAS RIGGED!" A wooden stadium chair flew over their heads, landing just inches away from them and exploding into shards.

"I LOST ALL MY EARNINGS ON THAT BLASTED HORSE!"

"WE WANT OUR MONEY BACK!"

Jules' eyes flew open, and she jerked away from Rand. Booing and jeering followed shouts of the race being fixed and how everyone had been cheated. They both looked out into the stands, realizing that most of the people in the stands had placed their hard-earned dollars on a horse that should have easily come in first, but instead came in third. There were a lot of people who lost their money at the very moment when Smooth Ivory stumbled and Galileo crossed the finish line.

The crowd turned wild, ripping wooden bleacher seats from the stands and dumping them over the railings and into private boxes. Mad throngs were climbing over the fence and streaming onto the racetrack. Fistfights broke out with men wrestling one another, punching at anyone standing near. Even the women revolted, pulling at each other's hair and slapping one another.

"Wait! Stop!" screamed Jules, twisting around, watching the riot grow. "You mustn't do this!" Her words were lost in the uproar. The crowd intensified, and she heard glass windows breaking near the clubhouse.

Frantic, Jules turned toward Rand. Rand? In the melee, he'd disappeared! Jules spun around, searching everywhere for a glimpse of golden hair. Just as Jules thought she should run away as well, someone grabbed at her, tearing a pearl necklace from her throat. "Stop that man!" she yelled, her words lost in the din. Alarmed and with her legs shaking, Jules searched for the exit, ready to flee.

Pfheeeeeee! A piercing wolf-whistle cut the din of the rioting crowd. Along with the crowd, Jules looked to where the sound had come. Ten yards away, Rand stood atop the bandstand, his two fingers still in his lips. *Pfheeeeeeeet*—this time sharper and louder, and the crowd silenced as police sirens sounded from the far distance.

"FREE BEER!" Rand waved his arms above his head and pointed to the exits. "MR. AJ PARKER APOLOGIZES FOR THE LAST RIDE OF SMOOTH IVORY'S CAREER. ANYONE HOLDING A TICKET STUB BETTING ON HER CAN PRESENT IT AT THE OLYMPIA BEER GARDEN FOR FREE BEER ALL DAY. COURTESY OF MR. AJ PARKER!"

A cheer went up from the crowd. Men and women stopped brawling and instead pushed at one another, eager to be the first in line for free beer at the Beer Garden. Jules' jaw dropped. She watched the stampede of people rush to the exit gates. They stepped over the wreckage they'd caused, kicking the debris aside in their hurry to get to the beer garden. Her eyes scanned the crowd, trying to count the number who would be partaking in Rand's offer. It seemed that hundreds were crowding at the exits.

She felt someone grab her arm and twisted around to find Rand, wearing a huge grin, standing next to her once again. Jules' eyes flashed, and she pulled back her hand and slapped him solidly across the face.

"How dare you!" she screamed.

Rand's eyebrows rose, questioning. A red palm print bloomed on his cheek.

"Who gave you permission to give away free beer?" Jules continued. "Who gave you permission to speak for my father?"

"*Your father?*"

"Yes," Jules replied. "Of course!"

"*AJ Parker is your father?*" Rand said, incredulous.

"Of course he is. And now your little ruse of free beer has just cost him hundreds of dollars!"

"That's a smidgen to a filthy rich, low-down dirty bastard like AJ Parker." Rand turned and spit. "But it's a fortune to the people who just lost a few months' worth of wages."

"Smooth Ivory's losing wasn't my father's fault," said Jules, drawing her shoulders back. "And it wasn't his fault that all those people bet on her and lost." Jules' eyes narrowed. "But, come to think of it, most people did bet on Ivory. There were only a couple of people who didn't—one in particular who bet on an unknown horse with 35:1 odds, name of Galileo. Surely that person won a lot of money." A boozy cheer echoed from the Beer Garden as another keg was tapped.

Jules raised her chin higher. "Tell me, Mr. Buckley… where did you learn of Galileo's sudden capability… and what else did you know… that no one else did?"

"Your horse balked," replied Rand. "You and I both know that Galileo won that race fair and square."

"Do we?"

"I'm going to pretend," said Rand, his voice cold. "That you didn't just suggest that I had anything dishonest to do with that race."

Their eyes blazed at each other. Then he reached out and grabbed Jules by the shoulders, pulling her into him. He wrapped his arms around her slight body and buried one hand in her hair. His other hand reached lower and caught hold of her bottom. With his lips parted, his mouth roughly covered hers, and he kissed her passionately.

Just as Jules' legs went weak, Rand wrenched away. "And now, if you'll excuse me, *Jules Parker*," he said, his voice husky. "I hear they're giving away free beer in the Beer Garden."

And with her lips still tender, her skin still burning where his hand had been, Rand Buckley walked out of Jules's life in precisely the same way as he'd walked in.

Chapter 16

Earlier that morning, Jules meandered around Butte on her bicycle, cruising from copper mine to copper mine. She'd started out at the Diamond, the familiar smell of blasting powder and machine oil bringing her comfort, and had remained for over an hour, thinking back to the day before.

At first, her thoughts had run to the riot and how angry the crowd turned when Smooth Ivory had lost. But then, Jules remembered how Rand had subdued the mob. Begrudgingly, Jules appreciated what Rand had done—it really was a clever move. Rand Buckley. Rand Buckley. She got shivers thinking of him. Was it real, or did she imagine the shared attraction between them?

Jules' mouth still tingled from Rand's kiss, and her tongue peeked out, tracing her lips. She'd never been kissed like that before. Even though her relationship with Ted had progressed quickly from acquaintance to one of familiarity, their kisses were still a bit chaste. Jules could never imagine Ted fervently kissing her and grabbing her bottom all the while. Jules felt a blush creeping up her neck.

She rubbed at her cheeks, trying to disperse the color. Jules had come here to the Parker Copper offices to tell her father something that she felt was important.

After leaving the Diamond, when she'd ridden her bicycle around the other mines, she'd stopped at the Metis because something hadn't felt right to her at that particular headframe. She'd tried to put her thumb on it, but had come away with nothing but a troubled feeling. Everything had looked fine to her, but maybe the sound or the atmosphere or something around the mine was just a bit off. She'd ridden directly to Parker Copper to talk about the Metis mine with her father.

When she'd arrived, the door to her father's office was slightly ajar. Jules stood with her hand on the door handle and had just about pushed it to enter when she heard the voices inside—her father and Ted.

She peeked into her father's office and spied Ted seated in a leather chair facing AJ's desk. Jules clenched her hands with fistfuls of her skirt. Ted was sitting in her chair—the one she'd occupied ever since Gus died, and she had taken his place in joining AJ in his office each day. It was her chair, and it drove Jules crazy to see Ted perched on what was rightfully hers.

But AJ had not budged on allowing Jules back into the mines, and instead had embraced Ted with both arms into the operations of Parker Copper. So now, instead of inside her father's office discussing the mines, Jules was outside a closed door eavesdropping, the way Celeste might.

"…and the Venturer continues to provide the highest output," Ted was saying. Jules lowered her eyes to the floor, listening to the conversation going on inside the office.

"Excellent," replied AJ. "We are lucky that mine has such incredibly high yield—it makes up most of our production. Right now, if anything were to happen to it, we'd be in bad straits."

"Yes, sir, I couldn't agree more," said Ted.

"And what of the Metis?" asked AJ. Jules raised her head.

Ted's pants rustled as he crossed his legs. "Fine," he replied. "As are all the Parker mines. Everything is in order." Jules frowned. Wasn't Ted going to mention the peculiar sound at the Metis? Didn't he realize, too, that something was amiss?

"I am grateful you were here to take care of business while I was in Helena," said AJ. "The mining operations seem to be running smoothly."

"Thank you, sir."

"Now, tell me of this fiasco at the race track," said AJ, sitting back in his leather desk chair. "And how I managed to incur a $500 debt to the Olympia Brewing Company."

Ted sat forward on his chair and recounted the details of the race. "And as you know, I wasn't there at the track, but Arvid Malone informed me that some fool name of Buckley called out the free beer offer in your name."

"Buckley?" AJ said. "Would that be one Random Ferris Buckley?" Jules leaned closer to the open door.

"Why yes, do you know him?" asked Ted.

"Know him? I booted the mudsill out of this very office just a week ago!" AJ stood and began pacing behind his desk. "The damn bastard came in here suggesting that Parker Copper Mining Company should swap out all our headframes from timber to steel. He claimed that by employing steel, our headframes would be exponentially stronger and we could increase our loads tenfold. But I told him that our timber headframes are top-notch. Why should I spend good money, let alone shut down days of operations on the mines, to replace perfect, top-rate headframes with new frames out of steel?" AJ pounded his fist on his desk. "Timber headframes have always served us well."

"Right you are," agreed Ted. "Timber is sufficient. Who is this Buckley to tell you, the eminent AJ Parker, differently?" Jules heard the scorn in Ted's voice. "What kind of expert is this Buckley, anyway?"

"None in mining, from what I can tell. Seems he's been traveling across the West, to the larger mining communities, trying to convince them of the superiority of steel. He was even over at Hailey Mines a few days before coming here."

Ted coughed. "Hailey Mines, you say."

"Hailey himself told me when we ran into each other at the Union Club Sunday afternoon. He said I should expect that Buckley would be contacting me next," said AJ. "When Buckley claimed to me to be an engineer from Chicago, I'd already found out that his uncle built the first Ferris wheel a few years back at the World's Fair."

"So Buckley claims he is related to George Washington Gale Ferris?" laughed Ted. "That's rich!"

"Yes. He must have been, what, seven or eight years old at the time of Chicago's World Fair? He was just a boy," replied AJ. "And probably still hiding behind his mother's skirts."

Ted's voice pitched low, and he said softly, "Well, he's certainly grown up now. Malone also claims Buckley keeps company with a particular, ahem, woman called Ruby Paradise."

"The high-paid prostitute in the Cabbage Patch?" exclaimed AJ. "Buckley seems to have expensive taste."

"But does he have the money to fund those expensive tastes?" asked Ted, disparagingly.

"Well, that is why he's come here—to make money off the mining industry by pushing a conversion to ferris wheel steel." AJ's voice had that criticizing tone, the one he had when he spoke to Jules about her place at Parker Copper Mining Company.

"I hope you threw the scoundrel out on this tail," Ted exclaimed.

"Of course I did," bellowed AJ. "After all this time in business, I think I can smell a liar out."

Jules' lips pursed. Rand kept company with a prostitute! Could he really be such a cheat and a liar? Of course, he could—she really didn't even know him, did she? Besides seeing him at the train station and then again at the racetrack, what did Jules know of Rand Buckley?

"I'm certain that he is the worst kind of man," said Ted. "A *con-man* trying to cheat men out of their money and women out of their virtue."

Jules drew in a sharp breath. Her mouth opened in an "oh" and her eyes went wide as she thought about how Rand had tightly held her while passionately kissing her. It was true! The liar and cheat had groped her and then had gone and drunk beer paid for by her father!

Jules fiercely shook her head, dispelling the memories. She felt dirty, kissed by the very same man who spent time—and money—with a prostitute. Jules was enraged at falling for his lies. Hadn't he said that he'd never met anyone who had so stolen his thoughts and captured his heart? Another lie. She was glad at this point that she hadn't accepted a date with him. Jules shuddered and wiped her coat sleeve hard across her still-tingling lips.

Rand may well be a fraud, but Jules was no fool. No, she wouldn't again be conned by the likes of Random Ferris Buckley.

Chapter 17

Jules knocked lightly on the office door, then pushed it all the way open. Ted stood from his chair, a smile already showing his dimples.

"Hello Ted," Jules leaned in and offered her cheek to Ted for a kiss. "Father, how are you?" Jules turned to AJ.

"Jules, it seems like months since you've visited my office," said her father.

"Yes, I agree," replied Jules. She moved a stack of newspapers from a nearby ottoman and sat down. "I wouldn't have imposed, but I wanted to tell you something…"

"It's not an imposition, my dear," said AJ. "In fact, I've been wanting to talk with you."

Ted cleared his throat. "I should think to take my leave, sir."

"No, please stay, Ted. You can hear this too."

AJ leaned forward over this desk and opened the burl-wood humidor. He selected a cigar and then twirled it between his thumb and fingers.

"Care for one?" he asked Ted, as if an afterthought.

"Thank you, but no," replied Ted. "I'm not an enthusiast."

AJ nodded, then bit the tip off and spat it toward the ashtray on the desk. "So, Jules, my dear," AJ began. "I know it has been hard on you, being banned from our mines. But I want to remind you of why."

Jules lowered her chin and gazed at the floor. "I do not need any reminder," she said.

"Fair enough. Perhaps that even shows me more that you carry the weight of your responsibility with you each and every day," said AJ. "And that is why I wanted to tell you how proud I am of you these past weeks. You have proven that you heard what I needed you to hear, and you have been quite responsible in your actions."

Ted sat forward in his chair. "If I may say so, sir," he added. "Augustina has been eager and devoted in introducing me to the area. And she seems to know more about your company than anyone else I've encountered. She has been invaluable in providing me with information on Parker Copper." Jules smiled with appreciation at Ted.

"I could see that," replied AJ. He looked at Jules over the cigar smoke. "And that is why, Jules, I'm reconsidering allowing you back into the mines."

Jules jumped up from her seat. "Father, really? Do you mean it? Because I came here in the first place to tell you about the…"

"Not so fast, Jules," he said. "I said I am reconsidering it. That does not mean…"

"Even still, I…"

"It means that you will still be on a kind of probation until the Vice Director deems the appropriate time."

"Me, sir?" asked Ted, taken aback. "Do you think that is wise?"

"Of course it is. In addition to you keeping tabs on Jules, I will be giving you additional responsibilities here at Parker Copper." AJ puffed on his cigar. "You are ready to move up in the company."

Jules' jaw dropped. Ted was getting a promotion? And he was accountable for her? It was even worse than when she'd first arrived at the office. Not only was Ted in her chair, but he was also in charge. She sat down hard and rubbed at her temples.

AJ pulled his chair close in and reached for his ringing telephone. "Now, Jules, you said you had something important to tell me." He stubbed his cigar out.

"Never mind," she replied, dejected. "Suddenly, it no longer seems so important.

Chapter 18

Jules lay in bed, her eyes wide open. Day had not yet broken, the outside of her windows just brightening with the periwinkle light that came between night and day. Something had awoken her, but she didn't know quite what. Even after she'd finally fallen asleep past midnight, she'd slept fitfully, a strange, faraway sound permeating her dreams.

An air horn blasted, the sound vibrating the glass in her bedroom windows. *Six o'clock, shift change.* Yet even through the loud horn blast, Jules could still hear, no, maybe feel that very same groaning, moaning sound that had kept her awake all night.

But now it felt different.

Jules' hair on the nape of her neck prickled. Her eyes searched the dim light in her room, and she pulled her bedspread aside. She swung her legs over the side of her bed and…

CRASH!

Jules' head snapped up. The Metis! Something had happened at the Metis. Somehow, she just knew. Jules ran to her window and threw open the sash, where she immediately heard yelling.

Grabbing her robe, Jules dashed out of her room and down the stairs to the front entryway. Her father was already at the door in his shirtsleeves, his suspenders not yet tight across his shoulders.

Jules ran to AJ. "Father, what's happened?"

"I've no idea," he replied. "But it looks like it's coming from the Metis—and it's not good." They stepped out onto the mansion's front porch. A plume of dust rose into the sky, blotting the morning sun. Emergency sirens blared over the hills. "Go fetch Hazel, Jules. Tell her to have my auto brought around immediately." AJ turned and strode into the quiet entryway, calling over his shoulder, "I'm calling over to the Metis right now."

Jules rushed into the kitchen. "Hazel!" she cried. "Where are you?" She scanned the empty kitchen, then crossed to the sink where water still flowed from the tap. She turned the faucet off, and from the window, spied the housemaids all standing in the backyard, looking out over the mine hill. She quickly rapped on the glass.

"Trudy, where is Hazel?"

Trudy cupped her hand around her mouth. "She ran to the garage to send up Mr. Parker's car."

Jules nodded, then turned from the window. Leave it to Hazel to be one step ahead of everyone. Jules leaned against the icebox, her hands covering her face. She had been one step ahead and should have said something when she had the chance. Jules had gone to tell her father about her uneasiness with something at the Metis. But instead, Jules had only selfishly thought about herself and how Ted was getting promoted and was sitting in her chair. She felt guilty.

Jules anxiously ran through the hallway to the library. Her father stood at his desk, the telephone tight to his ear. "The blasted telephones are down at the mine," he said. "I can't get through to anyone." He snatched his suit coat from the back of his chair. "But I can be there in 5 minutes."

They hurried back to the heavy front door, and AJ yanked it open as if it weighed nothing.

"Peterson! What in the blazes is going on?" yelled AJ. Jules stepped next to her father and saw Merle Peterson, Parker Copper's graveyard shift boss, jumping out of a truck, then running at a full sprint up their walkway. His face was twisted with panic.

"Mr. Peterson," called out Jules, her voice catching. "It was the main, wasn't it? On the Metis?"

Peterson pulled up short, his head bobbing up and down. "Yes'm." He wiped his sleeve across his brow. "Mr. Parker, Miz Jules is right. The Metis' main timber done broke clean through. We was haulin' the last load up and I hears a loud crack, louder'n I ever heard afore. When I look over at the box, just about level with the collar, the main timber just up and snapped in half!" Peterson took a breath. "Just like a little matchstick."

Jules' hand covered her mouth, her eyes wide with dread.

"That heavy load o' iron ore went down like the devil done pulled it down hisself. And… and… Jack Hagan was ridin' the box and he… he…"

"Was he hurt?" interrupted AJ.

Peterson broke down and covered his face with his filthy hands, his shoulders shaking. "Yes, sir. Hagan's done crushed at the bottom."

Millicent joined them at the door. She slipped her arm around Jules.

"How did the main split?" yelled AJ. "Your men just repaired it. I ordered you to ensure that it was solid!"

Peterson looked up and wiped his fist across his eyes. He nodded once. "It was solid, Mr. Parker, no question about it. But now, when I looked at the split, well, it seemed too clean."

"Too clean?"

"Yes, sir, too clean. Like maybe it had been cut that way," replied Peterson.

Jules looked to her mother. Millicent's eyebrows were drawn together in question as Peterson continued.

"Like maybe that brand new timber'd been sawed partway through," he said, fretfully shaking his head. "I think somebody done it on purpose."

"Sabotage?" exclaimed Millicent, her hand covering her heart. "AJ, could it be, really?" Jules' father turned and placed his hand on her mother's arm.

"We thought something like this might happen eventually," he said under his breath.

"But I didn't really think it so!" Millicent's eyes filled with concern.

"I'll not let this go any further," AJ said. "We'll get to the bottom of it before any more damage is wrought." AJ turned to Peterson. "Get a hold of Police Chief Davies and tell him to meet me at the Metis. Immediately!"

"He should already be there, sir." Ted strode quickly up the front walkway. "I passed him on Montana Street and flagged him down. I instructed him to secure the area." He paused. "And then I came straight here."

"Ted, did you hear about Mr. Hagan?" asked Jules, tears pooling in her eyes. Ted climbed the steps to Jules' side and wrapped his arms around her, hugging her tightly.

"Dumb luck," he answered quietly. "Hagan was in the wrong place at the wrong time."

Jules had last seen Jack Hagan a couple of months back. At the time, he'd been in great spirits, stomping his heavy work boots along to the tune he played on his pennywhistle, the rest of the Irish band keeping time.

It was a Friday in March, after the dinner hour, when Jules had decided to deliver a small gift to Sarah Dugan, who was due to deliver her first child in a few weeks. Sarah's husband, Danny, was the young mine foreman at the Venturer, Parker Copper's most prolific mine, and he and his wife were well respected within their community of mostly Irish families.

The basket held a lovely pure white lambs-fleece carriage blanket and a rich teething ring made of mother-of-pearl with a sterling silver bell that jingled softly. Hazel had added in a darling off-white knitted mohair tam-o'-shanter, with its jaunty hanging tassel and center pompom, and instructed Jules to wish Sarah "*saol fada agus breac-shláinte chugat,*" which was Gaelic for "long-life and fair health to you."

Jules had settled the basket in the crook of her arm and walked out of Parker Mansion, east on Granite Street, and up toward Dublin Gulch. The nearer she got to the Gulch, the more crowded the streets became. Men and women stood shoulder to shoulder in the corner pubs, laughter echoing out into the street. Different music competed as it poured from the open windows of the many cafes—a lively accordion bleated like a chorus of goats, a harmonica bent up and over rushing notes. Much, much busier than the typical Friday night, Jules finally comprehended that she'd walked into an Irish neighborhood celebrating St. Patrick's Day.

Caught up in the mood, Jules had stepped lightly and had pushed through the crowds for the Dugan's house on Anaconda Road. Once there, she realized she had come right in the middle of a party they were hosting. The front room was packed with revelers joining in clapping and stomping and dancing to a spirited five-piece band playing, the fiddler leading them in an Irish folk tune. Jules had crept forward, watching the merriment from the shadows behind an old maple tree.

Just when she thought she should leave and just return the following day, a voice behind her demanded, "Whatcher think yer doin' back here, hidin' amongst the ghostly shadows? Come on outta there!" Jules had turned to see a very tipsy Matty Kelly two-fisting pints of brown ale, the one in his left hand sloshing over his wrist.

She'd stepped out of the shadows with a guilty look and had stammered, "Mr. Kelly, I do apologize! I...I..."

"You'll not get away without pitching in for the keg," slurred Matty, as he drank deeply from his glass. "The hat's over yonder." He nodded in the faint direction of the front parlor. Jules had stepped away from the tree and into the light of the moon when she saw the glimmer of recognition cross Matty's bleary eyes.

"Oh," he'd said. Then, without hesitating, he held out his full pint, shoved it into Jules' hand, and then turned and staggered away. "First pint's on me. But don't matter who yer be," he called out behind him. "yer still gotta fill the hat."

Not knowing what else to do with it, Jules had drunk the delicious, thick brown ale down to its last drop. And then with a big smile, Jules had walked into the Dugan's home with an empty glass and a basket full of baby gifts.

Sarah had waddled forward when she'd spied Jules and accepted the basket graciously. She pulled Jules close to the band and cupped her hand around Jules' ear, telling her to stay as long as she'd like and to make herself at home. And then Sarah had drifted away into the party.

Jules sat on the wood bench by herself, tapping her foot to the music. She'd felt people looking at her, unsure of how to deal with the wealthy daughter of AJ Parker sitting in the midst of them, but then, out of the blue, someone thrust another brown ale into her hands with a shout of "*Lá fhéile Pádraig sona dhuit! Happy St. Patrick's Day to You!*" And then ten minutes later, another full glass was placed in front of her. And then another.

That's when Jack Hagan had come over to her, but instead of handing her a glass of ale, he shoved something else to her—a mandolin. "C'mon, Miss Jules," he'd shouted. "Play along with us, will you?"

So, with the courage that came in a pint glass, Jules had wholeheartedly jumped up to the band and had quickly fallen in with them as they played "The Wild Rover" and "I'll Tell Me Ma."

Jack had whooped and hollered along while the fiddler's fingers flew over his strings and the bodhran player's tipper pounded on the drum. The guitar and accordion players kept time, occasionally shouting out a *"tiugainn!"* The clomping of the dancers on the wood floor reverberated up the walls, causing the overhead lights to flicker.

Jack's wife Katy had yelled out to Jules over the raucous noise, "How'd you know how to play the mandolin?"

"Ten years of lute lessons with Monsieur Jean-Pierre Barteau," shouted Jules. "But this is the first time that I've ever truly played!" She twirled and stomped her foot to the music. Katy grabbed her young daughter's hands and spun her around, both of their ribboned hair flying out behind them, as the floor crowded with others joining in. Jules looked out over the dancers and saw her housemaid, Trudy, skipping along to the music with her skirt lifted above her ankles. When Trudy saw Jules watching her, she slowed her dancing, looking uncomfortable. But Jules winked at the girl and yelled, "Show us how, Trudy!" who then beamed and joined in dancing once again.

A couple of hours and many songs later, Jules finally set aside the mandolin. Her fingers had ached from playing, and her face hurt from smiling. She thought of the parties she'd attended at Parker Mansion, with the imported champagne and string quartets, and all the boring talk from the rich businessmen and politicians, and society ladies. How different this party was, with the miners and laborers and housekeepers. And how much more fun it was! Jules hadn't seen such joy, let alone experienced it herself.

But exhausted, Jules looked forward to falling into bed. She called thanks to Sarah and Danny Dugan as she staggered out to the front porch, shivering a bit after stepping out of the thick and muggy air in the house. In the backyard, a group of men stood around the keg, wildly singing along off-key to the thin trill of Jack Hagan's playing.

Sighing with contentment, Jules looked up into the Saint Patrick's Eve moon, then turned toward the pitch-dark Anaconda Street. But before she could take another step, two sturdy pairs of arms grabbed hers from behind.

Startled, Jules turned to run, trying to pull her arms free.

"Miss Jules, we're to walk you home to Parker Mansion," a teenage boy said, holding tight and tucking her hand in the crook of his arm.

"Katy and Jack are our ma and pa," said the other boy. "They said we're to make sure you get home safe."

"And that you're welcome back anytime at all," said yet another teenage boy walking behind them.

Jules let out a long, unsteady breath and said, "Why, that would be lovely." And as the foursome walked down the dark street to Parker Mansion, with the sound of the music still carrying along behind them, Jules figured there was nothing more joyous in the world than a pint of brown ale and the serenading of a pennywhistle.

Jules looked out over the yard and wiped at her eyes with the corner of her robe. The sun glinted off the morning dew, making the yard look carpeted with diamonds. It was too beautiful a morning for such a tragedy.

Ted pulled her closer and kissed the top of her head. He tilted her face to his—she could see the concern in his eyes, although he seemed somewhat edgy, his normally so-sure façade cracked just a bit. "Augustina, all will be fine."

"But, what about his family?" Jules asked, her voice breaking.

"Let's not worry about them right now," Ted replied. "I want to make sure Parker Copper is unharmed." Jules' eyebrows knitted together, questioning what would happen to Katy and her children. Was Ted really putting the mine before the Hagan family?

Ted pulled away, turning toward AJ. "Please, Mr. Parker, we must get to the mine. My auto is here, I'll drive you."

AJ pulled Millicent into an embrace. His hand rested on Jules's shoulder as he said, "Thank god Ted is here watching over our company. We're very lucky to have him as part of our family." Ted seemed to grow taller as the words were spoken.

He turned to Jules. "Your father needs me. Why don't you get dressed? Then you can have your father's car bring you to the Metis."

"Yes, good idea," replied Jules. "I'll hurry and change, and come straight up to the mine. Then I'll go tend to Katy and her children."

"Oh, Augustina, my dear…" started Ted.

Jules's eye grew wide at the endearment. "Yes..?" She placed her hand on Ted's arm.

"…Don't wear that lavender dress you wore last week. It's unflattering." He brought her hand to his lips, then just as quickly dropped it and headed for his automobile.

Jules climbed the stairs to her room, her legs heavy. The Metis sabotaged? Who would do such a thing—did her family really have such enemies? AJ had told her that some people might want to harm Parker Copper Mining Company, but what about Hagan's death? Was it truly murder, or had it just been an unfortunate mistake, as Ted suggested? Was the real damage meant for the Metis headframe?

She entered her room and leaned against her wardrobe. The Metis headframe. Again, Jules felt ashamed that she hadn't said something when she'd gone to tell AJ that day. That day when she'd heard him and Ted talking about Rand Buckley. That's when she'd discovered that Rand had been thrown out of her father's office for trying to convince him to switch to Ferris wheel steel for the headframes.

Jules opened the wardrobe doors, running her hand over the dozens of hanging silk dresses. The clicking of the wood hangers almost masked the far-off ringing bells of the mine. Absent-mindedly, she pulled out a dress and smoothed the skirt.

Rand Buckley knew quite a bit about headframes, didn't he? Like maybe if a timber headframe had been sawed partially through, it would eventually snap under a heavy load. And then maybe someone like AJ Parker might consider changing all his hundreds of headframes over to steel. And then maybe someone who dealt with the steel might greatly benefit financially.

"No!" Jules placed her hand over her mouth. No, no, Rand couldn't be involved. Sure, maybe he was a con, after some quick riches—but a saboteur and a murderer? "No," she repeated, as if trying to convince herself.

An hour later, Jules stood in the shadow of the Metis headframe. Broken and strewn across the ground, the pieces looked like a huge pile of kindling. Unlike a typical day where most miners were underground, on this dreadful morning, groups of men sat huddled together, their caps resting on their knees, talking in low voices, their eyes darting over the broken headframe. All work had stopped, and workers milled about aimlessly, awaiting news about when they might be able to go back to their jobs. Policemen went from group to group, taking reports from all the miners who had witnessed the breaking of the main timber.

Jules watched a huge man in a pressed and starched blue uniform striding alongside Ted. A full head taller and almost 40 pounds heavier, Police Chief Davies was a well-dressed man with eyes of steel and a face hard as granite. He cut an imposing figure as they approached her from the crowd.

"Miss Parker," called out the Police Chief. He tipped his cap as he appraised her. "You look lovely—my missus' favorite color happens to be lavender too." As Ted neared, Jules saw a frown crease his lips and his eyes darken.

"Thank you," Jules said, smiling, remembering that someone else had called her lovely in the lavender dress. She glanced at Ted, who glowered. Oh, but that someone wasn't Ted, was it? Jules swallowed hard, recalling that he'd instructed her against wearing the lavender dress.

After hesitating, Jules cleared her throat, then asked, "And Chief Davies, how is your charming wife?"

"Fine, fine, thank you. I'll tell her you asked about her."

Jules placed her hand upon the police chief's arm. "I'm glad you are here. I need to tell someone about what has been bothering me these past few days."

Ted stepped forward. "Augustina, the police chief is incredibly busy and doesn't really have time for stories right now. Can't this wait?"

"It's okay, Mr. Jackson," said Davies. "After all this time, I've learned to listen to Miss Parker when it comes to Parker Copper Mines. She's the most knowledgeable individual about the mines—rivals even Mr. Parker."

"Speaking of Mr. Parker, I'm sure he needs me over..." Ted gestured in the vague direction of the crowd. "But please don't let Augustina waste all your time."

"Sure enough, Mr. Jackson. Why don't you go on, and I'll stay here and listen to Miss Parker's... story." Davies stood, his hulking body barely moving.

"Fine," replied Ted, curtly. "I'll be expecting your full report by the end of the day." He turned and strode away, kicking up angry dust with each step.

Davies pulled a notebook from his pocket and looked at Jules, his steely eyes inquiring. "Ok, Miss Jules. Tell me everything."

After she'd told the police chief of the noises and the uneasy feeling she'd been feeling over the past couple of weeks, Jules paused. She looked up into Davies' face.

Chief Davies pushed his cap back on his head. "And you say you've had this feeling for a while?"

"Yes, probably since, well, maybe since Celeste and I met Bradley when he came back home from Idaho."

"Didn't Mr. Hayes come in on the train? Was he the only one you and Mrs. Hayes knew?" asked Davies. Jules nodded. "Seems like unusual things have been happening ever since that train come in with that load of out-of-towners."

"Unusual, yes…" agreed Jules. She thought of the first time she had seen Rand, at the train station, debarking from that very train, his hair glinting in the sunlight. But Rand arriving on that train surely had nothing to do with the unusual happenings around Parker Copper, did it? But if he had nothing to do with the sabotage at the Metis, then who did?

Jules looked out over the crowd, growing larger with every hour. The area surrounding the broken Metis took on a circus quality with the curious coming to gawk at the damage wrought. She was troubled that perhaps the very person who had caused this tragedy might very well be out there, in that mass.

She scanned the swelling crowd when a feeling of being watched came over Jules. Her heart started beating quickly in her chest as she caught a glimpse of sun-bleached hair. From a part in the crowd, she spied the very person she'd been thinking of. Rand Buckley was staring at her. He caught her eye and indicated with a jerk of his head and a pointing finger that Jules should meet him near the hoist house.

Jules frowned and looked away. Was he out of his mind? What with how he'd treated her at the racetrack? She most certainly was not going to meet Rand Buckley at the hoist house, or anywhere else for that matter, regardless of how handsome and interesting she found him. Yes, regardless of how *exceedingly* handsome and *incredibly* interesting she found him. Unable to resist, though, she slid another look his way. Damn it all, how could she be so drawn to him?

Rand hadn't moved an inch and instead was staring at her like an eagle at a field mouse. The sun glinted off that blonde hair and cast shadows over his strong features. Jules saw him point again to the side yard. Her head tilted to the side, and she bit at her lip.

"I would advise against it, Miss Jules," said Police Chief Davies, still standing beside her, watching Rand as well.

Jules nodded, surrendering. "As would I, Chief," she said as she stepped away from him and turned toward the hoist house. "But what could possibly happen?"

She came upon him waiting for her in the shadows of the hoist house, his hands tucked deep in his pockets. "Listen," he said under his breath. "I have something I need to tell you. Let's go someplace quieter." Without another word, he marched off. Jules cocked her eyebrow, presuming he expected her to follow him. She felt certain Rand wanted to discuss their last encounter. He probably wanted to ask her forgiveness because, of course, he was embarrassed at his actions. No wonder he wanted to be alone with her where no one else might hear his admission. She tagged behind Rand, around the mine yard, wandering in and out of the crowd until he got to a spot that was far away from the activity.

"All right, now that we are alone," he began as he pushed his hair from his forehead. "I wanted to tell you that..."

"Oh, Mr. Buckley," interrupted Jules. "Apology accepted! I am so glad you are being forthwith about all that at the racetrack." She tucked a lock of hair behind her ear and clasped her hands in front of her. "What with the kiss and all."

Rand just stared at her and said, "I wanted to tell you that..." He raised his eyebrow. "...I think something dodgy is going on here at the

Metis."

"Oh," exclaimed Jules, her face reddening.

"I don't seem to be in good graces with your father, so I thought you could relay the information for me."

"You want me to tell my father something for you?" asked Jules, incredulous. "Like a mere... messenger."

Rand quickly nodded. "I mean, I took a look at that split timber and it seemed as if it'd been cut partway."

Jules' eyes narrowed. "And just when would you have had a chance to get a close look at the main timber?" She stepped close to Rand. "Or are you telling me this because you might have been the one to actually cut it yourself?"

"That's ridiculous. Why would I do that?"

"Perhaps so you can convince my father that you can *help him bring new technology to an old industry*," Jules replied, mimicking what she'd heard Rand tell AJ weeks ago in his office. "And reap a tidy sum for yourself when he swaps out the wood Metis headframe for steel."

"You were eavesdropping?" Rand crossed his arms over his chest. "And now you've brought the police?" he said, disbelief in his voice. Police Chief Davies, with a frown across his face, slowly approached them.

"Oh, don't get all in a huff. Yes, I was eavesdropping—I can nose around my father's office whenever I'd like," answered Jules. "And no, I did not summon the police."

"That's a deplorable trait, being a sneak."

"And what trait do you possess that makes you so special?" Jules asked.

"Me? Well, I am... I am honorable," replied Rand.

Jules thought of how Rand had abruptly grabbed her in a tight embrace and kissed her until her legs went weak. She shook her head, saying, "Honorable my a–"

"About that… kiss…I truly do apologize," Rand interrupted as if reading her mind. A small smile played at his lips. "You have my word, it will not be repeated."

And just as Davies got within earshot, Rand turned and walked away from Jules, calling over his shoulder, "Unless you want it…" She saw his shoulders move as he chuckled and called out louder, "Again."

Again? Did she just hear Rand Buckley correctly—that he assumed she'd wanted him to grab her in the middle of a crowd and be kissed like that? He was making a mockery of her again!

Chief Davies stepped close and held his hands behind him. They looked out over the mine yard, both of them studying the swelling crowd. Still irritated with Rand, Jules watched him sneak through the crowd, separating himself from her and Davies.

Rand positioned himself next to a group of miners standing with their caps crushed in their hands, shifting from foot to foot as they waited for any news. He stood still, his hands in his pockets, his handsome face in shadow. Jules continued to watch him, and when she caught his gaze as he leaned out of the shadow, their eyes locked. She saw him smile, then Rand raised his hand to his mouth and blew her a kiss, above the heads of the crowd in the Metis mine yard. Jules raised her own hand to her chest, feeling a flood of blood creeping up her neck and into her cheeks.

She didn't know how he did it, but Rand Buckley could get under her skin like a Rocky Mountain wood tick. And his bite was just as sharp.

SCREEEECH!

Jules jumped and flinched, looking to her right where the police were pulling up the metal hoist from the mineshaft. The twisted metal scraped against itself, as if loath to be pulled up to the surface. Ted stood next to the mine collar, directing the operation, looking authoritative and forceful. After the mangled hoist had been laid next to the broken timbers, Ted seemed to bark an order to the men, instructing them with hand signals to move onto the hoist house. All of the men took off at a run.

Jules saw Ted cross his arms over his chest and rock back on his heels. Then he looked down at his feet, finding a fist-sized rock sitting at the mouth of the mine collar. Ted slowly kicked the rock into the Metis's shaft. And when the rock fell 1800 long feet down, and struck the bottom of the mine with a sharp thud, he never even flinched.

Ted glanced up to see Jules watching him from across the field, and he smiled, his dimples deep upon his face. Jules' eyebrows screwed up, unsure if a smile from the Vice Director of the company was appropriate at a time like this.

She turned back to the crowd, searching for Rand, but he'd disappeared and was nowhere to be found. Jules sighed. Maybe by way of skulking off, his actions showed that he *was* responsible.

Police Chief Davies tucked his notebook in his pocket. They stood silently next to one another for what seemed like hours. Finally, he said, "Miss Jules, what business do you have with that fine-looking young fellow you were talking with?"

Jules' eyes widened, and she flushed pink. "Why, nothing at all!"

"You sure?"

"Absolutely. Why… why do you ask?" she stammered.

"Well, the way you and that fellow were looking at each other… seems like you're awful familiar."

"I assure you, Chief Davies, the only fellow I'm familiar with is the Vice Director of Parker Copper—and my beau—Ted Jackson," replied Jules, fanning at her face with her hand.

"Uh-huh." Davies nodded. "You see, the reason I ask is because your beau is the one who thinks that that other fellow might have something to do with this whole mess." Jules slid a sideways glance at

Davies.

"Is that right?" asked Jules. A ray of sunlight reflected off the windows of the dry house near the downed headframe, shining across their eyes.

"Yes, ma'am," nodded Davies, shading his eyes with his hand. "Mr. Jackson asked me to have him followed."

Jules studied the police chief. "And do you always do what Ted Jackson asks of you?"

Davies continued staring straight ahead at the mayhem, his hand still at his forehead. Almost inaudibly, he said, "I should think to ask you the same—do you?"

Jules brushed at the skirt of her lavender dress, then just blinked quickly in the bright light.

Part Two

Chapter 19

"Montana Senate Seat Vacant" shouted the headline on the front page of the Butte Standard. Jules blew across her mug, cooling the coffee she'd just poured while her father sat across the dining table, the open newspaper concealing his face.

"AJ, dear, when will you be leaving?" Millicent approached the table holding a bowl of strawberries. "Will you at least stay through dinner tonight? After all, it is your birthday."

"Speaking of…" called out Celeste as she opened the front door of Parker Mansion. In a flurry of diaphanous fabric, she flowed into the dining room. "…many happy birthday wishes, Father." She stepped to AJ and placed a kiss upon his cheek, a ribbon from her blouse dipping a bit into his coffee.

"Good morning, dear," replied AJ without looking up from the newspaper. "You are here early."

Celeste placed a basket of freshly baked muffins in front of her father. "I wanted to bring these to you while they were still warm. Huckleberry, your favorite."

"That is very thoughtful of you, Celeste. Thank you." AJ reached out and selected a muffin.

Millicent poured orange juice into her crystal goblet and asked again,

"Well, AJ, does that mean you will be staying for dinner?"

AJ looked up from reading the paper. "Yes, certainly. I'll leave after the gathering tonight." He shook the pages. "Nothing is going to be decided today anyway."

Jules sipped at her coffee. "Why are you hurrying off to Helena?" she asked her father.

AJ cleared his throat. "Well, now's a perfect opportunity for me to get into the Senate race earlier than I'd expected—what with the death of Jedediah Lynch," he replied.

"Senator Lynch has died?" cried Celeste. "But how? When?" AJ remained silent, reading the newspaper.

"Father, how did Senator Lynch die?" persisted Celeste. "He was such a nice old man. Was it a horribly violent death? Father, how..?"

AJ sighed behind his newspaper. "Moose," he said. "The creature came barreling into his home, crashed through a wall while Jed was sitting, enjoying a cigar."

"MY GOD," gasped Celeste. Her slender hands flew to her mouth.

Jules put down her coffee cup. "Good lord, Celeste. Of course, Senator Lynch didn't die from a moose mauling." She shook her head. "He died of heart failure. It was in the newspapers a couple of days ago—the funeral is tomorrow."

Celeste's eyebrows drew together, a pout forming on her lips. "Father! Why would you play a trick on me like that? I truly believed old Senator Lynch had been attacked by a wild moose."

"Celeste, dear," replied AJ kindly. "I can't always be the source of your information. Perhaps you should try reading the newspaper sometime. Isn't that right, Jules?" AJ's youngest daughter shrugged and reached for a section of the newspaper.

Millicent dabbed at her mouth with a linen napkin and looked at the paper that Jules held. "You're reading the politics section of the Standard now, Jules?"

Jules nodded. "I'm finding that it's an exciting time in Montana politics right now. I've been keeping my eye out for any news of Jeannette and her Equal Franchise Society," she said.

"Jeannette Rankin should do fine in Helena. She has the respect of many—even some men. She may need to learn political etiquette, but she has a keen intelligence," said AJ. Jules blinked in surprise. She'd never heard her father give such easy approval to anyone, much less a woman pursuing politics. "I'll be sitting in on a speech she is making early tomorrow morning."

"Ah, so that is why you need to depart so soon tonight," guessed Millicent.

AJ grunted. "That, and the fact that I certainly need to be campaigning with the Legislators even well before Governor Toole calls the special election to replace Lynch."

Jules frowned. "But what are you going to do about Parker Copper and the Metis? Are the police even close to catching the person who sabotaged the headframe?"

"I think finding the culprit is going to be easier said than done. The police have no witnesses. And without a witness, the mishap may as well not have even happened." AJ laid the newspaper on the table. "I don't need to be here in Butte while they are still carrying on the investigation. My time is better spent in Helena."

"But how long will you be away?"

"I'm not sure, Jules. It depends on when the special election takes place—it's June now, so perhaps throughout the summer. And if I am successful and the Legislature elects me, it will probably be even longer. If I want to establish my presence in Montana politics, it is essential that I be in the Capitol right now." AJ looked at Jules quizzically for a moment, then lifted the newspaper up before his face, essentially ending the conversation.

Jules took another sip. Her father was headed to Helena for an indeterminate time. So what did that mean for her father's company? Who would be running Parker Copper? Jules suddenly sat up, her hand jerked, and coffee sloshed over the cup rim.

This could be her chance to prove to AJ that she could run the company. He was already reconsidering allowing her back into the fold. He'd just said that she had matured in the time she'd been away from the mines.

Jules thought she could count on Ted to vouch for her. Hadn't he said that she seemed to know more about the company than anyone else he'd encountered? Plus, Chief Davies said that she knew more about Parker Copper than anyone besides AJ himself.

It was all true. And Jules was more than ready to get back in and run Parker Copper Mining Company.

She quickly pushed away from the breakfast table, her chair screeching on the wood floor. Would it really work? Jules needed some counsel, and quickly.

"Mother, I'm going out," she called.

"Jules, where are you going?" answered her mother. "Please don't be gone long. We're having your father's birthday dinner early."

Jules rushed out the kitchen door and into the brilliant morning sun. After rounding the side yard, she paused in front of the mansion and looked out at the Parker Copper headframes with longing. Then she took off down the hill at a brisk walk, her hair tangling behind her. Within ten minutes, she arrived at the Chang Noodle Parlor, the doors not yet open for business. Jules peered through the polished glass window and saw her friend setting the many tables for lunch.

"Balinda," Jules rapped on the glass. "Can you talk?" Balinda looked up from setting a small porcelain vase with daisies on the table. A smile brightened her face, and she nodded while pointing toward the back.

Jules went around to the back alley and entered the dim hallway, a delicious smell already coming from the vast kitchen.

"Hi there," said Balinda, entering from the dining room. "What are you doing here this early? I would have thought you'd be having brunch with…"

Jules hurriedly grabbed Balinda's hand. "He's leaving for the summer. This is my chance!" Jules' eyes burned with intensity.

Balinda took a step back, her eyebrow raised. "Who is leaving? What are you talking about?" she asked.

"My father. He's going to Helena to try for that open Senate seat," Jules said. "And with him in Helena, who is going to be running Parker Copper Mining?"

Balinda crossed her arms over her chest. "I don't know Jules. Who?"

Jules tapped her breastbone three times with her finger. "Me."

"And your father said that was okay."

"Well, no, but it's the perfect opportunity for me to prove that I can. Don't you agree?" Jules said. "Listen, Balinda, ever since I was a little girl, all I've ever wanted is to run Parker Copper. You know that. I want to make it the most successful mining company in the United States—maybe even the world."

"I do know that. And if there were anyone in the world who could run Parker Copper, it'd be you."

Jules smiled affectionately at her friend. "Father leaves for Helena today. I need to tell him this evening, before he boards the train. By this time tomorrow, I'll be sitting at the main office! The first thing I want to do is go over the production reports for all the mines. I just have a feeling that the Venturer could be outputting even more than it is currently." Jules started pacing. "Maybe I should even get The Only open again."

"Jules, Jules. Don't get ahead of yourself," replied Balinda. "You don't yet know if your father will agree."

"I'll bring it up at our family dinner this evening," said Jules. "What could possibly go wrong?"

That afternoon, they'd all gathered at Parker Mansion for AJ's birthday. June in Montana could be either warm and sunny or wrought with frost and hailstorms. And on this Sunday, the day wasn't any different than any other in June. Although it had dawned lovely with the scent of honey-sweet lilac in the air, dark clouds drifted far off, in the distance.

Jules' thoughts raced as she carried an armload of pastel-colored hyacinths across the porch. Her sister and mother stood at the wrought iron garden table, arranging elaborate floral sprays. Jules stood near them, staring off into space, lost in her thoughts.

"Hello?" Celeste rubbed a dandelion under Jules' chin, smearing yellow across her smooth skin. "What in heaven have you been thinking about all day? I swear you haven't said two words." Deep, male laughter came from the shade tree in the vast yard. Celeste glanced over to where AJ and Bradley sat in deep wicker chairs, sipping whiskey and puffing on cigars, while Ted stood towering in front of them. Jules blinked her eyes and followed her sister's gaze.

Dressed in a summer suit of fine linen, a straw boater tipped back on his head, Ted couldn't have looked more handsome. His suit fit him well, smoothed over his long legs and broad shoulders. Ted seemed easy and confident—something that was not easy to pull off around AJ.

"Ah, yes," replied Celeste. "That's where your thoughts have been—the charming Ted Jackson." She smiled. "He certainly would make an excellent husband."

"An excellent husband?" repeated Jules disdainfully. "Celeste, that may be the only thing you think of, but it hadn't even crossed my mind. Don't you think that I may be thinking of more, say, industrious ideas?"

"Oh no," said Celeste, under her breath. "I hope someone changed the lock on the gun safe."

But with a June breeze wafting the sound of the shift-change whistle blow at precisely one o'clock, Jules really was thinking industrious ideas. The Metis had been out of commission for three weeks and had no sign of coming back on line. The investigation into the incident had been ongoing, but the police were no further along in finding a culprit than they had been the first day. Jules had heard some talk around Butte and finger-pointing at a certain "newcomer," but there was nothing concrete.

Regardless of any evidence—slim as it may be—directed at Rand Buckley, Jules was still reluctant to place blame on him. If anything, she just wanted to forget about him and pretend she hadn't even met him in the first place. Ha. Met? That seemed a bit tame considering all that'd transpired the only couple of times they'd been near one another. Jules made a shallow snorting noise.

Jules caught her mother staring at her, a wistful look upon her face. "Jules, dear, would marriage be so very awful for you?" she asked. Millicent laid a handful of beautiful white roses on the table. "You know that your father and I do want you to be happy, but might you envision yourself eventually wed?"

Jules' shoulders slumped. She thought that she might have been so selfish in wanting to do great things for herself that she'd completely disregarded what her parents wanted from her. "Oh, Mother," she said softly. "Of course, I can see myself married. I so appreciate how happy you have been with Father, and I do want someone like that for myself."

"Do you think you might have met that certain someone?" asked Millicent, inclining her head toward the shade tree. Jules cast her eyes down.

"Perhaps," she replied, plucking at a faded rose petal.

"That makes me very happy, Jules." Millicent picked up the roses and began to place the stems inside an already crowded vase. Her face seemed to have lightened.

"Then I'm glad, Mother," replied Jules, not mentioning that when she'd answered her mother's question, it wasn't Ted Jackson's face that had fleetingly crossed her mind. Instead, it was a face with intense hazel eyes, surrounded by sun-bleached hair that looked like placer gold.

"Won't you men please come join us on the porch?" Millicent called out as she stepped back to study her floral arrangement. She nodded with satisfaction, then looked toward the shade tree as the men stood, about to head for the porch. The wind blew up, a portion of their conversation floating up, and Jules heard Ted say, "You won't be sorry, sir," as he stopped and shook hands with AJ.

Jules rubbed her arms, as if she were chilled, then tilted her head as she placed a lone prairie coneflower into her mother's arrangement, the native flower looking out of place next to all the perfect heirloom blossoms.

The dining room table was formally set with bone china and white linens. Each place setting was laden with twelve pieces of silver and three plates. The occasional faint sunbeam shone through the crystal goblets, playing rainbow prisms across the tablecloth. Delicate lace curtains waved at an open window, a heavy breeze blowing steadily through.

Her father was already seated at the head of the table, her mother opposite him at the other end. Jules stood next to her seat, to the left of her father.

Ted approached Jules, kissed her cheek, then pulled her chair out. He withdrew a handkerchief from his pocket and rubbed at her chin, the cotton material coming away with a smear of yellow. "Augustina, darling, you look very nice today," he said. Jules glanced quickly at him. *Darling.* He'd not yet called her that, especially not in the presence of her parents. Jules thought she saw her mother hide a smile behind her hand.

"Tell me, besides the art of flower arranging, what else did you do with your morning?" he asked as Jules sat.

"Oh, I read some pages of the Oliver Wendell Holmes poetry book you gave me this week," she replied. "What a thoughtful gift."

Ted smiled, his dark brown eyes crinkling. "I thought it might amuse you and help to pass your time. Have you enjoyed works by other poets?"

"Oh yes. I am fond of poetry. Most recently, I've taken pleasure in reading a few poems by a woman with the name of Emily Dickinson. Do you know of her?" replied Jules.

Ted nodded his head. "But I have better things to read than a handful of writings from a lunatic shut-in." He laughed. "Just goes to show you why some women shouldn't try to do the same as men. Imagine her competing with Browning or Longfellow. No wonder she's a bit mad."

"Well, I don't know if she was truly mad…" began Jules.

"And what of the upcoming weeks? What are your plans while I'm busy at the Parker Copper office?" interrupted Ted. "Perhaps you'll have another run-in with a wayward flowering weed?" He reached forward and caressed Jules' chin with his thumb. A gust of wind blew through the window, fluttering Jules' hair across her forehead.

She smiled and sighed. "Well, tomorrow I'll be meeting the girls for tea. Genevieve and Josephine leave soon to spend the summer in Paris, so I want to wish them *bon voyage.*"

"No horseback or bicycle riding?"

"No."

"Good. I prefer it when your day is filled with more delicate activities.

Especially when spent with the other society girls. I've always thought you should be friends with the Alder twins and Mrs. Fleming."

"Ted, I *am* friends with them. That's how *you* met them."

"You know what I mean, darling." He kissed her wrist. Again with the darling? Jules studied Ted through her eyelashes.

"Well, then, you'll be pleased to know that when Genevieve and Josephine are in France, Martha, Anna, Charlotte, and I will be spending time with the disadvantaged in the Cabbage Patch."

Ted looked aghast. "The Cabbage Patch, really?" he asked. "That slum area has some very rough people." Ted referred to the drunks, gamblers, and ladies of the evening living in the neighborhood. "I've even heard of newly arrived migrants putting down there."

"Well, drunks and immigrants are humans too," replied Jules. "And they don't have any of the basics that we now benefit from."

"Ah. Things like telephones."

"No, not just telephones. I'm saying no running water or electricity. Or working sewers."

"Good god."

"Most of the people in the Cabbage Patch are just down on their luck. That is precisely why we are going there to help." Jules gazed out the dining room window, watching dark storm clouds shift in.

Ted leisurely folded his handkerchief and then tucked it into his pocket. "Do be careful, Augustina. It sounds like the characters in the Cabbage Patch are quite unsavory."

Jules smiled. "I will be careful. Besides, I'm sure that not *all* the characters are unsavory."

"And it will just be the four of you?" asked Ted.

Jules nodded. "But come to think of it, I'll also invite Balinda to join us."

"The restaurant owner's daughter?" asked Ted, the shock apparent on his face. "The Chinese girl?"

"Yes, that's right. I haven't been able to spend much time with her lately. I thought…"

"Perhaps that is not such a good idea," Ted said, placing his hand on her knee. "I'm sure she's very, well, nice. But don't you think you should concentrate on relationships with young women who are your peers?"

Jules stared at Ted. "She's my best friend." She placed her hand upon Ted's. "You aren't suggesting that I stop being friends with her, are you?" Her head dipped, and she squinted at him. A flash of lightning lit up outside the mansion, and a clap of thunder rumbled immediately after.

"Well, yes." Ted removed his hand from under hers and spoke in a low voice. "Augustina, I'm expecting you to take into account your status in society, and what it means. You must choose all your acts with discretion. "

From the head of the table, AJ tapped his crystal goblet with his silver butter knife. "My dears, thank you for the wonderful meal and celebrations for the day of my birth."

Upset, Jules leaned in close to Ted and said, "Please, we must continue this discussion later."

"Certainly, darling." Ted kissed Jules's forehead. "We'll have all the time in the world to discuss it." He turned toward AJ.

"Please join me in raising your glasses," continued AJ as everyone settled. "I'd like to propose a toast."

Jules sat straight and gathered her thoughts. She'd waited all day to make her own proposal—the one she'd discussed with Balinda, who was her closest friend, regardless of what Ted said. After her father's toast, Jules would make her own statement clear and simple—that she planned on taking over Parker Copper Mining Company, running it in her father's stead, while he was away, focused on his political future. Jules raised her glass and took a deep, steadying breath.

AJ lifted his crystal goblet into the air. "I am the luckiest man alive to be surrounded by my loved ones. I look upon my past birthdays with contentment, and I look forward to my future birthdays with excitement. And to all of you, I give you my blessings and my love."

Everyone around the table clapped heartily as AJ continued. "For the good of my family, I am embarking on a new journey." He seemed to grow in height as he loudly declared, "I am AJ Parker—and I aim to be the next Montana state senator!"

"Hear, hear!" they called out, touching the rims of the glasses to one another, the clink of the crystal drowning out the heavy raindrops pelting the dining room windows.

And just like that, as her family relaxed back into their dining room chairs, the moment was upon her. Jules rose to her feet, her heart pounding in anticipation.

"I'd like to propose something as well," she said as she felt Ted stand up next to her. She looked to her left and saw him raise his goblet high.

"Mr. Parker, everyone, if you would allow me a moment to propose a toast," he interrupted, his face aglow. He put his arm around Jules's shoulders, hugging her tight but slightly behind him.

"Ted, I was about to say something…" Jules tried to go on.

"Augustina, me first. This is very important," Ted insisted. He faced Jules and tipped his glass to her, his deep brown eyes searching hers. "Actually, I'd like to make a proposal… of marriage. My darling Augustina, would you do me the great honor of being my wife?"

Her jaw dropped, all the while the rest of the table erupted in jubilation. Jules saw her mother, clapping wildly, her eyes filled with joyous tears. Next to Millicent, Celeste smiled so wide it seemed to encompass her face. And Bradley had already reached clear across the entire table and was pumping Ted's hand in congratulations.

But it was AJ who spoke above the din. "What do you say, my dear

Jules? Ted has already asked your mother and me, and we've given you both our blessing to wed." He raised his goblet and looked at Ted. "I couldn't have found a finer young man to join the Parker dynasty and marry my youngest daughter."

Jules stilled her breathing, and her eyes darted around the table. Marry Ted? A momentary thought of Rand Buckley drifted into Jules' head—of being held and kissed by him. But Rand was a con of the worst kind, wasn't he? Why would she even consider being with that cad? Why was she even still thinking of him? AJ was right. There couldn't be a finer young man than Ted Jackson. And he wanted to marry her and be a part of her family.

"But, I wanted to say something first," said Jules. "About Parker Copper…"

"Jules, what could be more important than being asked for your hand in marriage?" said Celeste from across the table.

Ted looked at Jules with concern. "Yes, what could be more important, darling?" She allowed Ted to draw her into an embrace as he said softly, "Augustina, please, will you marry me?"

Jules bit her lip and drew in a deep breath. "I..I'm.." Jules stammered. A crack of thunder exploded over Parker Mansion.

"Of course you will," said Ted, and he leaned over and kissed her, sealing the deal. Everyone at the table stood, applauding once more, rejoicing at the engagement.

"Ah, and one more thing," said AJ loudly, interrupting the celebration. "Jules, not only are you now engaged to a fine young man, but also to the man who will be running the company." AJ lifted his wine goblet high. "Everyone, raise your glasses to a newly promoted Theodore Jackson, acting President of Parker Copper Mining Company."

With that one sentence, Jules' entire world seemed to crash around her. Her father had promoted Ted! And he had given Ted *her* job—the only job she'd ever wanted in her life. All her years of longing and all her aspirations, gone.

Her job.

Jules closed her eyes and her chin dropped to her chest, completely defeated. She would not be running Parker Copper. Just the opposite of what she'd always claimed—Jules wasn't the heir apparent at all.

She was just the Copper King's daughter.

Chapter 20

The koi broke the surface of the pond, seeking the low-flying insects skimming the water's surface. Their mouths opened and closed quickly, as if they were trying to talk. Jules leaned over the bridge and propped her forearms against the railing. The last time she'd been here in the tiny Chinese garden behind the joss house, it had been a beautifully clear day, and the sun's reflection had glossed the smooth lake. But today, the sky was dark, covered over by storm clouds.

"Engaged," said Balinda, breaking the silence.

"Yes, quite," replied Jules. After getting over the initial shock of everything that had transpired the evening before, Jules hadn't slept a wink, trying to sort it all out. Jules figured that in some ways, by being married to Ted, she would be closer to running the company than she'd been before. Hadn't Ted said that Jules was invaluable and that she seemed to know more about the company than anyone else he'd encountered? Maybe she would eventually have a say—Ted trusted Jules, and AJ trusted Ted. And while not exactly ecstatic about getting married, Jules wasn't miserable either. Ted was handsome, intelligent, and honest. Jules was lucky to have someone like him.

She walked over the bridge and under the canopy of a plum tree.

Sheltered beneath was a flat stone buried in the gravel path. The mosaic's inlay of plum blossoms on cracked ice symbolized endurance and hope.

Balinda followed, and when she stood next to Jules, she asked, "Jules, did you hear what I said?"

"I apologize," replied Jules. "I must have been daydreaming. What was it?"

"You don't sound very convincing," said Balinda. "Are you happy to be getting married?"

"It's not that I'm unhappy—it's just that I was kind of thrust into it," replied Jules. "And I'm still getting used to the idea."

"Jules, that's ridiculous. You could have done something, said something to your mother and father."

Jules turned quickly to her friend. "But don't you understand? I couldn't have. They're all done listening to me, to anything I have to say." She threw her hands up. "The only person who even listens to me anymore is Ted."

Balinda stepped close to a wall made of intricately carved gingko wood. Embedded in the panel was a fist-sized gem, tiger's eye, which was known for its attributes of protection and honesty.

"I am suspicious of him." Balinda polished the golden smooth stone with her sleeve, then continued guardedly. "That man isn't the same inside as he is outside. He is hiding his true personality. "

"Are we talking about Ted?" asked Jules, defensively. "You are saying that after just meeting him once at the Noodle Parlor?"

Balinda nodded. "Once is enough to see through his mask."

"You've been reading too many fortune cookies," Jules retorted, staring at her friend. "Or you're starting to believe that nonsense your family says about your ability to read people."

"It is not nonsense," bristled Balinda. She leaned close into Jules. "How dare you say that." A yellow and red koi jumped out of the pond, then fell back into the water with a slap.

"Oh, I see now. You're jealous. You're jealous now that I'm to be married and you will be left by yourself, single."

"That is so far from the truth."

"The truth?" said Jules, her voice unkind. "The truth is that Ted wants me to make my social circle smaller anyway." She crossed her arms over her chest. "He thinks I should keep company with my peers."

"What does that mean, Jules?" said Balinda, offended. "Are you implying that Ted Jackson thinks that I'm not good enough to be with you and your friends? Why, he's a scheming…"

"No, it means that it appears we may be growing apart," interrupted Jules. "And if you don't like my fiancé, perhaps you should–"

"Perhaps," Balinda cut in, heatedly. "You and I should not be friends any longer." She turned and stormed away from Jules, her footsteps crunching along the gravel path circling the koi pond. She angrily kicked at a rock that splashed into the water.

All the fish frightened and darted away, their streaks of vivid orange wriggling below the water. All except one last koi, which remained at the pond's edge, its eyes unblinking and lips open and closing, as if gasping for air.

Chapter 21

As they motored along Mercury Street, Jules gazed out at the Boulder Mountains in the distance while the other young women in the auto chattered about the recent inclement weather. At least this conversation was more interesting than their previous one, which centered on letters Jules had already received from Josephine and Genevieve. The twins had written from Paris saying that they would be cutting their travels short and coming back to Butte early, in time to attend Jules' eighteenth birthday party. Oh, and by the by, did Jules' handsome fiancé Ted have any suitable single friends?

Along with the missus Martha Fleming, the misses Anna MacDonald, Charlotte McGuire, and she were on their way to distribute food and blankets to the needy in Butte's Cabbage Patch area. The rich young ladies had gone through their closets and pantries and gathered what they thought might make up sufficient provisions packages for those who had none. Their laps were piled high with bundles of spun-wool blankets.

What with the past few weeks' heavy rains, their own gardens overflowed with a bounty of fresh vegetables. Baskets filled with baby carrots, onions, and green tomatoes sat on the floor of the auto with jars of strawberry jam and garlicky pickled cucumbers resting beside them. There was even a smoked ham tucked between Anna and Charlotte in the backseat.

Against Ted's insistence that she keep clear of the slum neighborhood, Jules suggested the visit to her school-friends. They'd lit up and clapped their hands, proclaiming it community service, something they could boast about during the summer cocktail parties. Jules had not invited Balinda, which contributed to Jules' current feelings of wretchedness. She hadn't seen Balinda since their argument weeks ago. Jules felt kind of like she had after Gus died—a bit empty inside.

Jules had been feeling a bit out of sorts, antsy really, and hoped that their outing today would quell that feeling. Yet she found herself tapping her foot, silently urging Martha to drive just a bit faster. Good god, did everyone these days drive as if a full ore car were tied behind the rear axle?

The neighborhood was filled with lean-tos and shanties butted up against one another, in a precarious balancing act. Rusted tin roofs and windows missing glass panes completed the shacks, lending to the overall sense of desolation.

As they passed a shack, the door flew open and a man wearing a filthy undershirt and long johns stepped through, coughing violently. He hacked up a ball of phlegm and spat into the street, then remained at the doorway, scratching his crotch.

The raucous sound of children kicking a tin can down the street woke Jules from her reverie. She followed the sounds to see three boys, barefoot and filthy, one whose hair stuck up as if it had never been washed before. Two little girls followed, their skinny legs and knobby knees bare beneath their thin cotton dresses. A scraggily black and white mottled cattle dog nipped behind them, barking non-stop.

"What is that racket?" asked Charlotte. She leaned out of the auto. "Excuse me! You, ragamuffins! Must you carry on so?" She placed her manicured hands over her ears.

Anna nodded. "I've never been someplace that was as noisy as this. Why, I can barely hear myself think!" She pulled her hat over her delicate ears.

The four young women wore elaborate bonnets, tied securely with bright silk scarves—less to shield them from the sun, Jules suspected, than to muffle the noise. But as she tipped her face to the sky, Jules noticed heavy, dark clouds roiling in from the west, over the mountains. Perhaps the storm would turn and pass by, as the weather so often did in Montana, but still, Jules eyed the clouds with concern. A collection of crows cackled nearby, which seemed ominous, but Jules knew that the birds would be eerily quiet should the storm be very near. That was the thing about birds—they often told you things, if you just listened. Jules relaxed into the car seat.

Mercury Street narrowed and turned into a grimy dirt road. From the many shanties came the smell of boiling cabbage, an inexpensive and frequent ingredient in the meals prepared in the area, hence the designation given to the neighborhood. The shacks lining the road, made from whatever materials that might have been scavenged or even stolen from the mines, housed the characters that Ted disdainfully referred to as "unsavory."

"Oh my!" squealed Anna, wrinkling her nose. Another foul odor wafted into the open auto from the exposed sewer ditch running along Arizona Street. She yanked open her handbag, snatched up a perfumed linen handkerchief, and placed it over her mouth and nose. Jules peered over the side of the auto, her eyes following the gully up Cabbage Gulch, where the Butte Brewery was located, two blocks higher, then back down to Mercury Street. The sewer water pooled at the bottom, fetid and rank.

"Well, girls," said Jules. "We're here. Welcome to the Cabbage Patch." Charlotte looked around them, a look of repugnance on her face.

"Does one *choose* to live here?" she asked, her hand covering her mouth. "How utterly unfortunate."

Martha slowed her auto, and they idled in the middle of the intersection. "And where do you suppose these unfortunates would be located?" she asked, looking around. "Shall we just unload the food and blankets here, at the side of the street?"

"Martha, we're not tossing table scraps out in the pig pen," replied Jules. "We should find a proper place to deliver our supplies." She stood up in the front seat to get a better look. "There! At the end of Curtis Street, I see a steeple. The pastor will surely help us out." A large shadow crossed the front of the small church, enveloping the tall bell tower in darkness. Jules looked up again to see clouds moving in rapidly.

"Fine idea, Jules," said Martha as she pulled the auto forward. Jules sat down and leaned slightly toward the other girls in the car.

The two girls in the back had turned uncharacteristically quiet when Jules noticed Anna's hand clenched tightly onto the car door handle, her knuckles white. Charlotte stared straight ahead, blinking quickly.

Jules looked just to their right, along Mercury Street, at a 2-storey brick building. Dotting across the front of the building were the most doors and windows on any one building that she'd ever seen. Just a few feet apart, the dozen doorways seemed to open to small, tight rooms. Curiously, an obviously inebriated miner teetered, speaking loudly to a glass window. That's when Jules saw what troubled her friends.

An older woman wearing only a corset, her hair piled atop her head, better to see her red painted lips and cheeks, perched upon a tufted stool inside the window, her arms crossed, looking bored. She ignored the miner at the window until he reached into his pocket and withdrew some silver coins and laid them out flat in his palm. Still looking bored, she nodded, held up one finger, and inserted it into her rouged mouth, sucking. Then she withdrew the finger, crooked it three times, and pointed to the door. The miner scampered to the door and disappeared inside. Charlotte gasped.

"That was an interesting business transaction, wasn't it, girls?" Jules asked, chuckling. "Martha, let's go right here on Ohio and take a quick tour through the neighborhood."

"Really, Jules. Must we?" whispered Charlotte, her hand at her throat.

"We need to find out who our consumers are, you know, for the next time when we bring donations for the needy, don't we?" replied Jules.

She thought she saw Martha hide a smile as she directed the car down Ohio Street. Lined with similar shacks, all sorts of women stood in the doorways, in various states of dress, sweet-talking and calling to the men ambling past.

"Why, look at all those men," said Anna, her voice strained. "And in the middle of the afternoon, no less."

"Yes, shocking, isn't it? Imagine a man wanting a bit of solace when it's still light out," Martha laughed. "Don't forget that with the mines running 24 hours a day, some of these men have just gotten off work."

Anna looked woozy. "Well, one would think the men would want something a bit more pleasing. Maybe like satin sheets on a large, soft feather bed."

Martha snorted. "The men can still get pleased for 15 minutes and a few silver coins." Jules slid a glance at Martha, who was obviously enjoying the other's discomfort. Jules thought that perhaps she might have underestimated Martha's pluck.

"But, surely the women can't work 24 hours," replied Anna.

"Why, they're on the same shifts as the miners. Matching the shifts keeps the rooms full every possible minute," Jules added. "I read in the Standard that Butte has upwards of 1,000 prostitutes. No chance for beds to even cool down."

"Jules!" exclaimed Anna, her face glowing pink. "If your beau Ted heard you at this moment, he would be quite mortified."

Jules faced forward. "Yes, quite," she replied with a sigh.

Martha cruised the auto past a beautiful 3-storey red brick Victorian building. An elaborate cornice wrapped the entire top floor, crowning the building with what seemed like a tiara. Red rose vines climbed the face, twisting around the white wood window frames. Rich crimson-colored drapery hung in the windows and at the glass pane of the heavy, dark oak front door.

Spying the red light glowing dim from the overhead transom, Anna inhaled sharply. "Could that be the…" she whispered.

"Yes," Jules said, "it most certainly is." Gawking, Martha slowed their auto to a crawl, her head turned toward the quiet building known to be one of the most successful brothels in the United States.

But just then, the door of the Venus House opened and a striking young woman stepped out onto the veranda. Tall and slender with thick auburn tresses the color of fire trailing over her shoulders, and with smooth, milky-white skin, she looked like a Celtic goddess.

"My heavens," exclaimed Martha. "That's none other than Ruby Paradise. I've heard tell that she is the most highly paid prostitute." Jules quickly craned her head around to get a glimpse of her. As Ruby stepped over the threshold, she held open the door for someone trailing behind her.

A heavy-set man in miner's garb walked onto the veranda, his eyes quickly shifting back and forth. He looked up into the sky and shook his head, looking troubled. Jules didn't recognize him from Parker Copper Mining and supposed he worked for Hailey. Just as she was turning away, another man came through the door with his mouth set in a tense line.

Jules gasped. It was Rand Buckley.

He abruptly turned his back to the miner, then passed closely to

Ruby, took hold of her elbow, leaned in, and kissed her cheek. Jules' own cheeks burned, and she ducked her head down, acting as if the bundle of blankets on her lap had slid off.

"Please, Martha," she pleaded, looking across to the driver's seat. "Let's be on our way." Martha raised one eyebrow, but put the car in gear and pulled forward quickly.

"Jules," asked Martha out of the side of her mouth. "You're acting odd, almost like you'd seen a ghost. Did you know those men?"

"No, no. Yes…" Jules shook her head vigorously. "I mean no." She turned in her seat to see Charlotte and Anna's heads close together as they whispered to each other and pointed at the brothel. Jules sighed.

Martha removed one hand from the steering wheel and placed it on Jules's knee. She whispered, "I don't know what is going on, but I can assure you that I won't say anything to anyone." Jules silently mouthed *thank you*.

"But how you chose between two exceptionally handsome men—that blonde one and Ted Jackson—is beyond me," continued Martha. Jules dropped her head against the back of the car seat, as if it had suddenly become too heavy. Beside them, a raven's shrill laughter filled the air.

"Now, let's see about getting these goods delivered," called out Martha to Anna and Charlotte, who were still looking stunned in the back seat. She gunned the engine. "Ladies, we're going to church."

Chapter 22

Jules, her head still resting on the back of her seat, remained quiet as Martha drove to the small church. She still couldn't believe her eyes, seeing Rand with Ruby Paradise. Although she'd heard her father and Ted talking about it, somehow she hadn't really thought it true. But sure enough, she'd witnessed it now—Rand was involved with the highly paid prostitute. But why should it even bother her? She had decided long ago that Rand was a scoundrel and that she was better off forgetting him. Why, she hadn't even thought of him since, well, since the evening she got engaged to Ted. And besides, she wasn't even attracted to Rand Buckley any longer.

Jules finally opened her eyes and saw that in the short time since arriving in the Cabbage Patch, the weather had turned. The sky had darkened, the thick clouds heavy with rain. The air was charged, crackling with impending lightning.

Martha pulled the car to the side of the street and was studying the sky as well. "That doesn't look good," she said. "I think we should be getting back home." Just as Jules was about to answer, the first fat raindrops fell from the sky.

"Oh no," cried Charlotte. "Jules, Martha, let's get going." Anna tied her bonnet tighter around her chin.

Martha turned to the girls behind her. "Fortitude, ladies! A little rain won't kill us. It's been like this for weeks—you know what a wet summer we've been having."

"But this looks different. Could we please get going before it really starts coming down?" asked Anna. The black clouds blocked the sun, turning day into evening.

"But we're so close to the church," said Jules, pointing a half block away. The wind whipped at her linen duster. "We might as well just go and drop off the bundles."

"All right," reluctantly agreed Anna. "But let's do hurry." Martha curtly nodded, and they drove swiftly to the church as the storm swept in.

The wind gusted through the tight streets and alleys, occasionally pushing the auto a bit off course. Martha held tight to the steering wheel, her knuckles stretched white with effort. Anna and Charlotte ducked deep into the collars of their traveling coats, their hands gripping at their necks.

Once at the church steps, Jules craned her head back, looking at the top of the tall bell tower, 40 feet above. Even higher, the spire rose into the dark sky as black clouds raced past. Jules heard the wind whistling through the open arches, the first hard raindrops pinging against the cast metal bell.

"Come on, girls. Let's place everything here on the steps," Jules called out. She turned to retrieve her bundle and saw movement from the corner of her eye. A flash of sun-bleached hair racing behind the church caused her to freeze, holding the blankets in her arms. Was that who she thought it was, running rapidly behind them? And if it were Rand, what possibly could he be doing here? And why was he running so? Jules' eyebrows knitted together. Well, she was staying to find out.

"Jules, come on!" shouted Anna above the wind. The three of them had deposited their bundles on the church steps and were already in the auto, ready to leave. The wind grabbed at their bonnets, almost tearing them from their heads.

"You all go on," Jules replied loudly. "I'm going to bring these inside so they don't get ruined in the rain. Go on—I'll stay here until the storm passes."

"But Jules, you can't," yelled Charlotte, her eyes round.

"Yes, I can. You all get going." Jules waved them on. "Martha, send a car for me when the weather clears. Go on!" Martha reluctantly nodded but quickly pulled away from the church and gathered speed as she tried to outrace the storm.

Jules turned toward the church and ran to the front door. She yanked it open and threw down the blankets in her arms. Without pausing, she ran back to the steps and with a thunder crack that seemed to open the heavens, rain began pouring down just seconds after Jules had pulled the last bundle inside the foyer.

She stood in the doorway watching the torrential downpour hitting the dirt road. The wet spring in Butte had lasted long, with heavy rainfall continuing into early summer. So with the ground already full from previous rains, the soil couldn't possibly take any more and rapidly turned the streets into muddy creeks. Within minutes, the tiny brook running alongside the church had turned into a raging river.

Jules turned away from the doorway. "Hello?" she yelled into the dark church. "Is anyone here? Is everyone quite all right?" A pair of turtle doves cooed from a perch inside the portico. "Hello?"

Jules stepped into the foyer, her wet shoes squishing with each step. Not a person seemed to be around, the silence inside almost louder than the storm raging outside. Without lights or even a lit candle, the interior was like an abandoned copper mine, dark and chilling. It was too eerie. Jules took a tentative step back, her hand searching the closed front doors behind her for the feeling of wood.

Then, from the dark hallway to her right, she heard a door slam. Jules took another step back, her hand reaching for the door handle, when she heard footsteps running for the altar. A huge thunderclap crashed from overhead, and a flash of lightning lit up the room just as a young man with sun-bleached hair sprinted across, toward the door to the bell tower.

Cold air blasted into the church as the tower door opened. Jules heard the wind screaming down the tower staircase, just before the heavy door was pulled shut with a slam.

Jules was certain it was Rand Buckley running past. What in blazes was the scoundrel up to? She hurried to the tower door and threw it open. Without thinking, she hauled up her skirt and raced after him.

As Jules neared the top, the wind blew so fiercely into the stairwell that she had to pull herself up with the ancient wrought-iron handrail. Her hat had blown off about 30 steps earlier, and her long hair whipped out around her. She stepped out onto the tower portico and was immediately drenched, her hair plastered against her cheeks and neck. Rand stood at the tower's low stone wall, intensely gazing out past the city.

"You! What do you think you're doing here?" shouted Jules over the wind.

Rand turned around with a look of shock. "Me? What in the hell do you think you're doing here?" His drenched clothes clung to his lean body.

"I saw you running up these steps and knew you were up to no good."

"Me? I'm up to no good?"

"Stop repeating me and answer me properly!" yelled Jules. "What are you doing here?"

Rand strode to her and grabbed her arm tightly. "Listen to me. This storm—it's dangerous. It's going to kill people."

"What are you talking about? It's just another storm." A thunderclap boomed above them.

"It's too much. The rain is coming down too hard, too fast," said Rand, his eyes wild.

"You're nuts! Rain doesn't kill people," Jules said, her face incredulous, the rain dripping from her nose.

"It does if a defective dam can't keep it back from flooding." Rand pulled Jules roughly to the wall of the tower. They braced against the strong wind. "Look! From up here, you can see the Hailey Mines dam—what is it, a couple of miles or so away?"

Jules put her hand to her forehead, shading the rain pelting her face. "I see it," she replied.

"Well, when that dam was put up by Hailey for his copper smelter, it was poorly built. He didn't use enough steel to hold back the amount of water that's building up behind it." Jules could see the water almost lapping at the top of the dam. Rand frowned. "That's holding back about 30,000 cubic feet of moving water."

"How do you know?" yelled Jules, turning to face Rand. "How do you know that the dam is faulty?"

"One of Hailey's engineers told me in confidence. He said he felt obliged to tell someone, but that he'd lose his job if anyone found out that he'd ratted," Rand yelled. "Good engineers all know of each other. He knows that I know steel—so he told me."

Rand jerked Jules back to face the dam. "And see how we're in a valley, the steepness of the hills just below the dam? Now follow the flood path," Rand yelled, tracing it with his finger.

Jules gasped. The path would take the flood directly into the Cabbage Patch.

Another huge clap of thunder shook the bell tower where they stood. "Believe me. That dam is going to crumble like sand. And every person in this low-lying area is about to drown."

"What are we going to do?" screamed Jules.

"We've got to warn everyone," yelled Rand. "And now."

They raced down the steeple stairs, slipping and sliding on the smooth stone steps, and out through the church door. The mud in the streets grabbed at her feet, slowing her, but Jules ran on, her heart pounding.

"Evacuate! Evacuate!" she screamed. "A flood is coming!" The deluge continued with heavy raindrops exploding on the ground and rooftops.

Rand ran up to the doors of the brothels, pounding and yelling. "Get out now! Everyone evacuate to high ground!" A few of the girls came to the doors and windows to see what the commotion was about. "Get to high ground," repeated Rand. "Follow the gully up." He pointed up to the top of Dublin Gulch. "The Cabbage Patch is going to flood."

Jules burst through the door at the Venus House. "Emergency! Flood!" she shouted, dripping water onto the expensive oriental carpet. Spying an oversized silver urn on a hallway console table, Jules grabbed it and started banging it with a walking cane she pulled from the umbrella stand near the door. "Everyone, get out! Emergency!" She heard screams coming from deep inside the building. Within seconds, dozens of girls in various states of undress went running past her, out into the rain. Some carried armloads of clothes, some dragged their clients, half-dressed with suspenders down around their waists, disbelief across their faces. And one girl of about sixteen years ran past Jules sobbing, hugging an infant to her breast.

"Is anyone still here?" Jules cried out, turning about in the entryway. The rain smacked at the front door, sounding like bullets. Momentarily taken aback, Jules took a moment and gazed upon the fine furniture and heavy velvet curtains covering the high windows. So, this is what a brothel looked like inside. The Venus House's well-appointed interior rivaled many wealthy businessmen's homes.

"Jules! Come on!" she heard Rand call from the street. She gave one last look into the parlor, dropped the urn, then ran out to him. He stood in water up to his ankles and threw his hands in the air. "I can't get anyone out of O'Brian's Pub. All those guys are three sheets to the wind. You've got to help me!" They ran splashing to O'Brian's and then stood dripping at the doorway.

From far off, they heard something sounding like a huge *CRACK*. "It's the dam!" yelled Rand. "It's broken. We don't have much time." Jules looked to Rand, horror in her eyes.

"The Cabbage Patch is going to flood," yelled Rand over the din of the pub. A huge thunderclap sounded overhead. "You've got to evacuate!" Most of the drunks barely looked up. When he tried lifting one off his barstool, the drunk mumbled "put me down" and swung his fist wildly in the direction of Rand's head. Rand took advantage of his position and returned the swing, catching the drunk in the middle of his gut. "Ooooph!" he wheezed, stepping back.

"Solar plexus," grinned Jules at Rand as she grabbed the drunk by his suspenders, pulling him outside. Once in the pouring rain, the drunk rubbed his face with his hands, then looked down the street at all the people climbing uphill. As if he'd just awakened, he wagged his head back and forth, then ran after the crowd. Once she was sure he was headed in the right direction, Jules ran back into the pub.

Rand was standing on a table yelling. "A flood is coming to wipe out the area. You've all got to leave and get to high ground." No one moved. Rand looked to Jules, his face panicked.

Jules took stock of the men in the bar. She guessed there were around 50, most of them drinking draft beer.

Draft beer.

In a flash, Jules was standing on the table next to Rand, her hands cupped around her mouth. "Gentlemen," she hollered so loudly she thought her voice would break. "FREE BEER!" Rand looked at her, then bent over and began laughing.

"O'Brian's has run out of beer," Jules yelled. "The first 50 of you to get up to Butte Brewery can have free beer for the rest of the day!" Bar stools pushed back from the bar as Jules heard "free beer" repeated over and over. A stampede of drunken men staggered as fast as they could out of O'Brian's Pub. In between fits of laughter, Rand pointed up the hill and choked out, "Follow the gully up. Follow the gully."

They jumped off the table and followed the last man into the street. It was working! People were leaving in droves and heading to higher ground.

And then, without warning, a 12-foot wall of water appeared at the far end of Wyoming Street. The filthy brown water foamed and tumbled rapidly toward them.

"Holy hell," yelled Rand. "Run!"

He twisted around, looking for Jules, and found her frantically tugging at the halter of an aged brown and white cow standing next to a hitching post. Beside her, on unsteady legs, stood a grizzled, white haired old geezer.

Jules screamed, "He says she's his only possession in the world—his only friend. And he's not moving without her." Rand bounded up the crooked wooden steps, his face just a few inches away from the old miner's. "Don't you understand? We're going to drown!" The old miner sighed, knocking Rand back with the smell of whiskey coming off his breath.

"Ain't no reason to live if ol' Debbie here ain't with me. She's my best friend."

"Rand!" shrieked Jules. "Behind you!" The wall of water rushed down the center of Wyoming, headed in their direction. Rand's eyes grew huge, and he ran into the pub. "Coward! You can't leave me!" screamed Jules.

"Never." Rand came back clutching a bottle of whiskey. He thrust the bottle into the old man's hands and said, "Here's your new best friend. You take that up to the top of Dublin Gulch, and this beautiful young lady and I will deliver your friend here to you." The man's eyes lit up, and he grabbed the bottle from Rand.

"Hurry," yelled Jules as she pulled the old man uphill. Once Jules saw he was headed steadily to higher ground, she turned and ran back to Rand.

The first wave barreled into her, throwing her off her feet and pushing her to the muddy ground. She scrambled back onto her feet, the swift water tugging at her skirt.

"Grab onto the cow," yelled Rand, reaching out his hand. Jules caught hold of Rand with one hand, and with the other, yanked the cow's halter to her chest mere seconds before the rest of the flood poured into the street.

"Mmmmrruuuh," bellowed the cow holding its head above the rapidly rising water.

"That's right, baby, we're moving," yelled Rand, pushing his hair from his eyes. The rain continued to pelt them, and water swirled around their legs, lifting them from the ground.

As the fast-moving water pulled them downstream, away from O'Brian's bar, Rand grabbed the sash of Jules' drenched dress and tied it to his arm. His eyes bore into hers. "I won't leave you."

Pulled underwater, Jules struggled and gasped, "Promise me!"

"I promise," yelled Rand. "Now kick!" They both kicked their feet to keep afloat as the fast-running water tore at their arms and legs and threatened to pull the cow under.

"Swim," yelled Jules. "Come on, Debbie, give me a little help here." She took a deep breath and pushed the cow's hind quarters like she'd never pushed before. The cow started moving her legs and was soon swimming, her head peeked above the rushing water. "She's swimming," choked Jules with a laugh. "She's swimming."

Dragged along by the current, they banged against debris floating past them: uprooted trees, the storefront from Brown's Hardware with its windows still intact, and a wagon filled with dirty laundry.

Jules focused on keeping her head above water. The occasional wave crashed over her, and she'd sputter, trying not to sink further down.

"Keep holding on," Rand called out. "I'll help you."

Through the surging water, Jules saw Rand, his muscles straining to keep her and the cow afloat. He certainly wasn't acting like a murderer, in fact, just the opposite. What kind of man risks his own life to save anyone or anything from the dregs of society? Jules knew the answer. A man of honor. A man of integrity. A man… she could love.

"Jules! Over there!" Rand pointed to an area in front of them. She nodded vigorously, and together they pushed and pulled the cow to a shallow area situated below Butte Brewery. From a few blocks above, Jules could hear shouts and laughter coming from the brewery.

It took them half an hour to navigate to the embankment, fighting the floodwater that still towed them along. With her energy finally fading, Jules gave one last tug on the cow's halter as the clouds briefly parted, and a sunbeam lit upon her face. The rain had at last stopped its torrential downpour.

Once her feet touched solid ground, Jules dropped the halter and crawled out of the water. She lay panting on the edge of the flooded river, the grimy water lapping at her legs. Her shoes were gone, her dress torn and filthy. Her long black hair matted and hung in her face, covering her closed eyes.

"We made it," she said, breathing heavily. Jules lifted her head. "We made it, Rand." She raked her hair from her eyes and saw nothing but flood remains. "Rand? Rand?" Waterlogged barrels piled against the shore next to a woman's frilly nightgown choked with barbed wire, and a rooster flapping pitifully in the mud, its wings bent backwards.

"RAND!" she screamed in terror and pulled herself to her feet. Her hands groped around her waist for her sash, but when she pulled, it came away torn, the other half that had been attached to Rand, gone. And he was nowhere to be found.

"NO!" Jules thought of the way he'd looked at her when he'd tied the sash to his arm. He couldn't be gone! She twirled around, madly searching for that sun-bleached hair.

"He promised he wouldn't leave me," she screamed. A sob escaped her throat as she fell to her knees. "He promised… he wouldn't…leave me." Jules scanned the floodwaters for him, but all she saw was the laundry wagon filling with brown water and slowly sinking under.

On her hands and knees, Jules crawled to the beached cow, the heifer's chest rising and falling with labored breath. "He promised he wouldn't leave me," she repeated. "Oh god, no…" Jules lay next to the cow, her face lying flat in the mud, her hot tears mixing with the filthy river water.

"Jesus, get off me."

Jules' head snapped up, and she jumped to her feet. She ran around the cow to find Rand, on his back, his leg pinned by all 1,000 pounds of Debbie. Jules rushed to Rand and cradled his head in her lap.

"I thought you'd drowned," she choked, running her fingers through his disheveled hair. Rand reached out and caught her hand in his, clenching it to his chest.

"I told you I wouldn't leave you," he said, his eyes searching her face.

"I know," replied Jules, raising their clasped hands to her cheek. "I know." Her eyes burned into Rand's, and she slowly leaned forward. Her face neared his, and she parted her lips.

"Mmmmrruuuuh," the cow bellowed. Jules jerked back as Debbie thrashed, attempting to stand.

"Ahhhh! Jules, you gotta help me," said Rand, pain crossing his face. "This damn cow is crushing my leg." Jules reached out to calm the cow. "Get her off me, Jules. Before my leg breaks!"

"Oh god," replied Jules. She ran to the cow's backside, placed a hand on either side of her tail, and pushed. Nothing. Jules darted to the front of the cow, grabbed her halter, and pulled with all her might. Nothing.

"Come on, Jules," cried Rand. "This is killing me." He groaned.

Even as Jules pulled harder, the cow resisted, pulling back on the rope, eyeing Jules madly. Jules threw the strap of the halter over her shoulder and tried climbing up the slope, her feet slipping in the slimy mud. The cow pulled back, refusing to budge. After what seemed like hours of tugging the cow's neck, Jules fell to the ground, exhausted.

"Jules, honey," called Rand. "You gotta do this—I'm losing feeling in my leg."

Jules crawled to where Rand lay and clawed at the ground around his leg. "You are not losing that leg. I'll get you free." She reached down and dug, her arms plastered with sludge up to her shoulder. She flung the mud aside frantically. Then, bracing her bare feet in the mud, she tried pushing the cow again, her muscles straining with the effort. And yet the cow remained lying solidly on her side, Rand's leg eternally pinned.

Drained, Jules fell to the ground. "It's not working." She covered her face with her mud-encrusted hands. "I'm sorry, Rand," she whispered.

Rand's head dropped back, his face growing pale. "Jules…" She could barely hear him.

Phweet-weetle! A whistle trilled from higher up the embankment. Debbie raised her heavy head. *Phweet-weetle!* The heifer labored at lifting her bulk and gradually got to her knees. She blew hard through her nose and then, like a clumsy giant, stood up on her four legs. "Woo-hoo, come to me, girl!" Debbie's head tilted up, and she finally spied him. The old miner sat perched on a tree stump, 100 yards above them, a half-finished bottle of whiskey in his hand. "Mmruuuh," said the cow as she slowly lumbered up toward him.

Jules reached across the mire and grabbed Rand, pulling him to her. "Your leg?" she asked. "Is it okay?"

"It's…" Rand grimaced while he gingerly moved his leg. "Yeah. The blood is moving now. I'll be fine." Jules wrapped her arms around his neck and buried her face in his hair.

"I was worried about your leg," she murmured. "But what really frightened me was when I thought you'd drowned, swept under, and couldn't breathe."

Rand reached his arms around Jules and drew her in even closer. "You are the air that I breathe." With one hand in her hair, he pulled her head back, then leaned in and kissed her passionately. She clung to him, returning his kiss, pressing her body against his.

Rand rolled over, pinning Jules to the ground, his knee between her legs. He grabbed her hands and raised them above her head, then kissed up her neck and behind her ear. Jules moved her face, her lips searching for his. She returned his kisses as drops of river water ran down his forehead and onto her cheeks.

And then, without warning, Rand chuckled. Jules pulled back and stared at him, unbelieving. "You seriously can't be laughing," she said.

"I'm sorry," he choked out. "But did that old cow just get up and go to her owner at his whistle?" As she lay under him, Jules could feel Rand's laughter bubbling in his chest.

She couldn't help but grin. "Just like a trained dog," she replied. "Sit."

"Roll over."

"Debbie, shake."

And at that, they both burst out laughing, rolling around in the mud so that every inch of them was covered. They laughed and laughed some more—only to start up again when Rand softly whistled through his teeth.

Suddenly, Rand turned his head to the side, "Ah-choo!"

"Bless you," said Jules, kissing him on the neck. "I'm surprised you aren't sneezing up a storm, like the last time I met you."

Rand chuckled. "That was because of horses. Debbie is a cow." He pulled Jules tighter against him. "Or are you such a city girl that you don't know the difference?"

Jules rested her head on his chest. "I've just never been around anyone allergic to something as exquisite as a horse. I should think it makes a person seem a bit weak."

"You're saying that I'm weak because I'm allergic to horses," said Rand, cocking his eyebrow. "So what does it mean if I'm also allergic to bears?"

"Bears?"

"And camels."

"Bears and camels?" laughed Jules. "However would you even know that?"

"If you travel as much as I have and have to stay in the kind of sketchy places as I have, you'd get to know what you're allergic to."

"So you just sneezed. Should I be on the lookout for a grizzly?" asked Jules, slightly worried.

"Jules, honey," said Rand. "Sometimes a sneeze is just a sneeze." He grabbed her and pulled her closer. Trapping her arms to her sides with his strong arms, he ran his nose under her chin, tickling her with small nips just above her shoulder. Struggling with all her might to get loose, she choked back a shriek, a wide smile across her face as Rand whispered into her ear. "And I'm anything but weak."

When Jules' laughter had finally died away, she found herself lying on top of Rand, her head tucked under his chin. She'd never felt so comfortable in her entire life—they fit together almost like they were made from one piece. She could feel his heartbeat, strong and slow, against her breast. The gentle sound of Rand's even breathing soothed her, as did the nattering of the old drunk and the contented "mmmrruuuuh" reply from his best friend, echoing from higher up.

"Miss Parker!" came a shout from across the floodwater. Jules jolted, her head snapping up. "Miss Parker, is it you?"

"Here! I'm here," Jules called out, pulling herself off Rand's chest. She jumped to her feet and waved her hands in the air. From the other side, a lone policeman cupped his hands around his mouth.

"Are you quite well?" he hollered.

Jules stood silently, surveying the damage that the flood had caused. Although the rain had stopped, a large river still ran through the middle of the Cabbage Patch. Houses had been swept from their foundations and lay crumpled against the banks of the flood river. Even an automobile had been caught up and deposited overturned, its wheels still spinning in the air.

"*Miss Parker, are you quite well?*" the policeman asked more forcefully. Jules felt Rand come up behind her.

"You should answer him." Rand's voice sent a shiver down her back.

Jules' head bobbed up and down. "Yes, quite," she replied, with a feeble wave.

The policeman called out again, "The entire police force has been out searching for you…"

"..for hours," a low voice called from behind the policeman. "All 150 of Butte's finest. I'm sure your father will be paying handsomely for their time." Ted stepped around and stared at Jules from across the water. Impeccably dressed in a white linen suit, bright silk tie, and luxurious cordovan leather loafers, he stood out against the disaster mess like a peacock in a chicken yard.

He placed his hand over his heart. "Augustina, thank god you are alive. Do not move," he called out. "They're rowing me over to you. Stay right there." Ted turned and quickly followed a group of policemen to a rowboat anchored near the embankment. Before entering the swaying rowboat, Ted stooped and removed his expensive shoes, handing them to a policeman seated in the boat. Ted rolled up the cuffs of his pants and shrugged off his suit jacket, folding it neatly over his arm.

"Are you quite ready?" Jules heard from the policeman in the rowboat. She saw Ted's eyes flash, his mouth twisted in anger.

"*Do not ever* address me in that tone of voice," Ted threatened. "Those shoes you hold cost more than your entire monthly salary." He stepped into the boat. "And I have a closet full of them." Ted sat on the bench, glaring at the policeman. "Now row me across this mess to Miss Parker."

Jules stood still and stared out at the swirling brown water. She could feel Rand still standing quietly behind her.

"Who is that pompous jackass?"

"That..." She closed her eyes. "...is my fiancé."

A hand clasped her shoulder and spun her around, tearing her eyes from the dozens of policemen milling around the embankment.

"Augustina," said Ted. "Thank god you were not harmed."

"Ted... I... I..." Jules' mouth opened and closed. "How did you find me?"

"Well, in the middle of the downpour, Miss Fleming, herself drenched to the bone, ran into the Parker Copper offices blabbing that you were still in that god-forsaken Cabbage Patch and that the Hailey Dam had failed, flooding the area."

"Martha..." stammered Jules. "I'd asked her to send a car..."

"And then, because of the flood, we couldn't get close to the area. We had no idea where you were."

"I was at the church and O'Brian's Pub and the Venus House..." Jules said softly, thinking back to the places she'd rushed into. "Oh no! Were they wiped out? Please say no, tell me they are still standing!"

"The Venus House!" repeated Ted, his eyes wide with abhorrence. "A Parker in a house of prostitution?"

Jules grasped Ted's arm tightly. "Why, it's beautiful! The draperies, the polished wood… It's as lovely as any home on Park Street."

"Don't be ridiculous," Ted replied. "It's certainly not that attractive." He reached both hands to Jules' shoulders and took a step back. He surveyed her from arm's length, taking in her torn clothing and her mud-matted hair.

"My word, you look hideous," he said, his eyes traveling the length of her body, ending at her bare feet. Jules hung her head, her arms limp at her sides. Ted snapped his fingers at a young police officer standing nearby, holding a thick fur blanket. He snatched the fur from the officer and draped it over Jules' shoulders.

"You're going straight to Parker Mansion to get cleaned up. Lord knows we don't want anyone seeing you look like this."

"But, but…we rescued people," Jules desperately said. "Does it matter what I look like? People were going to die." Ted held out his hand.

"It was only the Cabbage Patch—perhaps the loss wouldn't have been that consequential," he murmured. "Come along." Ted began walking away, drawing Jules behind him.

She twisted her head about, her eyes searching for Rand. She found him standing silently, shivering and mud-covered, his arms folded tight across his chest.

"Rand!" she called out, her voice catching. Jules stumbled as Ted dragged her along. "Rand! Tell them how we saved those people. Tell them, Rand!"

Ted halted in his tracks and turned slowly, his eyes narrowed to slits. "Rand?" He dropped Jules' hand. "Might you be Random Buckley?" he asked in a low voice.

The two men stared at one another, the tension between them high.

"I might be," Rand finally answered. "And who might you be?"

Ted raised his chin. "Theodore Jackson, President of Parker Copper Mining Company."

"Acting president," replied Rand with a slow blink of his eyes.

"Pardon me?" scowled Ted.

"Acting president. From what I hear, you won't be full president until…"

"…Until we marry," Ted said, finishing Rand's sentence. He reached for Jules' hand.

She moved aside, clasping her hands in front of her, and said, "Ted, darling, you go on ahead. I'm just going to stay for a minute and thank Mr. Buckley for… saving me." The men looked hard at each other again. Breaking the stare, Ted turned away.

"One minute, Augustina. No more." He walked toward the rowboat.

Jules made for Rand but stopped short when she saw the coldness in his eyes. She approached him slowly, unsure of what to say.

"Rand," she began. "I…"

"Don't, Jules," he said, shaking his head.

"But…" Jules started reaching out until she saw Rand's eyes narrow, and he gave one final shake of his head. Jules was taken aback. How could he be so cool toward her? Especially after everything they'd just been through together. "Rand, please…"

"Go to your fiancé, Jules."

Jules flushed and covered her mouth with her hand. Fiancé. Of course, Rand was right—she was engaged to be married. What was she doing, kissing another man? She'd just been thinking that Rand had integrity, and now he was proving it. That he was honorable made Jules feel even more intensely drawn to him.

She looked down at the filthy ground. "What will you do?" she asked softly. "Where will you go?"

"Where will I go? Well, I hear they're giving away free beer up at the Brewery," answered Rand, scorn dripping from his voice. He finally uncrossed his arms from his chest, reached into his pants pocket, and pulled out the other half of her sash—the one he had tied to his own arm to keep them together in the flood. He let it drop to the muddy ground.

Without a word, Rand turned to walk away. Her heart broke, sensing that this time it was final. And just as Jules choked back a sob, she felt the clouds open up again, streaming rain from the heavens like the tears from her eyes.

Chapter 23

Jules arrived at the Parker Copper headquarters at the appointed time. Ted had made clear that after she'd had 24 hours to recuperate from her ordeal, she was to meet him to talk. What was the word he used? *Consult.* That's really what he had said. She stood before a door to the large corner office, staring at the frosted glass pane. *Theodore Jackson, President,* was painted in gold letters across the glass. She glanced at her reflection and adjusted her hat.

Why were her palms so clammy? After all, she was meeting with her fiancé, the man she was to marry. But Ted hadn't said anything to her after fetching her from the flood. Had he seen her kissing Rand? She could kick herself for what Ted might be thinking of her. He wasn't planning on calling off the engagement, was he?

Jules did care for Ted—really, he was the only one who truly listened to her, who needed her. So that morning, before she was to *consult* with him, Jules had taken extra care in dressing, and she had Trudy curl her hair. Jules drew in a deep breath and rapped on the door.

"Enter," a low voice said from within the office.

Jules stepped into the office and was immediately hit with the scents of cigars, fine leather, and newsprint. Her father's smell.

"Ted, darling," she said, hurrying through the doorway. He sat deep in a leather chair, behind an enormous oak desk, with his fingertips steepled under his chin.

"Good afternoon, Augustina. Please, won't you have a seat?" Ted asked, his voice quiet. Jules hesitated. She noticed that he hadn't returned her endearment. Jules approached the twin leather chairs opposite Ted's desk, a lump forming in her throat. Before she had a chance to sit down, a voice boomed from the back of the room.

"My dear Jules. You're looking lovely today." AJ laid down a stack of papers he'd been reading, strode to Jules, and wrapped her in a hug. He kissed the top of her head as she clung to him.

"Father," she whispered. "We weren't expecting you back in Butte for a while."

He released her from his hug. "I hadn't planned on being back."

He pulled out a chair and nodded to Jules to sit, then joined her in the opposite chair. After crossing his leg and adjusting the hem of his trousers, AJ settled into the chair and frowned. "Jules," AJ said. "Ted sent for me."

Jules slid a sideways glance at Ted—he hadn't moved.

"I entrusted Ted to look after you, to care for you. You are making it impossible for him to do either," began AJ. He removed a cigar from his jacket pocket and struck a match against his shoe. AJ twirled the cigar in the match flame, an orange ember finally glowing at the tip. At last, he puffed out a cloud of smoke, then sat deeper in his seat. As if a second thought, AJ reached back into his pocket for another cigar, offering it to Ted. Ted shook his head, then shifted in his seat.

"I am concerned," AJ continued. "I am concerned with your recent behavior and what it means to the Parker name." He set a steely eye on Jules. "I've repeatedly told you that I will not allow you to tarnish my name and jeopardize everything that I've put into this family."

"But, Father…"

"No, Jules. Do not speak. Listen," AJ continued. "Firstly, I understand that even prior to my leaving for Helena, you were seen picketing in favor of women's rights. That you were actually heaving a placard and yelling in the streets." Jules lowered her eyes to the floor. "And if that weren't bad enough, when you'd been, well, accosted by an inebriated Timmer Foley, you entered into a fist-fight with him." Jules scrunched her eyebrows together. How did her father find out that?

"Secondly, even after your mother pleaded with you to be more feminine, you decided it was a good idea to take a leisurely afternoon horseback ride dressed as a miner." Jules held her breath.

"And finally, this business in the Cabbage Patch." AJ uncrossed his legs and leaned forward in his chair. "I don't like it one bit, Jules. I've not even mentioned the fact that I recently banned you from the mines for just these kinds of behaviors."

"Father, I can explain everything," replied Jules, leaning forward as well.

"No. I do not want to hear excuses." AJ held up his hand. "I am intently working at becoming the next Montana state senator, Jules. But because of your actions, I had to abandon my work in Helena— during an extremely important week for me—and come back to tell you that your appalling behavior stops immediately."

"Listen to me," said Jules loudly. "All of this can be…"

"NO. YOU LISTEN TO ME, DAUGHTER!" bellowed AJ. He jumped to his feet and slammed his fist on the solid oak desktop. "One more improper incident from you and not only will you be cut off from the mines, but you will be cut off from the family." Jules sat, pinned to the back of her chair.

"I am prepared to send you away. Just one more incident, and you will go live in Idaho with your mother's aged aunt. You will not receive any monetary support whatsoever. You will not be recognized by this family, and…" AJ's face pulled into an angry mask. "You will give up the Parker name so as not to sully it any further. In my eyes, you will have ceased to exist altogether."

Jules gasped, horror-struck. She could not imagine being stricken from her family. Her whole life revolved around being a Parker. What would happen to her if she lost everything she loved dearly—and only because of her reckless actions?

"Do you understand?" AJ asked forcefully.

Was anything really worth being cut off from her family? No, of course it wasn't. Jules resolutely raised her head and set her shoulders. She stared her father in the eye. "I understand."

"You also know that your actions affect Ted as well. He's put too much work and effort into Parker Copper—and into your relationship—for you to soil it with your behavior, " said AJ. "You understand that, correct?"

"Yes, Father." Jules slid a glance to Ted, who sat stone-faced.

"Wholly?" asked AJ.

"Yes. Wholly and completely," she replied, laying a hand over her heart.

"Very well then, Jules. Welcome back into the Parker family." Her father rubbed his hand over his face, as if wiping the worry from his brow.

AJ chewed on his cigar and walked to the window. He gazed out, lost in thought, as the mid-day shift-change whistle blew, rattling the glass panes, while the rowdy voices of the miners carried up as they went to another day's work for Parker Copper Mining Company.

AJ leaned against the wall next to the window. He nodded to Ted, who had remained silent throughout her father's diatribe. Ted rested his hands atop his desk, and he studied his trimmed and buffed fingernails.

"Now, about this man you were found with the day before yesterday, Augustina," he said. "A certain Random Buckley."

Jules looked away and tucked a stray tendril of hair behind her ear.

"I'm so sorry, Ted," she said. "Rand means nothing to me." She bit her upper lip.

Ted blinked twice. "I should hope not," he replied slowly.

Jules remained still as Ted continued. "He is quite well known to be an unsavory character. We've gotten multiple reports from the police that he is immoral in the worst way."

Jules saw her father nod once as he said, "I want you to really hear this, Jules."

Ted leaned forward, resting on his arms. "Augustina, a man was found dead the day of the dam flood."

"Just one?" asked Jules. "Why, if only one drowned, then that must be considered quite fortunate." She remembered Rand and her running through the streets, evacuating the area before the flood hit, and how many people had headed for higher ground.

"No, this couldn't be mistaken for a drowning. The man's head had been crushed by a vicious and fatal blow—he was found murdered," replied Ted. Jules inhaled sharply.

"Have the police identified the victim?" she asked, shocked.

"Yes, he was a mining engineer at Hailey Mines," replied Ted. "And he was last seen leaving the Venus House with the very person, Random Buckley." Her hand flew to her mouth, and Jules shook her head. "The police have every reason to believe that Mr. Buckley is a murderer."

"No!" cried Jules. "It can't be!"

"You better believe it, Jules," said AJ in a firm voice. "That young man is no good. We're still investigating his involvement with the Metis' failed headframe. If Mr. Buckley was involved in that as well, he'll be charged with double murder."

Jules' head began to swim. Rand a double murderer? She thought back to when they had been together during the storm. She'd been with him on Wyoming Street the entire time after they'd run out of the church.

The church! When she was with the girls at the side of the street, debating whether to deliver the bundles before the rain came, there was certainly time to kill a man between when she saw Rand leaving Ruby Paradise and when he arrived at the church. In fact, Jules had seen him running toward the church—running almost as if he were guilty of something. She really didn't know Rand Buckley at all. Why would she think that he was not capable of murder, only because he had kissed and held her tight? Even murderers would be happy to do that, given the chance.

Jules closed her eyes and started shaking. Again! What was that saying? *Fool me once, shame on you. Fool me twice, shame on me.* Jules had been taken for a fool once again by none other than Random Buckley.

She wanted to scream. Her hands clenched, her fingernails digging into her palms. She opened her eyes to find her father and Ted watching her.

Jules raised her chin and pulled her shoulders back. "Well, that is certainly news worthy of note," she said after taking a deep breath. "I have no reason to think that I would run into Mr. Buckley again."

"Let us hope not," said Ted, leaning back into his leather chair.

"Yes, let's," she replied.

Chapter 24

"I can't believe it's the middle of summer already," Millicent said as she leisurely rocked on the back porch, the sound of her rocking chair hypnotizing. "After that horribly wet June, I'm pleased with this hot, dry July we're having." Jules could feel her mother's gaze even though she had her eyes closed and her arm covering her forehead.

"Um-hm," she replied.

"And just think, dear, your birthday is less than a month away."

"Um-hm." Jules stretched further across the wicker sofa.

"And as the birthday party entertainment, I've hired dancing bears, live cobras, and a swarm of mosquitoes."

"Um-hm."

Millicent got up from her rocking chair. "Really, Jules! You are driving me crazy with your lying around all day. Why, you've been like this for weeks!"

Jules leaned up on her forearm. "You're right. It has been weeks and I've already tatted a half dozen lace collars, painted three watercolor landscapes, and read the entirety of Father's library," she said. "Do you know that New World vultures are not closely related to Old World vultures? New Worlds have an excellent sense of smell that they use

"

to find carcasses to feed upon. The Old Worlds have better sight." She lay back down. "There is only one species in Montana."

"I don't understand what's happened to you," sighed Millicent. "It seems that you've lost all sense of purpose."

"Perhaps I have," replied Jules. "Isn't that what happens when one marries?"

Millicent shook her head. "Dear, dear Jules, you're not married quite yet. Get up—let us take a stroll."

"How about we walk up Continental Street? I'd like to see how far the construction has gotten," Millicent said as they walked out the back gate of Parker Mansion, away from town.

"Good idea," said Jules. "I haven't been past there in a while. Jules thought about the last time she'd walked on Continental Street—when Spirit had bucked her off and had galloped home, rider-less.

They walked without talking, with her mother setting a brisk pace. Millicent transferred a small picnic basket from one hand to the other, then reached out to link arms with Jules. "Mother, please," Jules said. She slid a sideways glance at her mother and crossed her arms around her chest.

"You used to like to walk arm in arm with me," Millicent said.

"That was years ago," she replied.

Jules examined her mother—she didn't seem at all winded, even with how fast they strolled. Jules did the mental math—her mother and father married when Millicent was eighteen. Celeste was twenty-one. Why, her mother wasn't yet even forty years of age; she was still quite young.

As if reading her mind, Millicent said, "With your birthday next month and your wedding at the end of the year, you and I will have married at the same age."

"Yes, eighteen."

"It seems dreadfully long ago," smiled Millicent.

"Does it?" asked Jules, finally smiling back. "Have you and Father changed so very much since?"

"Oh yes," replied Millicent. "Back then, your father and I were poor and in love. Now look at us."

"Wealthy and in love?" laughed Jules. Millicent chuckled.

Jules turned to her mother. "That must have been difficult, scratching out a living, trying to build a life together with nothing more than your smarts and hard work. Do you think you might do it all again, if you had to?"

"Yes, I would certainly do it all again. AJ and I had the time of our lives back then." She shifted the picnic basket to her other arm. "Although I'd love to hear how AJ feels about the subject." She laughed. "I was a bit of a handful for him."

Jules stopped in her tracks. "You were a handful?" she repeated, staring at her mother with her stylish clothing and perfectly coiffed hair.

"Oh, yes, yes, yes," replied Millicent. "There were many a time I thought your father would kick me to the side of the road, he'd get so aggravated. I'm sure he thought about it more than I care to know."

"But why? What would you do?"

"I'd test his patience by just doing what I felt like doing. If AJ wanted me to turn right, but I wanted to turn left, I would turn left. If I thought we should eat liver, we'd eat liver for days. And your father hated liver." Millicent shook her head.

"But I suppose the time that he got the most annoyed with me was when I insisted on working. I was tired of sitting at home tatting and painting and reading boring books." Millicent glanced at Jules, and they both smiled.

"So you worked?"

Millicent nodded. "Oh, I didn't just work, I helped AJ run his company."

"Mother, you didn't!" exclaimed Jules.

"Yes, dear, I did the books for Parker Copper. Saved your father quite a bit of money doing it, too. That man couldn't balance a ledger to save his life."

"Father must have appreciated that."

"Well, yes and no," her mother replied. "See, Jules, AJ had a hard time reconciling what was right by *society's* ideals and what was right by *his* ideals. Even though we worked well together, there were no other women at the time employed as bookkeepers—especially in the mining industry." Millicent shrugged. "AJ knew it didn't matter whether it was a man or a woman doing the work, he just always wanted the best person."

"He still says that," replied Jules.

"But back then, certainly, no one else agreed with him."

Jules shook her head. "But you two continued to run the company."

"No, dear," replied Millicent. "I quit."

"You quit?" exclaimed Jules. "But I thought Father was fine with you working. And you liked doing the job, didn't you?"

"I did, and I was really quite good at it. But I couldn't bear seeing your father with this internal struggle every time someone made some comment about how women belong in the home," said Millicent. "So I made the sacrifice and gave up what was important to me. I did what was right for your father. For our family."

Jules studied her mother and asked, "Do you have any regrets about your sacrifices?"

"Regrets?" Millicent sighed. "No. No regrets. I just had to find things that gave me a sense of purpose and made me feel whole as a person." She started walking again and called back to Jules after a few steps. "Have you *seen* the elaborate floral arrangements I make?"

They reached the top of Continental Street and, shading their eyes against the bright sun, looked out over the entire city. The view was amazing. Laid out in an imperfect grid, with thousands of churches and houses and shacks placed haphazardly on the lots, Jules thought it seemed a kaleidoscope pattern, twisting each time she looked from a different direction.

Just to the west of where they stood ran Main Street, the major thoroughfare lined with restaurants, stores, pubs, banks, theaters, and office buildings. Of course, one stood out amongst the many, occupying half the block—Parker Copper Mining Company.

Her mother had been involved in creating the company whose headquarters they looked down upon. They watched the electric trolley stop directly in front of the main entrance, discharging dozens of Parker Copper employees. Millicent could have been one of those striding into the office, but instead, she gave it all up for her husband, devoting her time to making his life happy and comfortable. Jules felt her mother move away to the street's edge, lost in thought, humming softly to herself.

Construction on the street had not progressed as far as Jules figured it should have. Just as it had been when she was last walking along the dirt road, small boulders still lay to the side, waiting to be cleared. Jules thought that if she were the foreman of the road construction crew, Continental Street might have been completed weeks ago.

Loath to interrupt her mother's reverie, Jules moved to a pile of boulders and lowered herself to the ground, leaning against the largest sun-baked rock, warming her back. She studied the activity below, the hard-working miners scurrying around the many headframes, hoisting precious iron ore from the depths of the earth.

Jules missed being at the mines. She missed the dry smell of dynamite after a blast, the sounds of drilling coming from deep underground, the low rumble of the earth as a hoist hauled a huge bucket of iron ore to the top platform. Jules squinted at a little glimmer coming from around their largest mine, the Venturer, the flicker looking like a sun reflection off something shiny. No matter. The mines no longer concerned her. She leaned her head against the boulder and sighed.

"Jules! Don't move!" Jules quickly opened her eyes when she heard the alarm in her mother's voice. She knew something was terribly wrong when the hairs prickled on the back of her neck.

Just then, a dry rattle whirred near her outstretched legs where a huge, coiled rattlesnake stared at Jules, its raised tail flicking rapidly. Jules' heart pounded in her chest, and her mouth dried.

"Mother?" she whispered.

KA-BLAMMM!

As if in slow motion, Jules saw the snake flip into the air, ripped to pieces, its blood spraying her dress, the droplets catching the sunlight like scarlet-colored rain.

In one fluid move, Jules leapt to her feet and scrambled onto the boulder, her mouth open in a silent shriek, her eyes wide in horror. Jules twisted and looked at her mother, twenty feet away.

Millicent stood with a Smith and Wesson revolver still clenched in her hands, pointing to the bits of rattlesnake scattered across the dirt road. Tipped on its side, the picnic basket lay at Millicent's feet, a squashed strawberry tart spilling out.

"Holy hell!" yelled Jules.

Millicent lowered the gun to her side. "Yes, quite," she replied.

Jules' heart still skipped as she and Millicent walked single file in the middle of Continental Street. Occasionally shuddering, Jules couldn't seem to escape the briny smell that seemed to come off her blood-splattered dress. They hadn't said a word since Millicent had stowed the gun back in her picnic basket, and they'd picked their way past the gore.

Jules scurried to catch up with Millicent, who had resumed their earlier brisk pace. Pulling up next to her mother, Jules slipped her hand around Millicent's crooked elbow, and they continued, arm in arm.

"Mother, I had no idea," said Jules. She looked at her mother with a whole new appreciation, the one-time headstrong young woman who had helped create one of the most powerful companies in the United States.

She saw a small smile play across Millicent's lips as she patted her daughter's hand. "Yes—you aren't the only good shot in the family, dear."

Chapter 25

The violet sky bent around the Venturer, the headframe looking like some kind of prehistoric animal in the deepening shadows. Jules breathed in and savored the dusty, smoky smell as she climbed the hill. She heard nine bells ringing from the hoist house and knew that a cage was being lowered, probably with supplies. At this time of day, just before dusk, when others were settled in their drawing rooms with a glass of brandy, miners were already down below drilling and digging.

She crested the hill and smiled when she saw she was right. A cage full of dynamite was slowly dropping below the collar of the shaft. They must have come across a new vein of precious iron ore. Jules crossed her fingers as she approached the large supply house close to the headframe. She looked around to make sure no one was watching, then crept inside, closing the door quietly behind her.

Jules ducked her head as she stepped out of a large window on the second floor onto a flat area of the roof that ran across the back of the supply house. She'd been coming here for years, after she'd discovered that she could sit her in the murky darkness, unnoticed.

She sat, leaning back against the wall, the rough wood scratching at her back. Her head tipped back and her eyes closed. Jules knew she was no longer allowed at the mines, but she wasn't *inside*. She so missed being here.

Listening to the familiar squeaks and screeches of the workings of the mine, Jules could name the meaning of each sound. There—that deep strumming? That was the drilling at about the 1500 level. That high-pitched screech? That was the ore train's brakes as it headed downhill, full of ore. That *taptaptap*? Jules' eyes flew open. She tensed at the unfamiliar sound coming from the eaves of the supply house. Quietly, Jules got to her feet and peeked around the corner.

Atop an overturned bucket stood the infamous Rand Buckley. His hands reaching high overhead, he tottered on his toes, affixing something under the building's eaves. His hair glimmered in the early evening light, and his muscles flexed beneath his thin cotton shirt. A breeze wafted his unmistakable scent of sandalwood and ambrette to Jules. She closed her eyes and inhaled.

But Jules couldn't forget who she was dealing with—a murderer. A double murderer! And she could only be a fool if she was attracted to a double murderer. An angry fool.

"You!" she whispered, irate.

Startled, Rand toppled back, landing on his backside. His head whipped up in surprise. A slow grin played across his mouth. "Well, if it isn't our very own copper heiress. Good evening, Miss Parker." He leisurely got to his feet and then bowed low, sweeping his arm in a wide arc.

"Stop that," Jules said sharply. "What are you doing here?"

"Well, Miss Parker, I could ask you the same thing."

"I own this mine. I am fully allowed to be here," said Jules. "But you. You are trespassing—I'm alerting the authorities. Get down on your knees right there until the police get here."

"Ahhh, I would appreciate it if you didn't do that," replied Rand, holding his hands up and kneeling, a smirk played across his face.

"Miss Parker."

"And stop calling me that!" Jules' eyes flashed.

Rand raised his eyebrows. "How about I address you as Mrs. Jackson?" asked Rand, with sarcasm. "Or is there something else you'd rather I call you?"

Jules remembered when she was trying to free Rand's leg from beneath the beached cow and he'd called her *Jules, honey.* But that was before she knew he was a double murderer.

"Stand up," she ordered. "You are under citizen's arrest—I am taking you to the police station."

"What? What for?"

"Double murder, of course!"

"Don't believe everything you hear, Jules," replied Rand

She paused, taking into account what Rand said. But then she shook her head and demanded, "I told you to get up!"

"Make up your mind, Jules honey," Rand taunted, still kneeling.

Jules darted to Rand, grabbed him by the shirt collar, and pulled up with all her might. Her arms tugged at his weight, and her legs heaved, pushing against the worn wood floor. Was he heavier than she remembered? And did his hair have to glint in the setting sun like that, partially blinding her? Jules inhaled Rand's heavenly scent again, faltering.

She yanked up with a concerted effort, but stunned by the palpable electricity flowing between them, the charge she always felt when they were close, Jules weakened, and her arms dropped just as they came eye to eye.

"You better not..." started Jules just as Rand wrapped his arms around her, pulling her into an embrace. Unable to resist, Jules clung to him.

"I better not," he said, but clutched her tighter against him, enveloping her.

"You better not."

"I won't," Rand repeated. He paused, then buried his head in Jules' hair.

"Good," Jules replied. "I'm glad you…"

"I give up. I'm completely mad about you," he whispered, right before tilting her head back and covering her lips with his, kissing her like she'd never been kissed before.

Rand sat back against the supply house wall, pulling Jules into his lap. "You don't really think that I'm a murderer, do you?" he asked, his hazel eyes serious. When Jules didn't answer, Rand stiffened. "Come on, Jules. I did not murder those men. And you are well aware of it."

"Yes, I suppose so," replied Jules. "But the talk about town is that you were spied in the area when the Metis main timber broke. And you were also the last man seen with the engineer from Hailey Mines."

"Damn it," said Rand, shaking his head. "There must have been a dozen other people around during those same times, too. Why am I being singled out?" He grasped hold of Jules' hand. "Tell me you believe me."

Jules studied Rand's handsome face, searching his eyes for some sign that he was the liar and cheat that she'd been told he was. "I believe you."

Rand let out a big sigh. "Thank you."

Jules gripped Rand's hand tight. "I'm telling you right now that I believe you," she said. "Don't make me out to be a fool. Do not mess with me, Rand."

"Me mess with you?" Rand asked, incredulous. "I've seen firsthand what you do to men who mess with Miss Jules Parker."

Upon hearing her name, Jules stiffened and tried pulling away. But Rand tightened his arms around her. "What? What did I say?"

"Oh, Rand, I *am* Miss Jules Parker," said Jules, bitterly. "You've got to let me go." She loosened his arms from about her then moved off his lap, sitting far enough away that they didn't touch at all.

Jules covered her face with her hands. "I am Miss Jules Parker," she spat. "Daughter of the powerful AJ Parker. Fiancé to the next president of Parker Copper Mining Company." She pulled her knees to her chest and rested her forehead on top, listening to the sounds of the mine yard below them.

Jules spent the next half hour telling Rand about what had happened after the flood—about her conversation with her father and the ultimatum she was given. She explained how she had to keep actions under control, and that Ted was even expecting her to be a certain way.

"And you're just going to do it?"

Jules nodded.

Rand ran a hand through his tousled hair. "Huh. I guess I just thought you were this free-spirited girl. Someone who did what she really wanted."

"So did I."

"Well, what happened to that girl? The girl who is obstinate and determined and quite pig-headed…"

"Quite," she replied, raising one eyebrow.

"…And strong and intelligent and intense," Rand continued, his eyes searching her face. "And beautiful."

"That girl doesn't exist anymore. She left when she was almost sent to Idaho. " Jules hung her head. "Or maybe, when she got engaged."

Above them, on the warm evening air currents, a bald eagle soared, its massive wings spread wide. They sat quietly, watching it fly off into the distance.

"Maybe I should leave, too." Rand stretched his legs out in front of him, crossing them at the ankle. "It's funny how different it is here than I thought it would be." He stared out over the Venturer, the grooved sheave wheel turning steadily atop the headframe. "I thought because Montana was considered the wild west, that people would be more, well, wild."

"But it turns out that most people you've been dealing with have been tamed," said Jules. "Only doing what they're supposed to—what has already been prescribed. Back when the first pioneers dug up gold over in Alder Gulch was really when they were wild. That's when they took chances trying to get rich." She looked south, imagining men striking a rich vein.

"Like your father," said Rand. "You know, when I was looking for my next stop in my travels, the only place I considered was Montana—Butte in particular. This city was known to be the richest city above Salt Lake. Last I heard, $16 million came out of the mines here, and that was mostly from earlier silver mining. Then, when I heard about the amount of sweat involved in copper mining, I was astounded. And it was mostly because of someone of the name AJ Parker." Rand raised his chin. "I knew I had to meet him. Get him to swap out all his old wood gallows frames for steel. He'd be able to go deeper and bring up much more rock—and make thousands, if not millions, of dollars more. I thought my proposition couldn't lose. And once Parker Copper started using steel, other mines across the West would too. But he didn't even consider it."

"Do you think that steel is so much better?"

"Yes, it certainly is. The rigidity of structural steel is incredibly strong. I don't know why your father didn't go for the idea. I mean, he had already swapped a couple of the gallows frames out." Rand waved his hand out in front of him. "Like the Venturer. Your father somehow knew that this mine would be a mammoth producer, so he put up the steel headframe in anticipation."

Jules nodded, looking out over the massive structure that loomed over them, its steel girders backlit by the setting sun.

"And then when he suspected another huge load over in that other mine on the outskirts of Butte, he put up a steel headframe there too," continued Rand. "What is the name of that mine?"

"The Only."

"Yeah, that one was the only other steel headframe Parker Copper built. No more after that." Rand shrugged. "And then, all of a sudden, it closed."

"It's been closed for over a decade," said Jules. "The Only is where my brother died."

"Oh." Rand shook his head and rubbed his hand over his jaw.

"It wasn't you. It wasn't your ideas," said Jules. "It's my father's long-held grief. Gus was the only son, and he fell down the mineshaft and died. Father said he'd never open The Only ever again."

Rand exhaled, his shoulders dropping. "I get it now. Because of the steel headframe, they could go further down, make the mineshaft deeper." They stared out over the Venturer. "Your brother probably fell 3,500 feet to his death."

"I'm sorry, Rand. I'm sorry you couldn't make it work with my father," Jules said quietly.

"Yeah, me too. I thought he'd see my way and I'd make my mark here, the way my father made his own mark in New York."

"You are from New York?" Jules asked. "I never knew."

Rand shrugged and said, "It's odd, but I've been branded this criminal even though nobody knows a thing about me."

"I don't think you're a criminal." She smiled warmly, glad at the change of topic. "Tell me more."

Rand matched her smile. "Well, even though my parents were in New York, I grew up living with my uncle in Chicago. He was an inventor, an engineer."

"He built the Ferris Wheel," smiled Jules.

"Yes. He did," Rand said, nodding, his eyebrow cocked. "But before that, Uncle Gale built steel bridges and railroads—he even dabbled a little in mining. That's how I got interested. But I was very young, so I took to following him around, listening and learning everything."

Jules nodded forcefully. "That's how I learned about the mining business."

Rand reached out and squeezed her hand. "So when I was old enough to go out on my own, I immediately headed west," he continued.

"Why didn't you go back to your family in New York?"

"Well, because my father was already quite connected around there. He was a well-known engineer, educated at Columbia. His own company had contracts from the U.S. government for building skyscrapers and bridges—and even canals. He may be in Central America as we sit here." Rand crossed his arms over his chest. "I think everyone expected me to come in and run it alongside my father. But, I had my own ideas, my own plans."

"Central America," exclaimed Jules. "That sounds so exciting—why wouldn't you go work for your father?"

"See, that's where you and I differ. You desperately want to take over your father's company. I wanted to get as far away from my father's as I could. I needed to strike out on my own because I feel that a person ought to make a name for himself," he said.

"I wonder if my brother might have felt the same." Jules frowned. "I guess my family will never know." She glanced over at Rand. "Do you ever see your own family anymore?"

"Yes, sure. I last saw them a few months ago when I attended the wedding of a family friend, Eleanor Roosevelt. You know how I said he might be in Central America even now? My father was recently appointed a member of the committee of engineers reporting on the Panama Canal by Eleanor's uncle, President Roosevelt."

"Your father knows President Roosevelt?"

"Jules, that's what I'm saying—my father knows everyone. And while I appreciate what he has done and the career he has built, if I had stayed in New York, he would have tried to convince me to follow in his footsteps. To do what he wanted me to. So now you can see why I came out west and why I want to make a name for myself."

Jules sighed heavily. "Oh, Rand, our fathers have such plans for us, neither of which we agree on. I understand completely."

"I'm sure you do, Miss Parker," replied Rand with a knowing nod. "I'm sure you do."

Rand tipped his head back, knocking it twice against the shack. "But presently I'm being blamed for murder and for sabotaging your mine," Rand said, resting his head and closing his eyes. "I've got to get some kind of evidence that I'm not the one committing these crimes."

"How possibly will you do that?" Jules asked.

Rand looked up, overhead at the object he'd been attaching under the eaves when Jules had come upon him. "I'm hoping with that," he said.

She had forgotten about the box Rand was attaching to the shack's eaves. "What is it?" asked Jules, climbing to her feet to get a better look. A small, plain dark brown box hung from the underside of the roof. "It looks like a photography camera."

"That is exactly right," smiled Rand as he stood. "It's a Brownie."

"But what are all those wires and straps?" she asked. "And is that a pocket watch?"

"Come closer, Miss Parker, and let me educate you on the way of spying of the future."

Rand upended the overturned bucket, holding out a hand to help Jules climb on top. He explained that the camera was pointed at the Venturer, framed so that anything or anyone would be in frame when the photograph was taken. Rigged so that the pocket watch triggered a switch that depressed the button, the camera could capture an image every 15 minutes.

"I have to come up here a few times a day and swap out the film, then go get the photographs developed," explained Rand. "It's tedious, and I haven't gotten any interesting pictures. Just a lot of miners coming and going during a regular day."

"But what a brilliant idea." Jules grinned and squeezed Rand's hand as he helped her off the overturned bucket.

"You see, people may lie, but photographs certainly don't. The police would never believe me if I simply told them I had nothing to do with the headframe failure at your Metis mine."

"Why are you setting up the camera here—shouldn't you be over there, at the Metis?"

"Jules," Rand said, suddenly serious. "The miner you mentioned before, the engineer from Hailey Mines?"

"Yes, the man who was found murdered the day of the flood."

Rand nodded. "Well, he told me two things that day." He held up one finger. "One, that the Hailey dam was faulty." He held up another finger. "And two, that he overheard a conversation at the Venus House that made him suspect that some kind of mishap was going to come to one of Parker Copper Mining Company's mines."

"Who had this conversation?" asked Jules, concern etched across her face.

"He didn't exactly know. He heard the conversation while passing through the hallway. There were two men in the drawing room, Silas Hailey and another gentleman he hadn't met."

Jules' forehead wrinkled. "And what kind of mishap?"

"He didn't know exactly that either," replied Rand. "Only that some kind of accident would happen at Parker's largest producing mine."

"The Venturer!"

"Yes, that's exactly what I thought too." Rand nodded. "He told me he would return to the Venus House the next day to try and find out more, say what or when, and give me the information so I could do something, warn someone. But we know he never made it back."

Jules covered her mouth with her hand. "That's why he was murdered."

"And now someone is trying to place the blame on me."

Chapter 26

"Someone is trying to set you up?" exclaimed Jules with wide eyes. But then her expression changed, with her brow wrinkling in question. "That's awfully suspicious of you. I'm not sure there is anyone that clever in Butte."

"I suppose it does sound far-fetched," replied Rand, shrugging and rubbing hard at his temples.

"Actually… It's not so very far-fetched," said Jules, shaking her head. "I mean, even I saw it with my own eyes. And I'm the one who believes you're innocent."

"What do you mean you saw it with your own eyes?"

"Well, that day of the flood, I saw you and that engineer leaving the Venus House. He looked nervous, and you looked angry when you split up," said Jules, uneasily.

"You saw me?" Rand exclaimed.

Nodding, she continued, "…And then you were kissing your…" Jules blushed. "Your…uh, girl…uh, friend… goodbye."

Rand raised his eyebrows. "My *girlfriend?*"

"Well, I mean, she is very lovely. And you certainly looked quite friendly. And I'd heard that you spend quite a bit of–"

"Of… what," asked Rand, his mouth breaking into a slow grin.

"Of…time together," answered Jules.

"So you saw me kissing my lovely girlfriend, Ruby Paradise," Rand said, still grinning. "How did you feel about that, Jules?"

Jules crossed her arms across her chest. "Well, I didn't like it one bit." She shrugged. "But, obviously, you can do whatever you'd like. You can court whomever you please."

"I can court whomever I please," repeated Rand.

"Why do you insist on always repeating what I say?" glowered Jules.

Rand burst out laughing.

"And now you're laughing at me," Jules cried. "I don't need to sit here, while the night grows deep, and just allow you to make a joke of me." She jumped up, kicking out at the overturned bucket.

Just as quickly, Rand was on his feet, reaching out and grabbing her hand. "Jules, honey, Ruby isn't my…" he choked a laugh back. "…my girlfriend. You are right, she is quite lovely, and she deserves a better life for herself. But she is just a friend who needed some help from me."

Jules looked at him with doubt. "What kind of help could you offer Ruby Paradise?"

Rand pointed up to the eaves again. "My Brownie. I'm taking photographs of Ruby so she can pack up and move to Hollywood. She heard from a client from California that certain actresses are beginning to become popular in their own right. Ruby thought she'd like to try a hand at the moving pictures, so she needs photographs to hand out to the movie studio people."

Jules, finally calming, allowed a smile at Rand. "Well, for someone who may be a double murderer, you certainly show a kindness to your fellow man. And, I suppose, woman."

A brilliant moon illuminated where they sat, the clear sky crowded with stars sparkling and winking. The Venturer below kept up an even hum along with the constant groans and shouts and bells.

"The stars look like diamonds," said Rand, his head tilted up.

Jules nodded, staring out over the headframe. "Some people think that there is no greater treasure that comes from the earth than diamonds. But when gold was first discovered here, over in Alder Gulch, they all thought gold was the greatest treasure." She sighed. "Then that ran out. And they found silver. And then that ran out."

"And then they struck copper iron ore," replied Rand.

"And that turned out to be the greatest treasure of all," Jules said, slowly twirling in a circle. "Who would have guessed that we would be standing on the richest hill on earth?"

"The richest hill on earth…" said Rand.

"There you go, repeating me again."

"That's what people call this hill?"

"Why, yes," said Jules. "When it started producing most of the copper in the country, people started calling it the richest hill on earth."

"The richest *hill* on earth." Rand chuckled and ducked his head. "All this time, after I found out you were a Parker, and I tried to ignore you, to forget about you, I thought they were always talking about you. Everyone, everywhere, talking about you, all the time. I kept hearing it, over and over."

Jules tilted her head and raised her eyebrows, questioning. "What?"

"I thought I heard," said Rand with his slow grin. "The richest girl on earth."

Jules dropped her head, her shoulders heavy. "The night has gotten late," she said. "I must be getting home." She moved away from the shack wall, the cool night air sending shivers down her back. Rand followed her, standing nearby, gently watching her.

"You know my friend I spoke of earlier, Eleanor? The one who got married? She's quite wonderful, all full of smarts and compassion," Rand said quietly. "You remind me of her." Jules allowed a smile.

"Although she was much older than you when she got married."

"Oh, she is not so much older. I'll be eighteen in just a few weeks," corrected Jules.

Rand lifted his eyebrows. "Well, then. You should find someone whom you might want to marry."

Jules looked at Rand, a question on her face. "But I have," she said. "Ted."

Rand barked a laugh and shook his head. "I mean someone who actually loves you."

In two strides, he had her in his arms, his lips covering hers. Jules moved tighter into Rand's embrace and returned his kisses, their lips melding. He held her tight against his warm chest, dispersing her shivers and reminding Jules of how well they fit one another. She clung to him.

But then, Jules pulled away, guilt playing across her face. She sighed. "Rand, didn't you understand anything I told you earlier? If I'm to stay in good graces with my family, I need to carry on with what they are demanding of me."

"Well, didn't you understand what I told you earlier? That you should do what you want—and that a person ought to make a name for himself?" he said, his voice low and strong.

"I did understand. And my name is Parker. And regardless of what I choose to do, or what name I take when I marry, I'll always be a Parker."

"You're just going to do what your parents want of you," Rand said bitterly.

"It's time for me to quit being so inconsiderate. I need to stop thinking that I can do what I want, with no regard to what it does to my family."

"Well, no one matters to me but you." Rand shook his head and reached for her. "I want you to be happy. And I want us to be together."

"No, I can't do it. I owe it to my family," she said. "Despite my feelings for you, I can never be with you ever again." She bowed her head, covering her face with her hands. They stood silent, the air chilling between them. Nine bells rang from the Venturer, and they heard the hoist slowly grind into motion.

"Maybe you'll never be with me again," replied Rand, moving Jules' hand and placing her wrist to his lips. "But you will always have my heart."

"Well then, that really does make me the richest girl on earth," she replied, her voice wavering. "Good-bye, Rand."

Jules turned away, a lump in her throat. But before she could take one more step, she turned back to Rand and crushed herself into his arms. Kissing him one last time, surrounded by the rumbles and groans of the mountain at work, a tiny click sounded from under the supply shack's eaves.

Part Three

Chapter 27

Jules and Police Chief Davies strolled down Main Street, nodding hello to the many people they passed. Jules had felt a need to tell someone what she—and Rand—suspected at the Venturer. So with a white lie that she needed to discuss a fundraiser for the annual Policeman's Ball, she got Chief Davies outside and on their own, where she was sure they would not be overheard.

After hearing what Jules had to say, Chief Davies replied, "Well, Miss Parker, I'm not quite sure what to do with your information." He scratched his chin. "Have you told Mr. Jackson, or your father?"

"I am reluctant to do that at the moment. You see, they are making me—ah, I should say—I am trying to step away from involving myself at Parker Copper," she replied slowly.

"Uh-huh," nodded Davies. "With what you know about that company, I'd say it's their loss." Jules placed her hand on his arm, a look of gratitude in her eyes. "Miss Parker, I'll certainly keep my eyes peeled for any suspicious behavior. And I am going to put some men on following that Random Buckley since he's our main suspect."

"No! Don't do that!"

Davies raised his eyebrows. "Uh-huh," he nodded again. "Because you don't have anything to do with that fellow."

Jules blinked innocently. "Of course I don't." They crossed the road. "But he didn't have anything to do with the sabotage at the Metis nor with anything adverse that might happen to Parker Copper in the future. So thank you for taking your men off him." She smiled widely at Davies.

"Miss Parker, you know me and my reputation," said Davies. "The minute I feel somebody's brought any trouble into my town, I'm not going to wait. I carry the law straight to them." They stopped outside Liberty Theater, the lights dark, a day-old playbill crushed at their feet.

"I wouldn't expect anything less, Chief," replied Jules. "That is why we all refer to you as Judicious Davies."

Davies smiled with a big, toothy grin. "You do?"

Jules laughed and stepped away from the theater. "Yes, Chief. We do because you are both sensible and wise. And you know everything and everyone in our fine city."

They continued walking, approaching a group of businessmen standing outside the Finlen Hotel who shouted out greetings to Davies, and reached out to shake his hand vigorously. But then at the same time, a jeer came from a passing electric trolley car, "Hey Davies, you miserable son of a…" the rest of the words cut off as the trolley bell loudly rang. Police Chief Davies raised his eyebrows, a grin playing over his lips.

"I guess not everyone thinks I'm so judicious," he laughed, with Jules joining in.

They arrived back at the bustling police station and stood at the steps. "I think this year's Policeman's Ball is going to be the finest in years," said Jules as she opened her handbag, withdrawing a prewritten bank check. Holding it out, she added, "And please remember our conversation about not following Mr. Buckley."

"Miss Parker, I know you well enough that I'm certain this is not a bribe," said Davies, his face now stern. "I'm not promising anything about Buckley."

"Of course it isn't. And of course you aren't," said Jules, her eyes hooded. She handed it to Davies and whispered, "But thank you anyway, Chief."

Back at Parker Mansion, Jules could hear two low voices coming from her father's library. She crept across the polished wood floor and peeked in the open door, spying AJ and Ted sitting across from each other on the dark leather sofas. Jules stepped aside and stood noiselessly outside the library door, listening.

"This is certainly a surprise, sir," Ted said. "We were not expecting you back for a few weeks."

"Well, things in Helena are a bit quiet right now," replied AJ. "All the Legislators are back on their homesteads cutting their summer wheat. It's the largest harvest time of the year."

Ted nodded, saying, "And the quietest for politics."

"Right you are. It is a good opportunity to be home for a spell. I've been feeling bad about the drubbing I gave Jules when I was last here," continued AJ. "I thought I should come spend time with her before her party. She is probably aghast at what her mother and sister are putting together."

Jules silently nodded, agreeing with what her father had said. Millicent and Celeste were busy planning Jules' eighteenth birthday party, with plans that included dozens of huge white tents, two bands, champagne imported from France, and six spits of roasting pork. She wouldn't have been surprised if her mother announced the confirmation of a group of dancing bears.

"And how is she?" continued AJ. "Does she seem at all tamed, matured?"

Ted snorted. "Augustina tamed and matured," he repeated. "I

suppose she is. Ever since the flood, she has been staying around Parker Mansion and not wandering off as she used to. Certainly, she's been very considerate to me."

"Well, she should," said AJ. "Considering you are her fiancé."

"Yes, quite," replied Ted.

"Tell me honestly," said AJ after waiting a beat. "…You do love her, don't you?"

"Why, yes," was Ted's reply. "As much as any man could."

Jules closed her eyes and leaned against the wall. Was she really that hard to love?

Indeed, during the past couple of weeks, Ted had seemed a bit different—much less considerate and complimentary than he'd been in the past. Jules couldn't remember the last time they'd actually taken a drive together, just for the enjoyment. And he'd taken to criticizing her dress, nitpicking the fit or color. At one point, he drove her to Hennessy's department store and selected new clothing for her while she silently stood to the side.

But at least Ted was attentive in all things related to Parker Copper. He seemed more and more interested in what Jules had to say about the company and its operations. He asked about how the mines were set up prior to a blast, what they did to prepare. More than once, he brought Jules with him when he drove past the Venturer, inspecting the headframe each week, as was required. He knew how fond she was of that particular mine, and Jules was thrilled to share her knowledge with him.

No matter what Rand had said that night at the Venturer, Jules was sure Ted loved her. Even if it were only as much as any man could.

Ted cleared his throat, then said, "But, being honest, I am not convinced that she feels the same for me."

Her father grunted a low laugh. "I know the feeling," he replied. "My daughter and I are often at such odds that I wonder sometimes if she loves me too."

Upon hearing a despondent tone in her father's voice, Jules covered her mouth with her hand, quieting a small cry that escaped her throat and feeling terrible at the pain and trouble she caused him.

"But if she has one love," said AJ. "It's Parker Copper." Jules nodded silently to her father. He was right.

Their shared love for the company seemed, at times, greater than the love they had for each other.

The grandfather clock in the library struck the hour, the long, resonant chimes breaking the spell between AJ and Ted. Jules heard AJ rustling in his jacket, then heard a match strike just before a waft of cigar smoke drifted into the hallway. Jules remained just outside the library doors as AJ and Ted continued their conversation.

"Care for one?" AJ asked Ted.

"Thank you, no." Ted cleared his throat again. "Mr. Parker, everything here at the company is well under control," he said. "I should think you would be better off back in Helena."

Jules imagined AJ eyeing Ted, their intimate conversation long past. "I should think I would be better off where I say."

"Yes, sir."

"In fact, now Ted, while I am here, let me inquire as to the Venturer."

"The Venturer, sir?"

"I've heard tell that you've been spending additional time down in the mine." Jules moved toward the library doors and peered through the slight opening. She watched AJ lean back into his seat and ask, "What is going on in that particular mine?"

Ted shifted in his seat. "Sir, the mine geologist felt they were close to finding another vein. A large one."

"Is that right? So that is why all the additional dynamite has been stored in the mine," said AJ. "I noticed another crate going down the chippy along with a load of wood planks."

"We are timbering, sir," replied Ted, referring to the shoring of the walls in anticipation of the blast.

"Well done, Ted," said AJ. He nodded once, then asked, "Are you sure there isn't perhaps something more?"

"Something more? No, sir," replied Ted. "Why do you ask?"

"I'm not certain." AJ puffed on his cigar. "It's just that I have a nagging feeling… Ah, I'm sure it is fine. What possibly could happen?"

"Not to worry, sir. I have everything handled," replied Ted.

Jules stood near the supply shack, looking down over the Venturer headframe. After listening to her father and Ted talk about it in the library, she'd felt a need to be once again at her special refuge. She'd taken the back roads to the mine, her step light but her shoulders heavy.

Jules thought she ought to be content, but instead she felt a bit melancholy. Maybe it was overhearing her father and Ted talk about her. Or maybe it was that she missed Balinda. Whatever it was, Jules hoped the Venturer would bring her solace, as it always did.

The sun was still overhead, hours still from setting, but the mine shift whistle had blown, announcing the day shift's end. Jules wondered why the second shift miners still stood in line, queued up. The last lift had come up the elevator with a group of weary miners holding their lamps and lunch pails, their faces blackened with dirt and grime.

Typically, as the cage came up and discharged a group, a group would board to take the cage down. But not now.

"Hello, boys!" came a call from around the headframe as AJ Parker and Ted rounded the corner. Jules smiled. Her father and Ted must have left Parker Mansion soon after she had. Funny that they would have ended up at the same place again.

"Mister Parker! Hallo, Mister Parker!" came the reply from the miners standing in line. "Looks like we might've found another vein."

"So I hear. You boys are doing a mighty fine job here at the Venturer. I'm proud to have you all working at our best mine." AJ neared the queue and began shaking hands.

The assistant foreman at the Venturer, Levi Weston, approached AJ and Ted. "Mr. Parker, I'd like to formally announce that, indeed, we've uncovered a vein that could be the largest deposit of copper we've ever come across. It's just sitting there for us to carve out and bring up to you." Weston turned toward the hoist cages. "I've been waiting for Danny to tell you, but he hasn't come back up yet. I just lowered down the last little quarter crate of dynamite—it's still sitting there in the cage with the timbering planks. The rest is delivered, all 1,700 pounds of it, at the 2600 Station. We expect to start blasting this evening."

"Fine work, Weston. Fine work." They stepped to the collar. Sunlight beamed down through the headframe, like a shaft of light focused on actors on a stage. "Were you the one who discovered the line?"

Weston ducked his head. "Well, yessir, me and Danny."

"I suppose you are a good team, with Dugan as mine foreman, and you as his assistant foreman," said Ted, his arms folded over his chest.

"Yessir, Mr. Jackson," replied Levi. "Me and Danny are like blood brothers. I'm godfather to his young 'un."

AJ turned to Levi. "Well, let me congratulate you on the discovery since you're here now. I'll catch up with Dugan when he comes up." AJ reached into his suit jacket and withdrew two cigars. He put one in his mouth and then offered one to the assistant foreman, who grinned like a Cheshire cat.

"Come on, Mr. Jackson," said Levi. "How about it?"

Jules saw Ted blink twice and a slow smile cross his face. "Why, don't mind if I do," he said. AJ cocked his eyebrow, then reached into his jacket, withdrew another cigar, and handed it to Ted.

Ted produced a box of matches from his pocket and lit the three men's cigars. They tilted their heads back and blew smoke into the air.

"Mr. Weston, I'd like to talk with some of your men," AJ said, turning toward the miners still in line. He and Levi Weston walked away, leaving Ted standing at the shaft collar, peering down into the abyss.

Jules closed her eyes and lifted her face to the sun. She thought about the last time she saw Rand, at this very spot—it seemed so very long ago. She sighed deeply. When she opened her eyes, Ted was quickly walking away from the shaft, trying to catch up with AJ and Levi.

Without warning, a thunderous *BANG* blasted from the elevator shaft. A bright flash burst out of the mine entrance.

"What in the name of God?" shouted AJ. He clasped Ted's shoulder, steadying himself. Quickly, he turned and headed for the shaft. "There is a load of dynamite and wood planks on that deck! If it's destroyed and drops the dynamite on the floor bottom…"

Bells began clanging. Miners standing in line started shouting.

Jules cried out, "Father! Don't…" when a second, massive explosion roared out of the shaft, throwing AJ back, sending him into the air like a feather in a gale wind.

Smoke poured from the shaft. Dirt and gravel rained from the sky. Whistles screamed, the shrill sounds piercing through the shouts of men near the mine. Bells rang with urgency as men ran for help. The headframe erupted with a geyser of red-hot, angry flames.

"NOOOOO!" Jules screamed as she yanked up her skirt and began sprinting down the hillside—toward the firestorm that was the Venturer.

Chapter 28

She skidded down the last part of the hill, the sharp rocks scraping and digging at her ankles. Men were lying on the ground, moaning, limbs twisted at odd angles. Blood poured from their heads, arms, legs…everywhere. Jules stepped over inert bodies, the haze of smoke causing her to cough.

"Father!" she cried, rushing to AJ's still body. "Lord, let him be alive. *Pleasepleaseplease.*" Sirens sounded from far away, muffled by the din of the intense fire.

AJ lay on his back, his eyes closed, blood flowing from his nose. Jules knelt down beside her father. She pushed away the gravel and jagged wood heaped on top of him.

"Father… Father," she sobbed, the smoke searing her throat with every breath. His trousers were matted with mud and gore, his suit jacket torn and bloodstained. Jules brutally brushed at the dirt surrounding her father, the sharp granite rock shards slashing her hands, when she saw his chest rise and fall. He was breathing. He was still alive. Grasping his hand in hers, she screamed, "SOMEONE GET A DOCTOR!"

Strong hands gripped her shoulders and pulled her back. "Miss Parker, move aside. Let us get to your father." Jules looked up through her tears and saw the mine doctor kneeling beside her. Coughing, Jules tried standing, only to find her legs too weak to hold her. She landed on her hands and knees, her head hanging. Slowly, Jules tried crawling away from the smoke.

"Augustina," came a whispered plea from behind her.

Jules raised her head, looking for Ted through the smoky haze. She found him, crumpled, 15 feet away. A large gash on the side of his head spilled blood into his eyes and matted his dark hair. "Oh, Ted!" Jules cried, crawling quickly to him. "Are you quite alright?" She knelt beside him and pulled his head onto her lap.

"Darling," Ted replied as he reached up, his hand searching for hers, and weakly grasped hold, their bloody hands sticky and cold between them. His eyes closed, and Ted lost consciousness.

Holding tightly to Ted's hand, Jules wept as she looked over the mayhem, her eyes darting from each group of injured men. Shouts pierced through the smoke that hung in the air like a dense fog. It seemed as if it were all a dream.

"WATER! GET THE WATER HOSE!" Uninjured miners rushed around the platform of the headframe carrying buckets of water to the open shaft. "THEM TIMBERS GONNA CATCH FIRE!"

And as if beckoned, the chemically treated, tinder-dry timbers making up the walls of the mineshaft ignited, sending fire exploding up the shaft. The steel headframe of the Venturer funneled the fire, and like a fountain of flame, shot scorching fire 50 feet into the air.

Jules turned her back at the flames, shielding herself and Ted from the inferno. The fire radiated against her back. She could smell the blistering metal and hear the groaning of steel under pressure. When Levi Weston came rushing past, his face was filled with horror.

"Danny's still down in the mine!" he shouted at the men tugging the water hose. "He never made it up yet!"

"Levi, are you saying that Danny Dugan is trapped below?" yelled

Jules.

"I do! And we gotta save him!"

"Is he alive?" she asked.

"I'm sure of it! I was waitin' on him to come up in the cage. Him and another 20 of our guys. He just rung nine bells, tellin' the hoistman to bring up the cage, right after the first small blast. Then after the second big blast, we got another nine bells, so I knows he was at least ok."

"Then why didn't you raise the cage?"

"The timbers caught fire by then!"

"Oh god, you're telling me that those twenty men are still down in the mine? In that hellhole?" Jules cried as she watched fire leaping from the mine shaft, ash billowing out on a storm of smoke.

"Miss Parker, thank god you are unharmed!" Police Chief Davies strode quickly to Jules, his normally pressed uniform now disheveled and filthy. "Please, you must come with me. Your father is being loaded into the ambulance right now. It's waiting for you."

Ted's eyelids flickered, and a groan escaped his dry lips. Jules brushed his hair off his forehead. "Darling," she said hurriedly, "come, let's get you into the ambulance with Father." Ted nodded once and slowly pushed up to a sitting position. Jules put her arm around his shoulders and slowly pulled him up, his weight heavy on her. Chief Davies rushed to her aid and helped Ted limp toward the waiting ambulance.

"I sent an officer to Parker Mansion to fetch Mrs. Parker," said Davies. "And your sister as well. They should both be at the hospital before we reach it."

Ted climbed into the ambulance and sat next to AJ, who was laid out on a stretcher, his breathing uneven. Ted leaned his head back and closed his eyes again.

"Chief, send an officer for Sarah Dugan," said Jules, her hand tight on Davies' arm. "Her husband is still below, trapped with other men.

She'll want to be here."

Davies nodded and beckoned to an officer nearby.

"Oh, and Chief, have your man go up to Parker Mansion and fetch Trudy first! She should go to the Dugan home to take care of the baby while Sarah is here."

"Right away, Miss Jules," Davies said. "Now, go! Take care of your father." He closed the door to the ambulance and pounded on the side. "GO!"

The ambulance bounced down the dirt road, swerving to avoid the debris that lay in the way. Jules gazed at the two men in her life and thought back to the conversation they'd had just hours before.

The Venturer. What possibly could happen?

Chapter 29

Night fell at the hospital. Pandemonium at each turn, the doctors and nurses were stretched thin caring for all the injured who'd been brought in from the mine explosion. Jules had attended to her father and Ted until Millicent arrived. She wanted to be with her mother when the doctor explained about AJ's condition, his being in a coma.

There was nothing they could do for AJ but let him rest and keep him as comfortable as possible. Millicent had sobbed and held her husband's hand to her cheek, wet with countless tears. AJ was covered with many bloody wounds and bruises, already turning an angry purple. The doctor said that despite those injuries, AJ was lucky to still be alive and would probably come out of it in his own time.

Ted was relatively unharmed. The gash in his head had required ten stitches, but other than that, he would be fine. When Jules last looked in on him, he was asleep, his closed eyes flickering and his breathing uneven.

And now she'd come back to the chaos. Even from the hospital, she could see the fire on the hill. The inferno, feeding off the wooden timbers of the mine shaft, soared high through the steel headframe, looking like a candle atop a birthday cake.

A crowd had gathered at the base of the hill, the families of the men still trapped below at the forefront. Jules walked amongst them, offering her support and trying to reassure the wives that their husbands would soon be found safe. Children clung to their mother's legs, their eyes wide and unblinking, but bloodshot from the smoke in the air. Although she didn't know it for sure, she had to give them something to hope for. "All will be fine," Jules promised. "Just wait and see."

Sarah Dugan stood off to the side, alone, staring unblinking at the blaze. Her profile, with her strong chin and too-large nose, belied the beauty that she was. She was as smart as anybody that Jules knew and had compassion unrivaled, but was as quiet as a church mouse. Not one for chatting and socializing, Sarah was thought to be overly serious and perhaps a bit intimidating to most of the other women of Butte.

Sarah and Danny had only been married for a year before he was promoted to mine foreman. It was auspicious timing, considering that they'd just found out Sarah was pregnant with their first child. Since then, Danny had proved to be a superb foreman, working alongside his men and keeping the Venturer's copper output the highest in the nation.

And now, their son Daniel, Junior, was four months old. Celeste had told Jules that he was a strapping boy with ruddy cheeks and a shock of white, blonde hair, but without Sarah's telltale nose.

Jules approached Sarah and stood silently next to her, their arms just touching. Men rushed past, stirring the haze and smoke around them.

"Miss Jules." Sarah did not look away from the fire.

"Sarah," replied Jules.

"Thank you for sending Trudy to the house. Daniel was just going down for the night, but he's not yet sleeping through."

"I'm sorry I haven't been to the house yet to see him. I've just been…"

"Not to worry, Miss Jules."

"I just… I…" Jules said. After an awkward silence, she continued, "Who do you think he looks like?"

Sarah finally turned away from the fire and looked at Jules, her mouth a hard, thin line, her eyes filled with disbelief.

Jules cringed. What a ridiculous thing for her to ask—how thoughtless could she be?

"I'm sorry, Sarah. I don't know what to say… what to do."

"Me neither, Miss," said Sarah and turned away.

Jules mentally kicked herself as she walked away from the other women, waiting anxiously for their husbands. Jules needed to get away from them, in case she opened her big mouth again.

Parker Copper Mining Company's Safety & Rescue squad stood nearby, their equipment at their feet. The men had received formal training from the Bureau of Mines, although they all served as volunteers. The captain of the crew, Norman "Cap" McGuire, chewed on a toothpick, studying the fire.

"Cap, do you have any news?" asked Jules as she approached.

"Not yet, Miss Parker," replied Cap. "We gotta let her burn herself out some. Only then can we go in and look for men." The smoke rolled out of the mineshaft's opening.

"You have to wait? But how long will it take?"

"Not sure. This fire's got a life of her own. I'm aimin' to get in around day break."

"Another five hours?" asked Jules, appalled.

"Sooner if we can, Miss Parker, but sure not before then. You'd best send the women on home to their kids. Tell 'em to come back at first light. That's the soonest."

Jules surveyed the crowd, looking for Sarah Dugan, their conversation still fresh in her mind. *"I don't know what to say... what to do,"* Jules had stammered.

Well, thought Jules, now she knew. They were supposed to go home.

After Jules had sent the wives home, she caught a ride with a passing laundry wagon that would be going past Parker Mansion. She'd entered the dark house, climbed the stairs to her room, and had fallen into bed, completely clothed, reeking of smoke. That was three hours ago, and now she was back at the Venturer, in a clean dress, but still smelling of the persistent smoke.

All of the other women she'd sent home were back too, all of them waiting for news of their husbands and fathers and brothers who were trapped below the burning shaft. But this morning, Sarah Dugan carried baby Daniel in her arms. He was swathed in a light blue flannel blanket, his face tucked away to his mother's breast.

Remembering her *faux pas* from just hours before, Jules kept away from Sarah and stood on the platform of the Venturer. Just as Cap had guessed, the fire had mostly burned itself out, the timbers within the walls consumed.

During the night, a nearby wood-built dry house had caught fire from the falling embers and now lay in piles of ash and firewood, crumbled and smoldering.

The hulking steel headframe looked tired and heavy, one of its legs bent from the heat of the inferno. Jules remembered hearing something, the feeling wakening her briefly, like a groan or a sigh. She thought it must have been the Venturer, giving in, losing the fight with the fire.

"Take it easy, men," Cap called down the mineshaft. "Don't rush it. And if'n you come up on shooting flames, ring the damn bell and we'll hoist you all up again."

Jules watched the cage lower into the smoky depths of the shaft, a rescue crew of six men wearing heavy helmets equipped with breathing equipment. They looked like they were going deep-sea diving, but instead were being lowered into the depths of a fire-breathing hellhole.

One of the men stood a head taller than the rest, his large torso tight against the rails of the cage. Behind his bulky mask, Jules caught eyes with Timmer Foley. His face was already black and grimy—a rivulet of sweat carved a trail down his temple. Although Timmer worked for Hailey Mines and was head of their own rescue crew, he was here at the Venturer, helping Parker Copper. Awed at his generosity of risking his own life for men he might not even know, Jules bowed her head and placed her hand over her heart, crossing her fingers. Nodding once, Timmer raised his huge hand and mimicked the gesture just as the cage lowered down and out of sight.

The rest of Parker Copper's mines were closed so that families could be together, either in their homes or at one of the dozens of churches that had opened their doors for the anxious and grieving. The telegraph office on Main Street had stayed busy since the explosion, relaying messages to the faraway families of missing miners.

But at the Venturer, they waited at a standstill for any signal, a bell ring, a shout, a whisper. No sound came from the crowd at the base of the hill, although there were hundreds gathered. Jules heard a baby cry and thought it might have been little Daniel Dugan.

The minutes crawled by as the morning sun struggled to peek through the surrounding haze and smoke.

They waited.

And waited.

And waited.

Until the hoist bell loudly rang and Jules flinched, startled. She stumbled back as a collective gasp came from the mine yard. The hoistmen began hauling up the cage, and the crowd surged forward, anxious to see what, or who, might be coming up in the cage.

They heard them before seeing them, the screech of the bent and twisted metal rubbing against itself. But once the cage crested the collar of the shaft, ten men came up into the daylight. Timmer Foley, his breathing mask hanging from his neck, held the shoulders of two miners, slumped over and barely breathing.

On the floor of the cage lay another couple of men, unconscious and unmoving. A cough triggered the mine doctor to rush onto the platform, stethoscope in hand, to check for a spark of life in the ones who lay still in the cage.

Men holding the corners of a stretcher pushed forward, ready to take any men to a waiting ambulance. But five men walked off on their own strength, their bodies and faces one color, black like the smoke that had poured from the shaft for hours the night before.

"Mr. Foley!" yelled Jules, standing on her toes. "The rest—how are the rest of the men?"

Foley released the two miners he supported into the waiting hands of the rescuers standing by. "Most everyone is alive," he yelled back. "Dugan built a bulkhead that sealed off the fire and smoke! It was so solid, took three of us to tear it down and get inside to these men."

The hoist crested again, dispersing another six miners, coughing and groaning. Four slumped back against the cage, their legs barely holding them up. One of them gasped out, "Dugan shored it up with his own hands. He yelled at us to shove our shirts into any cracks so's the gas and smoke wouldn't get into us."

At hearing Danny's name, Sarah was pushed forward to the front of the crowd. She clutched at the baby in her arms. "Danny?" she repeated.

"Yes, ma'am," replied Foley. "Danny saved all those men." Sarah's eyes searched the cage, looking for her husband.

"But where is he?"

Foley's eyes welled as the final hoist, the chippy, came up, carrying one last body, lying prone on the metal floor of the cage, his face covered with black so that his features were barely distinguishable. On the floor, lifeless, lay Danny Dugan.

After the ambulance had taken the rest of the miners off to the hospital, Jules stood mute near the body of Danny Dugan and his widow. Sarah wept quietly, her hand resting on Danny's arm. Someone had taken baby Daniel out of her arms when they'd laid out Danny's body on the ground.

The crowd murmured behind them.

"Dugan was a hero!"

"He stayed on the fire side of the bulkhead and saved all twenty men—but not hisself."

"Always knew he was a better man than most."

Jules also heard people muttering that the Parker mines were no longer safe. The Metis had failed and claimed a life, and now the Venturer was burned up and useless. Jules thought she'd even heard a call for the mines to be shut down. Who knew when it would be safe enough for either mine to be back on line?

Despondent, Jules went to Sarah, gently laying her hand on Sarah's shoulder. Sarah turned and threw herself into Jules' arms, clinging tightly. Taken off guard, Jules' throat tightened and she stilled herself to prevent her own tears from flowing. Then, finally, as if unleashing her sorrow, Sarah's body heaved with sobs, her cries deep.

They had only lost one life from the disaster, but what a life it had been.

"I'm sorry, Sarah," whispered Jules. "I'm so very sorry. He was a good man."

Sarah nodded and pulled away from Jules. They stood looking down at her husband's body, his face blackened from the soot and smoke. Sarah removed a linen handkerchief from her dress pocket and knelt next to Danny's head. She gently wiped the soot away from his closed eyes, clearing white circles from the field of black.

From the outskirts of the crowd, Trudy pushed through, in her arms, baby Daniel, quietly cooing.

"Miss Sarah," began Trudy. "I'm sorry! It's just that I was aholdin' Daniel here when one of the miners noticed it was your and Danny's little one. One of 'em asked to hold him, and even though his hands were so dirty and covered with soot from the fire, he went ahead and just took the baby outta my hands. That miner was cryin' and sayin' 'Your daddy's a hero' and he rubbed the babe's cheek."

Sarah bit at her lip, her eyes pooling with tears. Jules covered her quivering mouth with her hand.

"And then another miner says, 'lemme hold him!' And then another. And another. Until finally, when the last man handed baby Daniel back to me, he came like this. I'm sorry." Trudy held the baby to Sarah, his clothes covered with black grime.

And the baby's face, every inch of soft, white skin coated with black soot.

Sarah choked out a sob, her tears falling onto her son's grimy blanket. Jules reached out and gripped Sarah's arm.

"Miss Jules," whispered Sarah, her voice catching. Jules' head jerked up, and her eyes searched Sarah's. "...you asked me yesterday who lil' Daniel looks like..."

Jules nodded, blinking quickly. "I know, Sarah, it was completely insensitive of me. I shouldn't have..."

"Miss Jules. Daniel... he..." Sarah took a deep breath and wiped her linen handkerchief across her son's closed eyes, leaving white circles in the pool of black. "He... looks like his Pa."

Chapter 30

The coyote's mournful cries only added to the sorrow that Jules felt. She sat curled up in a wicker chaise on Parker Mansion's back porch, the night shadows hiding her.

For hours, ever since Danny Dugan had been pronounced dead, Jules had wandered the periphery of the Venturer mine. Finally, when her legs wouldn't carry her any farther, she'd come back home. But she couldn't bring herself to go inside, to see the immaculate order after all the chaos she'd seen earlier.

The yips of the coyotes grew faint as they traveled across the hills, moving away from the smoke. Where would they go next, what would they do? Jules sighed. Where would she go next? What would she do? Her father and Ted were still in the hospital, her mother and Celeste there with them. The people and the mine she loved, broken.

And that left Jules all alone.

A sob escaped, burning her smoke-raw throat, and the tears she'd kept bottled inside poured from her red-rimmed eyes. Jules crumpled over in a heap and finally cried. She cried for what had been—her time in the mines, her days running free. She cried for what would be—her adversity, her loneliness.

She cried for Danny Dugan. She cried for her father. She cried for her beloved Venturer. But most of all, Jules cried for herself.

Chapter 31

"I really don't feel we should be out, eating dinner in public like this," said Millicent, quietly. "With AJ still in the coma and with all the others still recovering… It's simply not proper."

Millicent, Celeste, Ted, and Jules sat on a large table in Chang's Noodle Parlor, the restaurant crowded but oddly quiet. Normally bustling, the restaurant was subdued. The patrons looked tired, with sallow faces and blank looks. An occasional fight broke out amongst miners sharing a table in the back, the topic of conversation focused on the fire at the Venturer.

Although it had been five days since the explosion, the town was still in shock. After all the injured had been treated and Danny Dugan had been laid to rest, with thousands of people showing up to pay their respects, some from as far away as Wyoming, there had been an emptiness with the people of Butte. The Venturer had been immediately closed, and a cleanup crew worked to tear down the burned timbers. No new wood had shown up at the hill, which made some wonder if the mine would even be rebuilt.

Levi Weston, the assistant foreman to Danny Dugan, had been approached immediately after the fire to take over the duties and get the mine back up and running. But sometime right after the first men were brought up the hoist, Weston had gone a little off in the head and could now be found sitting at the Butte Brewery, muttering to himself, something about the Ghost of Dugan walking about in the 2600 Level of the Venturer.

With no one to control the hundreds of out-of-work miners, the environment had turned toxic. Miners throughout Parker Copper threatened to strike. Others jumped ship and went to work for Hailey Mines. Politicians took advantage of AJ being out of commission, trying to oust him from favor in the Senate.

And now, miners who had gone from being stunned to sad were turning angry.

"We shouldn't be here. I mean, listen to what they are saying," Millicent said to Ted. From the tables in back, a miner shouted, "Nobody ought to risk their lives anymore. For what? A couple of bucks pay? Parker and them been exploiting us workers so's they can build bigger houses and buy more race horses!"

"Mrs. Parker, that is exactly why we *should* be here," replied Ted, pointing at the table where they sat. "People need to see that we are carrying on. That our lives must return to normal."

Ted retrieved a fancy box from under the table, the front embossed with Liberty & Co., an expensive and exclusive shop out of London. He handed it to Jules, saying, "Darling, I thought I'd give your birthday present to you a bit early. I know you have some shopping to do before your party."

"I do?" asked Jules, taking the box from Ted.

"Don't all girls?" he replied, waving toward the box. "Please, open it."

Jules lifted the top and pulled back the heavy ivory-colored tissue paper. Nestled inside looked to be some kind of dead reptile, the dark green-brown hide unmoving. "Oh my," she said.

"Go on, it won't bite you," laughed Ted. He pulled the tissue paper open further, revealing an expensive crocodile skin handbag. "Well? What do you think?"

"A handbag," replied Jules, staring into the box. "You got me a handbag?"

"For your eighteenth birthday," beamed Ted. "You'll be the first one in all of Butte to carry a Liberty and Co. bag. They are all the rage in London. Isn't it fabulous?"

"Ted," said Jules. "Thank you for the gift." She clutched the box to her lap. She would have much preferred a book or a bicycle, but as always, Ted was making choices for her instead of with her.

"There is another little something tucked inside," said Ted with a slight smile. "Something for soon after your birthday."

Jules reached inside the bag and withdrew a fine linen handkerchief in the palest yellow. In the corner was a monogram in dark blue thread—AJJ. Ted had given her a handkerchief with her soon-to-be initials. Jules ran her fingertip over the embroidery.

Millicent's soft voice came from across the table. "Isn't that bag terribly expensive?"

"Yes, quite."

"We're here talking about closing Parker Copper. The company is losing money by the minute. And yet…" Millicent's voice trailed off.

"That is exactly what I've been saying. Parker Copper is failing, *and yet*," replied Ted, his eyes flashing. "*And yet*, we continue to carry on." His nostrils flared.

"Well, I don't like it," Millicent said, pushing a stray hair from her forehead. Her face was pale with deep dark circles staining her cheeks, under her dull eyes.

Jules watched her mother become more upset, retreating into herself, going silently angry. Jules turned her gaze to her sister. Celeste sat quietly, looking past Millicent and Ted, out the window to the street. She gnawed at a cuticle on her finger, a tiny droplet of blood smeared around the nail. Jules saw that all of her sister's fingernails were bitten to the quick, an old nervous habit that Celeste had stopped doing the day she had turned sixteen.

"Frankly, Mrs. Parker, it doesn't matter whether you like it or not," said Ted, his voice unforgiving and severe. "Parker Copper Mining Company is hemorrhaging money. We are losing thousands every day the Venturer and the Metis are off line. The banks have already started calling, wanting reassurances that Parker Copper can pay back the loans we took out last year to expand the mines, which we can't."

Millicent stared blankly at Ted as he continued. "Parker Copper is already running in the red. The only option you have is to close the company, or else you'll go bankrupt."

"We mustn't do that. It will get better," Jules finally spoke up.

"Augustina, darling, don't be a blasted fool," spit Ted. "It can not get better." He slammed his hand on the table, making all three women recoil. "I AM TELLING YOU, YOU NEED TO CLOSE PARKER COPPER BEFORE YOU END UP IN THE POOR HOUSE!"

He jumped up from his chair and came within inches of Balinda, who stood behind him, her arms full with a tray loaded with food. She halted, her eyes veiled.

"Pardon me, Mr. Jackson," she said as she stepped around him and started placing huge, steaming bowls of noodles with sliced beef, shrimp, and vegetables on the table. Ted sat back down, fuming.

"Balinda!" cried Jules. "I haven't seen you forever!" Jules looked into her friend's face, eagerly.

"Miss Parker, how are you?" replied Balinda, coolly. She placed dishes in front of Ted, Millicent, and Celeste. "I'm sorry to hear of your father." She studied the remaining bowl on her tray, then slipped it in front of Jules.

Millicent interrupted. "What is this food? We haven't even ordered yet."

"Mr. Jackson took the liberty of ordering for you when he first arrived."

Ted folded his arms across his chest and leaned back in his chair. "Yes, I thought I would take care of ordering our dinner so you wouldn't have the bother."

"Well, it's really no bother," replied Millicent, pushing the bowl away. "But I couldn't eat a bite anyway." Millicent's dress hung on her frame, already too large from days with no desire to eat.

"Nor I," agreed Celeste, still staring out the window.

Exasperated, Ted turned to Balinda, "It seems that Augustina and I are the only ones eating. Just go ahead and draw up our bill, will you?" He snapped his fingers.

Balinda dropped her chin and blinked once. "I'll do it right away, mister, sir." Jules looked up at the retreating Balinda, sure that she'd heard her friend put on a fake accent, sounding like a Chinese servant.

"Pardon me while I powder my nose," she said to the table. Jules stood up quickly and stepped away.

Jules ran down the restaurant hallway, peeking into the kitchen and storeroom. She ran past the tiny office but double-backed when she finally spied Balinda. Her friend's quick fingers flew over a wooden abacus, adding up the bill that lay on the desk beside her.

"Balinda," Jules said slowly as she entered the room.

Balinda's dark eyes looked up. "Jules," she replied, then crossed her arms over her chest.

"Listen, Balinda, I'm sorry."

"Whatever for?"

"For everything," Jules answered. "For our argument. For snubbing you this summer. For not being around. For *that*." Jules waved her hand over the bill that Balinda had been adding. "You should be so mad at me."

"I am."

"It's just that once Ted and I got engaged, he expected certain things from me. Everyone expected things from me."

"I didn't."

"No, you didn't," replied Jules. "And I should have fought for you, to keep you in my life." She wandered to the beat-up wooden desk piled with invoices and picked up a small photograph in a silver frame. Inside was a photograph overlooking Butte, just before evening, the contrast of the light and dark making the headframes throughout the photo pop and come alive. Jules looked closer and in the bottom corner of the photo, she saw herself and Balinda, sitting side by side against the tree at the top of Park Street.

"You are my truest friend. You know me better than anyone." Jules stepped toward Balinda and took hold of her hands. "I am so very sorry. Can you ever forgive me?"

Balinda pulled the photo from Jules's hand and placed it on the desk. She leaned back against the wall. "Forgive the town's beloved Parker girl?" Then a smile played on her face, and she shrugged. "I guess I can forgive you."

"Thank god," Jules cried. She wrapped Balinda in a hug, squeezing her tight.

After finally catching her breath, Balinda said, her eyebrow raised. "Your fiancé is certainly a handsome fellow, but you know he's trying to kill you, don't you?"

Jules gasped, and she grabbed her friend's arm tightly. "Balinda! Whatever are you talking about?"

"Well, you know when Ted ordered for your table?" Balinda continued mysteriously.

"Yes..."

"He ordered the Parlor Special with the beef, shrimp, and vegetables."

"Aha," replied Jules. "That is why you slipped the separate bowl in front of me."

"Yes, the bowl with chicken," said Balinda. "If Ted really knew you, he'd have realized that the Parlor Special contained shrimp."

"Balinda, you've always had my back." Jules nodded, impressed that her friend remembered Jules' deadly allergy to shellfish.

"But seriously, Jules, what are we going to do once you're married? Will Ted let us still be friends?" asked Balinda.

Jules held her hands up. "All right, I'll admit it."

"Admit what?"

"Admit that you were right," replied Jules. "That day of our argument. You said that you thought Ted wasn't who he represented himself to be."

"And…"

"And, Balinda, as my truest friend, I will confide in you." They looked at each other. "Ted drives me batty. He chooses my friends. He chooses what I eat. He doesn't allow me to ride a bicycle, let alone my horse. He constantly criticizes the way I dress, even going as far as to tell me what I can and cannot wear." Jules lifted the hem of her skirt knee-high. "He would have a fit if he knew I was wearing these." Balinda chuckled when she saw the pair of worn-in, muddy miners' work boots Jules wore under her dress. "He just constantly tells me what to do. And sometimes I just want him to *shut the hell up!*"

Balinda's mouth dropped open in an "O," then the girls began laughing so hard, they had to lean against each other to keep from falling down in hysterics.

Jules sighed and finally glanced around her, at the restaurant office. "Something is different in here," she said. "Are these photographs new?"

A dozen framed black and white photographs hung on the walls. One picture showed an elderly Chinese man in the alleyway behind the restaurant, his head bent, hands clasped behind him as he shuffled along, the light from above the back door spilling across the pavement like a beacon. Another was in the kitchen of the noodle parlor, the cooks grinning while tossing the noodles with long, thick chopsticks, the white steam surrounding them seeming to float off the photograph.

"Yes, aren't they beautiful?" asked Balinda. She straightened a tilted photograph. "Sammy took them."

"Sammy!" replied Jules. "Why, I had no idea he was so artistic."

"Neither did we," said Balinda. "But while he was recuperating from the gunshot wound in his shoulder, he hung around the restaurant a lot. He found my father's Brownie in the storeroom, and he just started taking photos. He even develops them himself in this little closet he has…" Balinda pointed at the floor. "…you know where."

Jules stood before a photo of the train station with the passengers packed on the platform. To the side stood newsboys all hefting newspapers, with the exception of one boy who tenderly held a black puppy.

"This was taken the day I met Ted," said Jules softly. "It seems ages ago—so much has happened since then." Balinda raised her eyebrows in question. "I've got to tell you everything." They sat on the edge of the desk, and Jules tripped over her words, telling Balinda all that had happened in the months they'd been apart.

"Jules, I can't pretend to fully understand what you're going through. But I know that you are smart and a good person—you need to stay true to yourself." Balinda took Jules' hand in hers. "I've always thought of you as someone who did what she really wanted."

"So did I," agreed Jules, feeling confident for the first time in weeks. "Balinda, say that again, will you?"

"Say what?" asked Balinda. "I've always thought of you as someone who did what she really wanted?"

Jules nodded. It's exactly what Rand had told her.

Chapter 32

The office door banged open, and a busboy shouted in Chinese, his words stumbling out in panic. Balinda jumped to her feet. "Uh-oh! You'd better get back to the table, your fiancé is pitching a fit."

Jules ran out of the office and down the hallway to the open dining area. Ted stood near the table, red in the face, the vein in his neck pulsing. Millicent and Celeste sat at the table, tense, the untouched food cold in front of them.

"Where is my goddamn bill?" shouted Ted. "I ought to get this place shut down."

"Ted," cried Jules, rushing toward him. "Calm down, will you? I have the bill right here." Ted turned to Jules, fury in his eyes.

"Where the hell have you been?" he roared. "And don't you, woman, tell me to calm down."

"Fine, fine," replied Jules. She held out the bill on a small blue ceramic plate, four cookies of destiny lay on top. Ted snatched the bill from the plate, scattering the cookies across the tabletop.

"This is the last time I ever pay for food in this establishment," he said with disdain. "Get up. Let's go."

Ted threw money onto the table and angrily turned toward the door. He stopped and looked from Millicent to Celeste to Jules. "It is essential that I have your consent by the morning—in twelve hours' time—on closing down Parker Copper."

Jules started following Ted when she remembered the expensive handbag still in the gift box. She lifted it out with a roll of her eyes and draped the leather handle over her arm. What with Parker Copper losing money, she might have to pawn it on the streets just to keep the lights on.

Jules spied a cookie of destiny lying on the table. She picked it up, cracked it in half, and read the little slip of paper. *Lies and sorrow may float through the air, but truth and happiness are inside you.* Hah. Where was the fortune that read that Parker Copper would be fine and that all of this would pass?

SMACK!

Jules heard someone yell "Down with Parker Copper!" just as a rotten tomato's red flesh slid down the front windowpane. They all ran to the window looking for the culprit, in time to see a shock of sun-bleached blonde hair across the street from the Noodle Parlor.

In a heartbeat, Ted was out of the restaurant and into the street. Jules and her mother and sister ran after him.

"You damn scoundrel," Ted screamed at a retreating Rand Buckley. "You threw that tomato at us!"

"I did nothing of the sort," replied Rand, not even turning to face Ted. "I am merely headed to the Cabbage Patch."

"I SAW YOU."

"You couldn't have…" Rand's back still to Ted, his arms tense at his side. "…because I didn't throw it."

"You did throw it," said Ted with menace in his voice. "Just as you caused the explosion at the Venturer."

"I am sick and tired of being blamed for things I haven't done," said Rand as he finally turned around, swinging wide with his right fist.

Connecting with Ted's jaw, Rand leaned into the punch, slamming into him like an ore train. Ted fell fast to the ground, his legs crumpling beneath him.

Surprised by the attack, Ted sputtered. But quickly recovering, he scrambled to his hands and knees and lifted his head with a roar. Using his shoulder, Ted rammed hard into Rand, lifting him off his feet and slamming him into the front wall of the Noodle Parlor, the plate-glass window quivering with the blow.

Rand reached tight around, hugging Ted with his left arm and pummeled at his temple with his right fist. As if barely feeling the punches, Ted pried Rand off, pushing him an arm's length away. Cocking his arm, Ted swung at Rand, catching him square in the face, under his left eye. Rand tripped back but promptly came back with a wild swing.

Ted struck out with a punch to Rand's gut, and as Rand bent over, the air knocked out of him, Ted reached out his long arms and grabbed Rand's shirtfront. Bending his leg, Ted repeatedly knee'd at Rand's midsection, each blow lifting Rand off his feet.

Barely catching his breath, Rand grabbed out, catching Ted's leg on the upswing, then shoved hard, toppling Ted back. Rand threw himself on top of Ted, pinning him to the ground, and alternated his right and left fists, hitting Ted like a pendulum.

But Ted wouldn't give up. With his eyes blazing like a bull seeing red, Ted bellowed at the top of his voice and pushed Rand off of him. They staggered to their feet and rushed at one another, trading punches.

The sound of the violent street fight between the two young men filled the air, and a crowd began to gather. Miners coming out of nearby pubs, pints of Olympia beer sloshing over their hands, started shouting encouragement, egging Ted and Rand on. "That's it, boys! Give it to him again!" Laughter mingled with the shouts and jeers.

But then, from somewhere within the crowd, a woman screamed,

"No! Please! Stop!" At the sound of her voice, Rand momentarily looked up, and Ted took the opening to take one final shot, hitting Rand plum on the jaw, knocking him once more to the ground.

With Rand down, Ted stood above him with his foot pulled back and kicked Rand's head, the impact sounding like a ripe melon dropped from the back of a pickup truck onto a hard-packed road. Rand reached up to cover his head with his arms, but Ted lowered his aim and kicked again, landing a blow around Rand's kidneys.

"Halt, in the name of the law!" Police Chief Davies stepped out of the crowd. "What's going on here?"

Ted looked up, the wound in his forehead reopened, with blood flowing into his eyes. "Nothing—now." He stepped back and landed one more firm kick to Rand's side.

"Ooph," Rand grunted at the blow. He rolled to his back, his arms and legs splayed out across the street. "Jackass," he muttered at Ted, his eyes closed.

Chief Davies stood beside the two battered men, shaking his head as five policemen ran up, their billy clubs drawn. Davies waved off his men as he grumbled, "Even though Miss Parker paid me not to follow Buckley, it's a good thing that I'm never too far away."

"Augustina paid to have him *not* followed?" Ted yelled, breathing hard.

"Jules *paid* to have me not followed?" said Rand, his slow grin playing across his battered face.

"What I was saying…" continued Police Chief Davies. He bent over Rand and held out his hand, helping him to his feet. Rand stood bent at the waist, his arm wrapped around his torso, while Davies steered him a few feet away from Ted. "…is that while we haven't been following you, it doesn't mean that I'm not still suspicious of you. And of your actions—like this incident here."

"I didn't do anything."

"Good lord, what is it going to take to make you give up?" shouted Ted.

Rand peered at Ted through his rapidly swelling eyes. "How about a pretty please?" he said, batting his eyelashes at Ted across the empty expanse.

Ted sneered back. "How about this instead?" He reached to his waistband and swiftly pulled out a pistol, the dark steel glinting in the last of the day's sun. He pointed at Rand's head and flicked the safety switch off. "Go to hell, you son of a…"

"NO!" screamed two women in unison as they pushed their way out of the crowd, throwing themselves between Ted and Rand.

The mob went silent as Jules Parker and Ruby Paradise faced each other. A cat hissed from the alleyway while each woman studied the other, standing across from her.

"Miss Parker," said Ruby sweetly. "It is a pleasure to make your acquaintance." She held out a slim hand, her nails painted crimson red.

Jules stared at Ruby, at her thick auburn tresses cascading over her shoulders, an expensive hat still perched on her head from earlier, shading her fair skin from the intense Montana sun. Ruby's eyes looked like a cat's, emerald green with flecks of black, thick lashes outlining them. Her lips, also painted red, were shaped like small, delicate hearts.

"Miss Paradise," said Jules, reaching out and clasping Ruby's hand. The crowd made a collective gasp. "The pleasure is all mine."

Police Chief Davies stepped to Ted and grabbed hold of his arm. "Now, now, Mr. Jackson," said Davies, his eyebrow cocked. "You weren't really planning on using that gun on Mr. Buckley here, were you?"

Ignoring the question, Ted ripped his arm out of Davies's hand, pulled back his jacket, and sheathed the gun. "I demand that you arrest that criminal," Ted said, pointing at Rand.

"For what?" Davies placed his hands on his hips.

"For sabotage at the Venturer," replied Ted, hotly.

"On what basis?" asked Davies.

"On… on.." stammered Ted.

"Exactly, Mr. Jackson. We don't have anything on Mr. Buckley."

Rand pulled back his shoulders and brushed the dirt from his trousers. One eye was already swollen shut, and blood dripped from a cut in his lip. He spit on the ground, inches away from Ted's feet.

"And you never will, you goddamn piece of…"

"THAT IS ENOUGH," roared Davies. The crowd took a step back. Davies glared at Rand. "Regardless of whether we have anything on you or not, you have overstayed your welcome in Butte." Chief Davies rose to his full 6-foot-5-inch height. Leaning into Rand's face, Davies said menacingly, "Mr. Buckley, there is a ten o'clock train leaving for San Francisco." He jerked his thumb at the train station. "See that you are on it."

"You're kicking me out of town," Rand said, with disgust. "I had such high hopes for Butte. Why, this city is just about ready to burst with potential—to take on Chicago or St. Louis or Detroit. But it's not going to happen." He looked directly at Ted. "Not with all the stupidity and fraud. Butte is going to end up dead—a mining ghost town. Mark my words."

He looked over to Jules through his blonde hair falling over his eyes. "It's going to take a stronger person than me to right all that is wrong here." Jules stared at Rand, her heart beating hard and slow, and she bit her lip to keep from crying out.

"I said that is quite enough, Mr. Buckley," interrupted Chief Davies. "Now, get along before I assign a couple of my best men to help you make that train. And if I have to do that, I don't rightly care what happens to you." Ted smiled smugly and moved closer to Chief Davies.

Rand slowly tucked his shirt in and turned away. Without another look, he walked leisurely toward the train station, his head held high. Jules and Ruby stood still as Rand disappeared into the crowd.

"Rand didn't have anything to do with the sabotage that has been going on at Parker Copper," Ruby said quietly.

Jules gazed at her and asked, "How do you know that?"

"He told me," replied Ruby. "But without any proof, I suppose he can't prove his innocence." Her eyes filled with tears, making her look even more stunning. Ruby truly was a beauty—she belonged in the movies.

"He took pictures of you."

"Yes, but it meant nothing," whispered Ruby. "He was helping me, which is more than anyone else ever did."

"He took pictures of you," Jules repeated. Abruptly, she reached out, enveloping Ruby in a hug. And then she turned on her heel, running off, leaving Ruby alone, her exquisite mouth dropped open in surprise.

Chapter 33

The smell of smoke was still heavy in the air. It looked as if nothing had changed from the time of the fire and since the Venturer was closed down. The mine's surrounding area was quiet in the waning day, and with no one around to notice her, Jules walked directly over to the supply shack. She threw open the heavy wood door and raced up the stairs to the roof. Rand had said that he needed proof of his innocence—and that people may lie, but…

Reaching over her head, Jules balanced on the overturned bucket, felt under the eaves of the supply shack, and carefully removed Rand's Brownie—his security camera. She rubbed the dust from the lens with the hem of her skirt. Then she raised the camera to her lips and planted a kiss squarely on top before tucking it deep into the crocodile handbag still slung over her arm. Yes, he said that people may lie, but photographs certainly don't.

"I have no idea what is captured on the film other than the daily goings on and regular schedule of the Venture," Jules said, pulling the camera out of her bag.

"But that's exactly what you want," replied Balinda, eyeing the handbag with disbelief.

"Right, because none of the photos will have Rand in them."

"Because he was never there," agreed Balinda.

Jules nodded. "Do you think Sammy will develop the film for me?"

"Of course he will. Doesn't he owe you his life or something?" said Balinda. "He's in his darkroom right now—let's go down there."

They entered the alleyway behind the Chang Noodle Parlor and walked the few steps to the hidden door. Even now, Jules had a hard time seeing the outline of the opening in the brick wall. Balinda pushed the door open, then stepped into the gloom, her hand pressed against the cold interior wall. Jules followed, quickly closing the door behind her with a soft pull. After stepping down the wooden staircase, she stopped to orient herself, remembering the last time she'd been under the streets. It seemed such a long, long time ago.

Balinda led them to a plain wooden door, closed tight but smelling strongly of chemicals. They knocked and called for Sammy, who answered with a muffled reply. After a couple of minutes, he opened the door and stepped out of the pitch-black darkness. He stood before them blinking, his eyes adjusting to the dim light.

Jules handed him the camera, asking to get the developed photographs as soon as she could. Sammy hadn't asked any questions, but had just grabbed the camera and, in one move, turned back into the closet.

"I told you he'd do it," said Balinda as Jules leaned over to hug her.

"Tell him that I owe him a pack of cigarettes," smiled Jules. "But he may have to take a rain check since I don't know when I'll ever again be able to afford buying another pack."

"Oh, Jules, I am so sorry—everything seems such a mess," said Balinda, tenderly. "But whatever is going on right now, I know you will find happiness." She held out a slim bit of paper and said, *"Lies and sorrow may float through the air, but truth and happiness are inside you."*

"My fortune! You kept it?"

"Of course. I've been keeping all of them. Yesterday I got one that said '*Best friends are hard to find, harder to leave, and impossible to forget.*' It was when I read that that I knew we'd be back together soon."

Jules hugged Balinda hard and whispered, "Thank you, friend." She turned toward the wooden staircase.

"Oh," called out Balinda. "I also got another that said '*You will be taking a long perilous journey.*'" Balinda cocked an eyebrow. "So, maybe we ought to take the fortunes with a grain of salt."

Jules held up her crossed fingers, then climbed the creaky stairs, pushed on the door, and made her way into the alley.

Jules stepped out onto Main Street, where the street lamps had just been lit, the weak light flickering overhead. The city was calming into a quiet evening, and Jules could feel the hush that came with the business district concluding the workday. A train whistle sounded from the edges of town, a distant notice of its comings and goings, sounding forlorn in the approaching twilight.

Feeling forlorn herself, she sighed heavily and gazed up the street. Two blocks away, a single light glowed in an office on the top floor of the building on the corner of Main and Park streets.

Jules stood staring at the tall, impressive building. And then, as if beckoned, she quickly walked the block. Jules headed for the Parker Copper Mining Company offices.

The sole light came from the Tiffany lamp sitting on the enormous oak desk. Jules adjusted the tilted shade as she wandered about her father's office. Her heart was breaking just thinking about the company closing. But with both the Metis and the Venturer off line, how could the company survive? Looking out the large picture window, through the darkening evening, directly over the two silent mines, Jules' throat tightened. The headframes halted, unmoving, like paralyzed limbs.

Turning away from the window, Jules walked to her father's enormous desk. She glanced at the papers left on the desk, then moved them to the side. She sat in the deep leather chair and ran her hand along the worn arms. It had been weeks, months even, since AJ had sat behind the desk. But even now, his personal keepsakes sat where they'd always been. Ted hadn't replaced any of it when he'd taken over as president, almost as if he didn't care to call the desk his own.

Jules gazed at a photograph in the right corner of the desk, the light from the lamp glinting on the silver frame. It was a photo of her family—AJ and Millicent stood erect in the back while Celeste and Gus sat primly on either side of their parents. In the middle, atop a blue velvet footstool, stood Jules, her head tilted slightly toward her father. Their thick black hair looked stark against the pale background, separating them from the lighter features of her mother, sister, and brother.

Jules picked up the frame and studied the photo closely. Although she'd seen this very picture for years, she'd never noticed how much she resembled AJ. Besides sharing the same straight, black hair, their eyes carried an intensity that the camera had captured. It was almost like both father and daughter were anxious to get the photo done with so they could get on with more important tasks. Jules could almost hear her father saying, 'I am AJ Parker, and this is my company!'

But with her father still in a coma and with no way of knowing when—if ever—he'd awake, Jules wondered at the future of AJ's company. She leaned back in the leather chair and propped her feet on the desktop.

"Look at you. You almost look like the president of Parker Copper," Celeste said acerbically, as she pulled open the door. She leaned against the door jam. "I suppose you'll be lighting a cigar soon."

Jules remained still, her eyes narrowing to slits.

"Why, the only thing missing is your felt bowler hat and bushy mustache," continued Celeste. She leaned close to Jules, looking at her face, above her upper lip. "Oh, on closer look, make that just the felt bowler hat."

In one quick move, Jules tipped forward and jumped to her feet. "Celeste," she said, her voice low and menacing. "I do not have the patience for your foolishness at the moment."

Celeste inhaled sharply, and she paused, the seriousness of Jules' tone halting her.

"What are you even doing here?" demanded Jules.

"I... I..." stammered Celeste. "I guess I'm doing the same as you are. I've come to have one last look. And to say a kind of goodbye before tomorrow when Mother tells Ted."

Jules' forehead wrinkled. "When Mother tells Ted what?"

"Jules," Celeste said, her voice cracking. "Mother has decided to close the company."

"How can she?" cried Jules. "How can she just make that decision?"

"Someone has to, what with Father still in the coma," replied Celeste. "She feels that we should get out before more damage can be done to the Parker name."

"The Parker name," replied Jules, livid. "Is that all she's concerned about? Our reputation? Why isn't she thinking of the business, about how to get the mines back up and running? To pull it back together and start making money again!"

"Mother doesn't know anything about the business anymore," said Celeste. She sighed. And then her head tilted and her eyes brightened as if seeing her younger sister for the very first time. "But you do." Celeste approached their father's desk and leaned across it, looking intently into Jules' eyes. "You need to make the decision, Jules."

"Me?"

"Yes. It's always been your decision," said Celeste. "It's what Father always wanted."

"What foolishness are you talking about now?"

"Jules, I never told you this, but after you started attending Parker Copper board meetings, I overheard Mother and Father talking in the library. Father said that he had the bylaws rewritten, saying that when you turned eighteen, you would become a full partner. Even though Gus was gone, he said the company would prosper under you."

"What?" Jules' eyes screwed up.

"He said that if you could prove your mettle and continue on your brilliant path, that Parker Copper could grow to be the largest mining company in the world," replied her sister.

"Celeste, stop teasing right now. This is not in the least bit funny."

"I am serious, Jules. Even had Gus lived, you were always the heir apparent." Celeste reached out and grasped Jules' hand. They looked at each other, their eyes searching one another's. Then Celeste shoved the photograph in the silver frame at Jules, and they both looked down, studying the two with the dark hair.

"August Julian Parker. Augustina Juliette Parker." Celeste nodded her head, tapping at father and sister in the photograph. " It was always you, Jules."

Chapter 34

"Holy hell." Jules and Celeste stood outside the Parker Copper offices, the many pedestrians jostling against them, the auto and rail traffic buzzing past. "I never would have guessed at what Father thought. We were always fighting about it, about me being part of Parker Copper."

Celeste frowned. "That's from your perspective. Father always let you have your say, but you could never just leave it at face value. You always had to push, push, push. Like a damn bighorn sheep."

Jules looked out the side of her eye and snorted. "Yes, I suppose so." She thought of the countless times when she'd driven her father to anger with her arguing. But Celeste was right, Father had always asked Jules her opinion when it came to matters of Parker Copper.

With a deep reverberation, the clock tower above City Hall began to toll. "Well?" asked Celeste. "It is almost tomorrow. What is your decision?"

Jules sighed deeply and rubbed at her forehead. She looked up into Celeste's eyes and said reluctantly, "Mother is right. We need to close Parker Copper." She shook her head and rubbed her arms as if she'd gotten a chill. "I'm sorry."

Celeste tilted her head, her face poignant. "Me, too," she said. She reached out and pulled Jules close in a tight hug as passersby walked around them.

"Oh!" exclaimed Celeste as she pulled away from Jules. A young Chinese boy running past had bumped directly into them and then twirled away and continued running down the street. "Excuse you, young man," she sarcastically called out.

Jules clutched the expensive crocodile bag close to her, closing the top and reattaching the clasp as she eyed the boy scurry away. "I wonder what he could be up to, so late in the evening. I hope he's not up to trouble." The boy disappeared into the dark and gloom.

"Well, what now?" Celeste asked Jules.

"I'm exhausted. I'm going home," said Jules with a sigh. "And tomorrow I shall tell Ted that he can close Parker Copper." Her shoulders dropped.

Celeste bowed her head, a ringlet of her fine brown hair drooping over her forehead. "I'm going home too. Bradley is probably waiting, wondering where I am." She turned away slowly. "I'll come over early tomorrow to help you prepare for your birthday party."

Jules shook her head. "I shouldn't wonder if we might cancel the party, given what is going on."

"No, let's not cancel. It may be the very last party we have ever again."

"Well, besides my wedding at the end of the year," replied Jules, looking out over the quiet city.

The sisters walked away from the fancy building, lifeless, its windows dark, until they reached Granite Street. Celeste turned toward her house but stopped for a moment, and stood on her toes and leaned into Jules, kissing her cheek. "Good night, sis," she said. Jules squeezed Celeste's hand, then watched her walk away to her bright home and to her husband—someone who expected Celeste by his side when night fell, and who loved her for who she was.

As Jules climbed the hill leading to Parker Mansion, the sounds of Butte carried up to her. The clatter of the trolleys, the backfiring of an auto, a group of men, probably miners, laughing as they departed a pub. But the one sound that broke through all the hubbub and sounded clear to Jules was the far-off clanging of headframe hoist bells, signaling that a load of precious Parker Copper iron ore was ready to be brought up from the depths of one of the richest hills on earth.

Hazel had left a few lights burning, but all was quiet as Jules pushed open the heavy front door. While her body was fatigued, Jules' head was a whirl, her thoughts spinning wildly on all that had happened that day. Drawn to her father's library, Jules' footsteps echoed across the hardwood floor until she stepped onto the fine tapestry-woven carpet. She dropped her handbag onto the overstuffed leather club chair and went to the wet bar where crystal decanters gleamed in the overhead lamplight.

Jules poured two fingers of whiskey into a glass, raised it, and tossed it down in one gulp.

"Whew!" she blew out a thin breath. "So that's what everybody's talking about." She thought of her father, of how he always sealed a deal with a glass of whiskey and a cigar.

But after tomorrow, no more deals would be struck on behalf of Parker Copper. Everything she had ever known was through, exhausted, kaput. How could this have happened so quickly? Jules sat on the arm of the sofa and dropped her head in her hands. She pinched the bridge of her nose, unwilling to give in to her sorrow, yet one hot, angry tear escaped down her cheek.

Choking back a sob, Jules patted her empty pockets in search of a handkerchief. Remembering the new monogrammed handkerchief Ted had given her, Jules reached into the crocodile bag and yanked it out. Tangled within, a small packet of heavy paper tumbled out as well. Jules wiped her eyes with the handkerchief, then dropped it quickly aside as she snatched up what had fallen out.

Photographs! She held a stack of photographs from Rand's security camera. Just 2 inches square, the images were a bit difficult to make out, but they were certainly clear enough to see all there was.

But, more importantly, what wasn't.

The top picture showed the Venturer headframe, with miners walking about. Just a typical day—and no sign of Rand Buckley! She moved on to the next photograph. It was similar, only snapped a few minutes after. Again, no Rand. The next photograph was the same.

Jules smiled for the first time all day and held the stack of photos to her heart. They had it! If all these photos were the same, they had proof that Rand wasn't anywhere near the Venturer on the day of the explosion. Elated, Jules switched to the next picture.

Her breath caught in her chest, and her eyes widened. "What's this?" she whispered to herself.

In the middle of the photo stood two men in front of the Venturer headframe. Both were tall and imposing. Both wore expensive suits. Jules brought the photo closer and stared at their faces. Both wore cunning grins, but only one had dimples. And there was only one man she knew with dimples that deep. Jules stared at the picture of Ted Jackson shaking hands with Silas Hailey.

Chapter 35

She heard the far-off clanging of a hoist bell, speaking to her, urging her to see what might be next. Her hands trembling, Jules quickly flipped through a few more pictures until she came to another of Ted. But in this one, he was alone, peering into the open shaft of the Venturer. Alone…with a lit cigar dropping from his open hand.

"Holy hell," she gasped as she jumped up, spilling the photographs onto the leather sofa.

Police Chief Davies—Jules had to get hold of Davies and inform him at once. She'd call the police station and have them send Davies to Parker Mansion, where she'd show him the photos, the evidence. Jules quickly turned toward the telephone on the desk. But just as she reached out, Jules froze when she saw him standing in the doorway. A chill went down her spine.

"Augustina," purred Ted, leaning against the doorframe of the library. "I thought I saw a light on in here."

"You!" choked Jules, her voice breaking. "What in blazes have you done?"

Ted raised an eyebrow. "Why, I've done nothing."

"LIAR!" screamed Jules. "You're working in cahoots with Hailey!

You started the fire at the Venture! I know everything!"

"Hah, who would listen to you? You're certainly known for being rash and irresponsible," laughed Ted as he walked slowly to her. "You have no proof of anything."

Jules held up the two photos with Ted prominently featured. "Oh yes, I do."

Ted's eyes flickered back and forth, taking in the images in the photographs. His face darkened. "You damn hellion."

He lunged for Jules, his fingers raking across her shoulder, causing her to drop the stack of photographs. Quickly, she vaulted over the sofa back, landing softly on the other side.

A chilling chuckle came from Ted. "You can run, but you can't hide." He pulled his jacket aside and withdrew a revolver. Ted aimed the gun squarely at Jules. He waved the gun, indicating to Jules to come back around and sit down. Her heart pounding, Jules did as she was told. She sat near the arm of the sofa, as far away from Ted as she could.

As soon as she sat down, Ted moved slowly to his right and swept his hand across the side table, shoving a Tiffany lamp to the floor. Chards of multi-colored glass exploded across the tapestry carpet. Jules remained still, watching Ted with wary eyes.

"I am going to shoot you," said Ted with a nasty grin. "Then I'm going to ransack this room and make it look like a robbery has taken place." Ted yanked books from the shelves. "And you know who is going to be blamed *again*?" He laughed low. "That's right. Your boyfriend."

"You can't blame it on Rand. He's on the ten o'clock train to San Francisco," exclaimed Jules, her chin lifted high. "And that was an hour and a half ago."

"Oh, really. How do we know he actually got on that train?" sneered Ted. "You paid to have him *not followed*." He walked to AJ's desk and swept everything on top to the ground. "Buckley will be arrested for robbing Parker Mansion. Then of course, after they find you dead, he'll be tried for *three* murders." Ted walked to the window and jabbed with his elbow, breaking the glass. "And with no one running Parker Copper, I can finally close the damn company myself."

Ted kicked at an end table, toppling it over. "Thank god I don't have to actually marry you now."

Jules inhaled sharply. "You were only marrying me so you could get control of Parker Copper—and then ruin our company?" she yelled. "You dirty…"

"Now, now, Augustina. Must I remind you that a lady doesn't swear?" Ted crossed the library and ripped a painting from the wall, revealing a large wall safe. "It seemed an easy enough plan to Hailey when he hired me. Marry the incorrigible Parker girl, gain her father's trust to run the company, and then quickly run the company into the ground. Surely I'd be a disgrace to the great AJ Parker. And I'd be sent away, where I would then be able to join back up with Hailey."

"Hailey hired you? What does he get out of this?"

"Silly girl," replied Ted. "Hailey would quickly buy up the mines, at rock bottom—please excuse the pun—prices. Your precious little Venturer would then be making money for Hailey. All kinds of money. That mine still has so many resources just waiting to be dug up. Why, it may just be the richest hill on earth." Ted laughed again.

Jules despaired at the thought of her father's company—her company—falling into the hands of Silas Hailey. Her head fell back onto the back of the sofa, and her arms dropped to her sides with her right hand falling into the opening between the cushions.

Ted took aim at Jules, then turned to the wall safe and dialed in the combination. He opened the heavy door, reached in, and withdrew a huge stack of $100 bills. "Ah, unfortunately, it looks as if you've been robbed." He slipped the money into his coat pocket. "And you were shot dead during the robbery." Ted spun around and pointed the revolver at Jules. "Goodbye, Augustina."

Jules' hand, which had slipped between the cushions on the leather sofa, felt something cold and hard. And the split second before Ted could pull the trigger on his revolver, Jules, in a fluid move, pulled the loaded Colt pocket semi-automatic pistol from the place she'd hidden it so many months ago, stood, swiftly clicked off the safety, and promptly fired at her fiancé.

Ted's shoulder blew back, and he fell to the ground. His hand opened, dropping the revolver behind him. Jules rushed from the sofa to the gun and kicked it, where it spun away on the exceptionally polished wood floor, coming to rest under a heavy oak armoire.

She stood over him, her long, straight hair hanging in her eyes, the oil from the Colt semi-automatic slick against her hand. She raised her skirt and used it to polish the still-warm muzzle.

"What are you wearing beneath your skirt?" Ted asked, incredulous. "You have always been a goddamn mess."

Jules glared at the man who was to be her husband—the man who was to run her beloved company. "Ted," she said with quiet anger, "Shut the hell up."

The handsome young man lay his head back on the expensive tapestry carpet, blood flowing from the bullet wound in his shoulder. "Damn you," he said, spitting the words. "And damn your family." But before he could utter another word, Jules' mud-caked work boot lashed out, connecting with his temple, silencing him at last.

Ted lay prone on the floor, knocked out from her brutal kick. But Jules knew he wouldn't stay out for long. She looked around the library, searching for something to bind his hands and feet. She found nothing but books.

But when she spied the crocodile skin handbag on the armchair, Jules smiled and said, "Finally, something this is good for." Jules ripped the sturdy leather strap from the bag and hog-tied Ted's wrists to his ankles. Just the way she'd been taught during the summers on

Jeannette Rankin's ranch.

"Holy goddamn almighty hell." Jules fell back onto the overstuffed leather sofa, toppling the stack of photos that had fallen there earlier. She pushed her hair from her face and reached down to gather the photos. Her hand covered her mouth, and she swallowed a lump in her throat. The top photo trembled in her grasp as Jules stared at the picture of her and Rand Buckley.

It showed the last rays of sunlight shining through the girders of the Venturer headframe, glowing upon them, while they held each other in a tight embrace, sharing one last kiss.

Chapter 36

Jules stood at her father's desk, the heavy black telephone cradled in her hand, waiting for Police Chief Davies to answer her call. She gazed out the window at the darkness surrounding Parker Mansion when she heard the church bells peal. It was midnight.

"Happy birthday to me," she whispered.

Chapter 37

The next day, with Ted in jail and a massive birthday party about to begin, Jules entered a packed Parker Copper Mining Company boardroom. Board members surrounded the huge meeting table; the walls lined with labor union leaders and mine foremen, shift bosses, and engineers. It was pandemonium with everyone talking at once.

"We're ready to strike," yelled the miner's union leader. "The conditions at Parker Copper are still unsafe."

"What's going to happen to Parker Copper?"

"Well, no one is running the ship. Who knows when AJ will come out of his coma?"

"Maybe Rockefeller ought to get into the mining business."

"Can you believe Jackson worked for Hailey? I hope he hangs for treason."

"The banks are ready to call in their loans if we can't guarantee payment."

"Gentlemen," Jules said, standing at the head of the table. "Let's come to order."

"What's going to happen to Parker Copper?"

"Hailey's got the jump on us. Wouldn't be surprised if he's already got an offer in to buy."

"Nah, it's gotta be Standard Oil what's going to buy Parker Copper."

"Rumor has it that the mines are starting to flood."

"Excuse me, Gentlemen," Jules tried again. She cleared her throat, then took a sip of water from the crystal glass set before her. "Gentlemen…"

"What's going to happen to Parker Copper?"

"Can the company ever get out of the red?"

"Hasn't been a full ore train leaving Butte in weeks."

Jules raised her arm and violently whipped the crystal glass into the boardroom fireplace, shards of fine glass exploding against the stone hearth.

SMASH!

"THIS MEETING WILL COME TO ORDER," she roared, silencing the men around the table. Jules deliberately picked up a sheaf of papers and turned to the first page. "Now, let us begin by evaluating Parker Copper's financial status," she began. "Afterwards, we'll spend a good hour reviewing my plans to get the Venturer back up and running within two days. It is still the richest hill on earth."

Jules looked up from her papers and saw the men unmoving and staring, silent. "Gentlemen?" she asked, crossing her arms across her chest. "Is there a problem?"

The men continued to stare unmoving until board member Dell Fleming sneered, saying, "What the hell—you're just a girl. Why should we listen to you?"

Jules grit her teeth, and fury rose into her eyes. She snatched the sheaf of papers from the man sitting next to her and circled a passage in the bylaws that read:

"… on such day upon reaching age eighteen, my youngest daughter, Augustina Juliette Parker, shall be named Co-president and Partner in Full of Parker Copper Mining Company and its subsidiaries."

Then, with a flourish, she wrote across the front page: AUGUSTINA JULIETTE PARKER, and she whipped the pile across the gleaming polished boardroom table, the sheets shooting out like saw blades.

She squared her shoulders and leaned over the table, looking into the eyes of each man sitting. "I am AJ Parker. And this is my company."

Chapter 38

Once the men got over the shock, they were actually quite genial toward her.

"Hear, hear!" they shouted.

"Bully for you!" came from the end of the table.

It turned out that most on the Board had always assumed that Jules would someday take over the running of Parker Copper, and they knew they would most certainly be in capable hands.

"Quiet down, let's hear about Miss Parker's plans," one of the board members had yelled. Chairs pulled back in, and papers were shuffled into order and replaced in front of them. Then they all settled in to work with Jules in resurrecting one of the most successful companies in the world.

Jules told the board members that she'd already placed calls to companies in the east that could send steel to repair the Venturer headframe. There was one company in particular that was so keen on getting business from Western copper mines that they'd agreed to discount the shipping. Plus, they would throw in another load of steel at no charge. Jules was going to use that load to replace the Metis' wood headframe with steel.

Her second order of business was to see about partnering with a new player in town she'd heard of, with the name of Hugh Aston. He had recently taken out bank loans and started building an immense copper smelter in the nearby town of Anaconda, just twelve miles away. Jules planned on using his company to smelt their copper ore, thereby reducing travel time and expense of having to ship to Bingham Junction.

The board members had been ecstatic with her plans and new ideas. Over the course of the meeting, the atmosphere in the room went from anxiety to excitement.

But there were still two men sitting on the board who refused to cooperate with Jules and her plans to get the company back up and producing. Besides Dell Fleming, the other was Uriah Pelton, the solicitor for Western Pacific Railway. Jules pulled them both aside after the meeting and had politely explained that it would be "her way…or the highway."

The men quit the board immediately, freeing up two seats. And Jules replaced them within hours with her mother, Millicent, and with her clever friend, Martha Fleming, making Parker Copper Mining Company the very first company in the U.S. with women on its board of directors.

And now, after a full day at Parker Copper headquarters, Jules sat at a table loaded with china and crystal and silver, under a huge white tent, in the gardens of Parker Mansion. Large vases holding dozens of pink roses graced the tables and stairways. Shimmery white balloons floated overhead, tugging at their ribbon leashes with every tiny breeze. Two bands played, and the wood floors filled with people dancing. Jules's eighteenth birthday party celebration had been going on for hours already, with the revelers exclaiming what an incredible gala it was.

Finally able to rest, Millicent and Celeste sipped at glasses of champagne. They had gone to the ends of the earth to host the grand fête—even having trailered in all of AJ's retired thoroughbreds from Lewisia Stock Farms. Outfitted in their colored silks, the beautiful horses all wandered amongst the elegantly dressed guests. Jules looked round with a smile, undecided which were lovelier, the guests or the horses.

But the crowning marvel that had brought laughter bubbling from her throat and tears to her eyes was the group of dancing bears. How Millicent had actually found the trio of tutu-clad black bears, trained to dance on their hind legs, Jules would never know. Her mother was truly someone to be admired.

"Mother," began Jules, reaching out for Millicent's hand. "Thank you so very much for this. I am a very fortunate girl." She leaned over and placed a kiss on her mother's cheek.

"Well, a girl you are no longer," smiled Millicent. She stood, rose on her tiptoes, and snapped her fingers. The bands ceased playing their party tunes and immediately struck up the strains to Happy Birthday.

A wide swath opened in the crowd as a massive table wheeled forth, laden with an enormous white-frosted birthday cake. All of the lights and lanterns were extinguished so that it was completely dark under the canopy. The only light, eighteen candles sparkled in front of Jules, bathing her in a bright glow.

"Happy eighteenth birthday, sweetheart," said Millicent, bending down and kissing Jules. "See here, what I got you as a present." A bespectacled, gray-haired man, wearing a white coat, approached Jules.

"Oh no, Mother," said Jules, horrified. "You are not doing any more matchmaking!"

Millicent threw her head back, laughing. "Jules! Of course I'm not. This is Dr. Tabbish." The doctor stepped forward and bowed his head to Jules.

"Miss Parker, I'm here to inform you that your father, AJ Parker, has come out of his coma. He asked me to come bid you his love and fond wishes."

The crowd erupted with elation, the applause so thunderous that Jules was sure her father could hear it, even while still in the hospital.

"Oh, Dr. Tabbish, what wonderful news!" said Jules, clapping her hands. "I so wish he were here."

"Well, although he has fared well and we expect a full recovery, he does still need some rest," the doctor replied.

"So then, please tell him that we'll all come to visit him and wish him well." Jules looked out over the throng. "Well, maybe not *all* of us." Collective laughter boomed across the garden.

"Jules, your candles!" Celeste cried, gesturing to the birthday cake. "They're almost burned down. Quick! Make a wish!"

The crowd joined in with Celeste, chanting, "Make a wish! Make a wish!"

Jules placed her hands over her heart.

"I will admit that today has already provided for two of my wishes to come true." She glanced at her mother. "Parker Copper is on the way to becoming strong once again—perhaps even more so than ever. And now, my father is on the mend. What more could a girl ask for?"

But Jules knew. If truth be told, she really longed for one more wish—to be in the strong arms of someone with hazel eyes and hair like placer gold. Someone who'd been run out of town and whom she'd probably never, ever see again.

"Make a wish! Make a wish!"

Nearby, the dancing bears, caught up in the chant, twirled around, paws waving in the air as if they were fairy godmothers granting wishes.

Jules smiled, closed her eyes, and took a quick breath.

And just as she blew out the last flickering candle, immersing everyone into pitch darkness, from somewhere far out in the crowd came a hearty "AH-CHOO!"

Acknowledgments

My deepest thanks to my sister, Angie Wingett, for being the first person to ever read anything I wrote, and for believing in me from the start.

To my husband, Jeremy, who once found his way to Montana and fell so deeply in love with the state that he brought us back almost twenty-five years later. And even though we moved away again, we just can't seem to quit that state.

To Lee Avison, for the breathtaking cover art that perfectly captures the spirit of this story.

To Old Butte Historical Adventures, for keeping the stories of this remarkable town alive and showing us headframes and shops beneath Butte's streets.

And to Jenny White, editor and early supporter, who once told me: *If you write five pages a day, at the end of three months, you'll have a novel.* That simple encouragement changed everything and was the spark that started it all.

About the Author

Rebecca Jasmine is originally from Montana and holds a B.A. in Communications from the University of Montana. She began her career in apparel and merchandising in San Francisco before moving to Los Angeles, where she worked in television advertising.

After she and her husband, Jeremy Sauter, returned to Montana to raise their twins, Rebecca began writing novels inspired by her home state. They now live in the Palm Springs, California area.

In her spare time, she enjoys reading, tennis, mountain biking, and dogs. She has also worked as an official TSA PreCheck Enrollment Agent and appeared as a background extra in *Yellowstone* (Season 4, Episode 1). *The Copper King's Daughter* is her debut novel.

You can connect with me on:

🌐 https://www.rebeccajasmine.com

f https://www.facebook.com/profile.php?id=61571531910624

🔗 https://www.instagram.com/rebeccajasminewrites

Also by Rebecca Jasmine

If you enjoyed reading *The Copper King's Daughter*, I'd really appreciate it if you would leave a review on Amazon or Goodreads.

————————————

Also by Rebecca Jasmine: the Whisper Hills Country Club series

Read all of the books in the Whisper Hills Country Club Series by Rebecca Jasmine

Book 1: The Pickleball Girl Finds Her Match

Whisper Hills Country Club Romance

Featuring Endy's story

📖 Available in paperback and ebook

Find it on Amazon: https://a.co/d/8CkoVTR

————————————

Book 1.5: A Pickleball Girl's Second Chance Christmas

Whisper Hills Country Club Holiday Novella

Featuring Morgan's story

📖 Available in paperback and ebook

Find it on Amazon: https://a.co/d/aQiGakT

————————————

Book 2: A Pickleball Girl's One-Week Arrangement

Whisper Hills Country Club Romance

Featuring Maria's story — Coming Soon!

(A sizzling fake-dating romance you won't want to miss!)

————————————